The Line

William LJ Galaini

Cover Illustration Copyright © 2013 by William L. J. Galaini
Cover design by Christopher Michael Jackson
Book design & formatting by Upgrade Your Story (upgradeyourstory.com)
Editing by Amanda Mercer and Patricia D. Eddy

Note: All historical events represented in this fictional work were done so as respectfully and accurately as possible. Minimal changes or embellishments were taken.

To Shaun Carres, who pointed his finger at me and commanded me to write this book.

To Trish Nelson, Paul Page, Lisa Page, Susan Leviton, and my Mum ... best beta readers and cheerleaders ever.

To Gregg Hoffman; our brain-storming sessions on the school bus were vital.

To my wife Ginger, who would work out plot details with me during our showers.

And to Liam... I could not encourage you to pursue your dreams in earnest if I did not pursue mine.

Chapter 1

Mary wasn't certain what woke her up. Her body was long and taut like a firm rubber band, and in a sleepy haze she stretched out with a prolonged groan. Soon after, she pulled her tangled hair from her face and first one eye was purged of morning crusties, then the other. Curling her toes, tensing her calves, and stretching again, she placed her bare body on display. A childhood of ballet had carved her and leaned her down and now at college in her second year, she discovered her interests to be in the humanities, to the dismay of her mother's expectations and her father's bank account.

Flopping a clumsy, sleepy arm to her side, she felt the pillow next to her and found it to still be warm, but vacant.

Last night had been simply *amazing* and even the dreaded thought of calling her parents with the news couldn't dull her elation. She and Trevor had spent yesterday afternoon studying on the dormitory lawn, sprawled out in the fat blades of the Florida grass, and as the sun went down he had handed her a book out of his backpack.

"I know you like dark stuff," he had said. "It's by Victor Hugo. About a kid who is kidnapped, his face cut up, and raised as a circus freak. Don't worry, though. He kills everyone." Trevor presented it with his usual musing grin and Mary rewarded him with a snicker at his description.

"Well, the French love this writer so there it is," she said as she took the hardback novel from him. Quickly she realized it had a small lump in it. Shaking it upside-down, something fell out and glittered in the grass between her feet. Instantly Mary knew what it was and hesitated for a moment before digging for it frantically, tearing up green blades, dirt, and thick roots. Her fingers halted when she found it.

"Go on…" Trevor encouraged from somewhere above her. Mary lifted a simple gold band with a small solitaire diamond; a visually sad offering of a ring but the loveliest thing she'd ever seen. She began to cry.

"I read in one of your magazines that crying can be the best sign or the *worst . . .*" Trevor said, seeming anxious. "And don't worry about it being so small. I figured after we're married for a few years and have saved up I can buy you a new one and that little diamond *there* can be on the side or something."

Mary was crying full bore now. "Shut up," she squeaked as she grabbed him around the neck and held him in a loving grip. "Yes. Dear God, *yes*. Always yes. Yes a long *time* ago." After a few minutes of holding each other and rocking back and forth she added, "The ring is perfect. It's just *perfect*. I'd rather you save your money for down the road or something."

"My car needs brakes," Trevor confessed. His car was notorious for announcing its presence to every stop sign and stop light with a loud screech.

"Yeah, get your brakes." She laughed, trying to salvage her makeup while wiping tears away. Finally, she looked him dead on in the eyes. "Really?"

"Really. Marry me."

She bit her lip. "Okay, but I *so* have to fuck you like, right *now*."

Trevor mock sighed, and pretended to look about in search of a bush or trash bin to hide behind. After his pantomime was played out, they went back to her dorm room. Sometime between the giggling and the orgasms she managed to call her roommate and ask her to sleep elsewhere.

Pizza was ordered. His parents were called and they were delighted. The TV was on but was never watched. Drinks were mixed. Futures were discussed. Music was played and sung along to. And eventually they both slept naked, curled up in her small bed intended for only one occupant.

Mary rubbed her eyes while blinking against the morning sun that sliced through the blinds. Then she heard the shower, and assumed it was Trevor closing the bathroom door that had awakened her. She smiled, and pushed the thought of calling her parents far back into her mind. Sitting up, she looked about for her coffee that was left from the night before. "Trevor, have you seen my coffee? I had half a cup left somewhere around here."

There was no answer.

She started to wrap herself in the sheets to look around for her coffee, but with a whimsical chirp she stood out of bed, naked. "This is how I will dress when I'm walking around the house."

The dorm room was actually two rooms; essentially a sleeping area separated from a study area with two computer desks, a micro fridge, and a second TV. Mary stepped out of the bedroom into the study and gasped at how cold it was. She scampered back into bed with a squeal, her teeth chattering.

"Trevor, when you get back, bring me my coffee, it's in a mug on the fridge! From last night!" she called out. A muffled 'okay' came from behind the bathroom door while the shower turned off.

Mary's mind drifted toward more serious things. Would her parents pull her out of school because of Trevor? Where would they live? Who would actually pay for the wedding? Her parents certainly could, but would they? Who would the bridesmaids be? What kind of home could they afford? She felt the stress mounting, and wished Trevor would hurry out of the bathroom so that he could make everything better.

Chapter 2

Wyatt looked to the heads-up display that covered his face and saw that he was standing in Sierra Leone, West Africa, thirty miles northeast of Freetown. The year was 1994 and the sun stabbed spears of light through the leafy canopy overhead. The common thunderstorms of October had already passed, and the drier air made the leaves vibrant and the breeze less suffocating.

There was a serenity to the wilderness around him that was betrayed the moment he looked at the surrounding carnage.

Wyatt's feet were silent, even to the birds and insects about, and he softly toed his way among the spent shell casings and strewn viscera toward the table at the center of the abandoned rebel camp. Not a soul breathed except Wyatt and his partner, Rupert.

"We're clear," Wyatt said after clicking his com on with his tongue. Despite Rupert being a mere twenty feet away, it was the only way for them to verbally communicate. "I'm not seeing anything breathing within sixty yards of camp. What have you got there?"

With the hints of a crisp West Indies accent, Rupert responded. "I have a trophy table. I count twelve among the dead, but there are more trophies here than that number…so I suspect either prisoners were taken post-amputation or we're missing a stash of bodies…"

"There are tracks leading out of camp in several directions with blood and tar on the leaves. Maybe the assailants diced them and then dipped the wounds in one of the tar buckets and sent them on their way. Old Navy trick."

"Maybe …" Rupert replied skeptically. Wyatt looked about some more. Several of the shelters were built into half-dug mounds for keeping them temperate as well as disguised from the air, so he decided to explore one of those. Careful not to slip in the blood pools on the dirt-ramp that led down, Wyatt disappeared into darkness. "Looks like a makeshift armory," he said, as much for Rupert's ear buds as Wyatt's own records. "The usual. Some surface-to-air, AK's, kids' versions of AK's, mines, a lot of Russian made ordnance, but hardly from Russia … most likely diamond-bought from neighbors who in turn got them from the Ukraine…" Wyatt put his face as close as he could without touching the leaning rifle in order to try to read the serial number. "Yep, Ukraine. Made post-bloc and second or third hand."

Looking further, Wyatt found maps of the region on the wall as well as photos of various local women being gang-raped or beaten to death. A few pictures were of both at once. "These guys were RUF." Wyatt added finally.

"Clearly, given the year," Rupert said. "Check out the tent next to that building you're in and tell me what you think. After that, you'll really want to see what is on this table I'm looking at…"

"Wilco," Wyatt said, not unhappy about leaving the armory and its garish photography. Stepping back into the shafted sunlight, he could stand his full height, and spent a moment taking in the camp, as a whole, before moving on.

There were bodies *everywhere*. The black skin of the Sierra Leone rebels, in some ways, hid how much blood there really was. Blackened and baked, the bodily fluids had soaked into the ground and saturated the torn uniforms and casual clothes the RUF had worn. Some of the dead had their heads literally crushed into the dirt, collapsed with eyes bulging and tongues bitten off into the dust. Others had crumpled sternums, ribs crackled into spider-leg compound fractures jutting up from their chests toward the peeking sun. One man had his pants around his ankles with his genitals torn off and shoved into his mouth. It was clear that while under attack, they were in various stages of dress and preparedness. They had been taken completely off guard.

Wyatt was a veteran of many military and government sanctioned conflicts. Some of those conflicts never even had names. He had seen enough bloodshed and violence that he stopped wondering where his tolerance for it would stop. What he witnessed here was something entirely new. Trying to form the words to explain how astounded he was, Wyatt found that adjectives failed him. So he moved on to the tent that Rupert had indicated prior.

Instantly it was clear what the tent was. In the far back, at the center, was a small television. There were two rows of twig and straw beddings that lined the whole tent and all about were pornographic magazines, board games, empty wine bottles, and drug paraphernalia. Toeing around the bedding, tossed clothes, and bottles, Wyatt made his way to the TV and looked at the VHS cassette tapes. Rambo 2, various Jason and Freddy horror movies, and a few unlabeled tapes were present.

It was clearly a tent for training child soldiers, and at the center of it was a body crushed to the limit of human recognition, its spine bent almost ninety degrees.

Wyatt was familiar with the 'recruitment' process of snatching up refugee children, making them think their families rejected them, and desensitizing them through drugs, porn, violence, and cruelty. "Okay, but there are no bodies of kids anywhere." Wyatt walked through the back of the tent nearest the jungle's brush line and found a whole row of tiny tracks leading into the darkened depths of the distance. He was about to comment on how they clearly weren't running given the length between each footprint when he saw a new pair of footprints. They weren't boots. They looked more like bare feet. And the distinct prints were massive and deep compared to the small march of children's tracks. All led to the jungle.

Wyatt crouched down at the large prints to make sure his recording devices would pick up everything possible. He switched his HUD to heat vision, cycled through electromagnetic fields, and took a near-silent sonic 'ping' that would map out the dimensions of the print. The on-board computer displayed across his vision that the footprint had been pressed into the ground by over three hundred pounds of pressure at a whopping shoe size of eighteen or beyond.

Wyatt gazed out into the jungle, to wherever the large-footed person had guided those children, and wondered where and if he could see someone looking back. He allowed himself a moment.

"Okay, let me see this trophy table." Wyatt walked around the tent, always cautious of where he was stepping and how hard. To disturb anything *whatsoever* was a major concern. On his way, Wyatt found another print … large, perfect, and deeper in the front – as if the owner had stomped on the ball of their foot and pivoted… but there were no accompanying prints near it.

Mind still aflutter with the mental sketch of these large assailants, he wasn't quite ready for what Rupert had to show him. He stood across the table from Rupert, looking down at the large arranged pile of collected hands on top of it. Rupert was constantly tilting his head to allow his eye pieces to take detailed measurements and readings. Some fingers were broken and twisted, but nearly every hand was cleanly severed, some prior to death and some after. Wyatt sighed.

"This is the single largest act of anger I have ever seen. It's a bloody marvel."

He had finally found the words he had been looking for.

Chapter 3

Mary sat with knees together and both feet tucked sideways under her. She curled herself into the plushy red row of seats that looked beyond the brass railing toward the glass pillar at the center of the room. It was one of the taller rooms onboard Janus and at two stories high gave the illusion of being more open than most of the curved corridors on the station.

Dressed in sweatpants and an old FSU t-shirt, Mary's eyes were sunken with dark circles settled around them. She had been onboard Janus for five months, accustomed to no longer seeing the sun or having a sense of North, but the recent discovery had put everyone on edge. She sat alone now, staring transfixed into the shifting glow of the pillar before her while waiting to hear about Wyatt and Rupert's expedition.

"Yeah, I can't sleep either," Jack said, entering the room. He was younger than Mary by ten years, placing him in his early thirties. Handsome and pleasant, he had none of the stigmas one would expect from a mathematician. His mannerisms were neither rigid nor obsessive; instead he was social and physically fit. Handing Mary a cup of cinnamon coffee, he sat in the seat next to her to sip from his own mug. "I know that they went into the carousel and came out in the exact same second, so I can't fathom why we have to wait three hours to hear about what they found."

The carousel was the launching and recovery mechanism that was powered by the faux gravity distortion that the 'space' station Janus was built around. Within it, Rupert and Wyatt could drop out of null space-time, where Janus was located, and emerge at the targeted time in history in a specific alternate time line designated the 'Beta Line.' In this instance, it was Africa.

Mary was the archival historian on board, and Jack handled the math and programming of Oracle … the computer that read the timeline of Earth from afar and represented that timeline through digital imagery within the touch-sensitive glass pillar interface before them. Mary's job was to compare Oracle's data to her own compiled historical archives.

With a cautious sip, Mary tried her coffee. "While I appreciate how the lights soften during the evening hours here, I miss the warmth of the sun." Not wanting to sound like a complainer, she added, "But thank goodness for coffee. Thank you. I like the cinnamon."

"A poor man's method of getting around the bitterness. Anyway we should get Wyatt's presentation on that fracture in about twenty minutes." Jack leaned casually into his chair.

"Just so I understand …" Mary's eyes fixed on Oracle's interface that spanned the room's height. "Oracle spent the past five months scanning and doing the math for human history and found a bunch of …"

"… severe inconstancies."

"You used the idiom 'cracks' before."

"Mostly because they look like tiny cracks in Oracle's UI. See?" Jack said while pointing to a jagged little line glowing on the pillar. "*That* right there is 1994 outside Freetown Africa. It was one of the smaller inconsistencies that we found and there were no people present, so it was ideal for investigation.

"Has Oracle calculated my request yet?" Mary had found that one of the child soldiers from the specific RUF camp in question had grown up in North Virginia and had written a book about his childhood trauma. Mary wanted to know if, despite the anomaly, the book had still been written.

"Oracle can multi-task, but it might take a bit. I also cheated a little and told Oracle to look for the New York Times book review of that book you wanted. Least it will do is give us a quick idea if it was written. If the book *itself* changed at all … that would take more time and processor power." Jack took another sip of coffee. With a glance over his shoulder, he looked about to see if Ingrid or Gustavo were there. They weren't, but he still proceeded in a lower tone. "In all honesty, every request of Oracle is a long conversation these days. I think we had expected that once Oracle finished its full survey of the line, we would find it all highly familiar with only a few irregularities because of inaccurate historical data. Turns out we have all kinds of problems. Some *big* discrepancies."

"Like what?" Mary asked, wide-eyed. "More like the camp?"

"Wyatt and Rupert were going to address you and Ingrid on it, but might as well tell you now. There are entire generations missing. Literal generations *missing*. And in one instance so far I think we found a whole *town* that didn't exist in our line, but Orcale has it pegged."

"But how is that shocking? We're technically not looking at our timeline, just the one next door." Mary said.

"True, but given that each parallel line is only a fraction different than the one next to it, this is bizarre. Simply put, the only expected difference between this timeline, the Beta, and the one we come from should be a singular sub-atomic particle zigged instead of zagged *somewhere* in the universe. That should be all the warranted difference between one timeline, and its neighbor. Yet here we are, poking around in our nearest temporal neighbor and we find it is *vastly* different. And it isn't a smooth series of sequential events that lead to gradual differences … instead it is drastic."

"So what are you saying, Jack? What do you mean by drastic?" Mary could see where he was headed, but was impatient for him to get there on his own.

"Well, either time is not as stable a thing as we thought, suffering from internal 'time quakes' or maybe in a constant flux within each isolated time line. Given Ockham's Razor … I would suggest that we are hardly the only ones to develop some level of time travel. There could be other variables here."

Mary had nothing to say to that. She took another sip of coffee.

Footsteps on the carpet from behind gave away Ingrid's full-steam-ahead saunter. The woman was constantly working and always sporting a slight sweat, but she was never in a rush, only filled with purpose. Dressed in a worn Virginia Tech t-shirt and jeans, she took a third chair next to the silent Mary and Jack. She eyed them both, her vibrant cobalt eyes contrasting her olive skin and casual demeanor. Squat and broad, Ingrid was a weathered woman in her late fifties who had suffered too many insults and too many husbands to be upset by much of anything.

"Morning Mr. Miller … mornin' Ms. Forsythe." Ingrid's mild Appalachian accent twanged.

"Good morning, Ingrid. How are you?" Mary knew she sounded distant, but couldn't be bothered to feign more than a perfunctory interest.

"I'm curious. I'm guessin' you feel the same? Both of you?"

"I shared with Mary that little theory of mine," Jack confessed.

"Ahh …" Ingrid nodded in understanding, followed by a smile. "The evil-leaper theory?"

Jack showed a slight trace of resentment.

"Shame. Such a good TV show. Can't believe they had to jump the shark." She continued, "Anyhow, clearly since every timeline parallel to ours built Janus just as we did, it is clear that the universe is flooded with time travelers now. It is also highly probable that other nations aside from the US would one day gain the amalgamation of factors that would result in the construction of a similar station or a faux gravity-well like our carousel has. So whereas you are alarmed at the thought of fellow time travelers, I find it completely expected and honestly, a little comforting."

"Comforting? Entire populations have been shifted and many people no longer live! What if I had Oracle crunch *your* lineage? What if half your bloodline was gone?" Jack snapped in his defense. "These aren't tiny systemic changes that spawn larger changes over time … these are huge and cataclysmic left turns!"

Ingrid waved the idea off with one of her large, weathered hands. "People come and go. Whatever we experienced in our lives is what the Alpha Line projects. We are merely observing another timeline from a detached position between timelines. It's *going* to look bizarre. Think of how stupefied the first underwater explorers were when they saw deep sea volcanic vents? Or what the Spanish thought when they first saw an alligator, or imagine a Native American finding a T-Rex skull in a landslide seven hundred years ago… so what if it is more different than expected? There are still humans in this timeline, and the nations look the same and the weather, as well as the space program, humanism, etc. Life as we know it is fine in the Alpha Line where we hail from. Beta Line is the subject of our study."

A few moments of quiet went by, and Ingrid's disarming smile seemed to ease Jack's shoulders.

"Ingrid?" Mary asked. "Why would other time travelers comfort you?"

"Being alone is about the worst thing I can think of. Being alone in uncharted territory would scare me even more. If we make a mistake, like if Wyatt stomps on a butterfly in the Triassic, then hopefully someone else will fix it. And maybe we can do the same for others."

Mary looked down at her coffee. "Sometimes I honestly can't believe I'm here. I'm stunned that I was picked as one of the six people to do this and be here. It's … sublime."

Beyond the railing, below the three musing scientists, a door opened and Gustavo walked into view. He was a broad Hispanic man with scraggly facial hair and bright green eyes revealing a hint of Irish in his family line. "Heya, kids," he called out as he walked up to Oracle and placed his open palm on the pillar. It read his print and displayed his files on its smooth surface. With a finger he began flipping through them and with a double tap, he opened a file and the entire pillar illuminated a web-like series of points and connecting lines. After a few more double taps, a single point came into focus, reading 'Freetown, Africa 1994.' He opened that next, and began scrolling through the months, zooming past records of rainfall, wind direction and strength, animal movement, sounds of helicopters overhead, and finally a makeshift RUF camp being set up.

"That coding you used spruced up the crunch speed for Oracle's localized readings. This only took four days to compile. Pretty pro, Jack. Pretty pro, " Gustavo said casually with a pleased whistle. Gustavo Lopez was the leader of the other three sitting above him, and he had pioneered the physics of the gravity well which not only powered the station, but made time travel possible.

"How are Wyatt and Rupert?"

"They are good. They're washing off the suits now. Give them about ten minutes. I've been talking to them, and you know, it's never easy seeing a camp of that kind. They said it was pretty bad."

"Bad how? I checked the archives and that camp was reported to have been active for the entire following year. Did they get attacked? Oracle said it was empty—"

With both hands up in a mock motion of defense, Gustavo tried to slow Mary's questioning down. "Easy! We have a lot to discuss. The boys will be here soon and we'll hear what they have to say. And Rupert was his usual smiley self so no worries."

Gustavo nodded a motion of approval, and ducked back through the door. Taking a narrow passageway under the viewing balcony, he walked to join everyone in their plush seats.

"Maybe we're making a big deal of everything. What I mean is, I'm just an archivist," Mary confessed, trying to avoid sounding passively-aggressive. "It's just that this isn't following with the pacing guide we were given. We've lost a week and a half on this incursion."

"I think being at least cautious and vigilant with something like time travel is *well* within the realm of prudent," Ingrid reassured without being demeaning. Jack went to speak, but withheld his thought.

Gustavo entered from behind them, took his seat, and propped his feet up on the brass railing. Sensing the tension, he cleared his throat and spoke. "You know, I picked these chairs because my favorite movie theater in Austin had them. I even put the railing at the same height for our feet. I also picked wood floors everywhere to look just like their lobby."

Mary thought of how lovely Janus really was. She had initially expected a steel and concrete biodome—stark and sterile, but Janus had soft track lighting, a smart and visually appealing layout, comfortable wood furniture, and ornate patterned carpeting. Brass lamps hung in the dining nook and the kitchen was warm and accommodating. Each of the station's members had personalized quarters which catered to their needs and expectations. The image of a lovely Victorian cruise ship came to mind, and all that was missing were tiny port windows that would look out into the empty black beyond.

After some thought, this was the only room, the ops room, that felt like anything other than a lovely New England home. The domed ceiling, theater seating, and giant glass pillar dominated the atmosphere making it clear to Mary that she was very much away from Earth.

The door leading to the base of Oracle opened once again and the four in their seats fell attentively silent. Wyatt came out first. He was an unassuming man with minimal facial expressions and a simple, undefined physique. His eyes were gently alert, and each motion of his was simple, lacking gesture. Everything about Wyatt's immediate appearance, including his untucked, red flannel shirt lazily reached the sum of 'average'. Wyatt was an average looking man with an average demeanor.

Rupert Naseer, who was anything but average, followed Wyatt. At nearly a foot taller than Wyatt, Rupert flashed his winning grin at everyone; his white teeth contrasted against his onyx skin. Every inch of him was carved with physical discipline and training which lent to his confident swagger. He lit up the room.

"Morning everyone," Rupert chirped with sharp consonants. Wyatt stood by the pillar with crumbled paperwork in his hands. While Rupert spoke to the four above on the balcony, Wyatt thumbed through his documents and began poking around on Oracle. "We just came back from a ten standard-minute incursion into the line, and found considerable differences between that and our base line. The camp was empty and clearly there had been some kind of combat action. We still need to go over the gathered data, but there were a lot of shell casings on the ground and the firing pattern suggests that a superior force from multiple sides had attacked."

Wyatt brought up an image onto Oracle showing a distant and indistinct view of the RUF camp. Shell casings, bodies, and a few tussled chairs were the highlights. At the center of camp was a crisped body that had been burned beyond recognition.

"This is all clearly different from your findings, Ms. Forsythe. You said archives gave you a different story behind this camp," Wyatt observed.

Mary nodded, leaned forward to the railing, and pointed. "Not only was this camp active for another entire year, it launched several successful recruitment assaults on local towns. Did you find any child soldiers there, or a woman?"

Wyatt looked up. "Woman?" He recalled that all hands at the table were clearly adult male. "We saw no evidence of a woman. The children looked to either have been liberated or maybe they had escaped. Their shelter was relatively untouched."

"In Boubacar Baptiste's *Memoirs of Hell*, he described a woman at the camp with him. She was blinded and kept in a separate shelter for raping. I'm not sure where she would have been held, but he vividly described a long, off-white tent where he and the other boys slept. They were sometimes taken three at a time and taught to rape her as a group."

Wyatt shook his head as Mary spoke, but waited for her to finish before replying. "No presence of any non-combatants. No children or women were present at the time of our arrival until the time of our departure."

"So clearly …" Rupert cut in, waiting until all eyes were on him, "*this* timeline is different from our base line of origination. Much more so than any of us thought statistically possible." His bright white eyes, centers black like lightless voids, looked to Jack. "Could our mathematical approach to the contents of this line have been inaccurate?"

Jack sighed. He knew that his math work would be put on the spot. "For me to say 'no' would be foolish. But I still think the calculations are solid. This line should be as close to identical to ours as *possible* without technically being the same time line. I would even suspect its differences from us to be too small to measure. Other time travelers however, very much fit into our mathematical models as being highly probable."

Rupert nodded accommodatingly, but clearly didn't accept that cause. "Other time travelers are clearly a factor at some point, after all we developed time travel which means *others* have … but this doesn't hold any indication of that. And even if they swooped in, why would they attack a camp and possibly rescue civilians? With Oracle and The Carousel, change could be brought more subtly and far more effectively. Change someone's location. Make them sleep in an hour later. Slip a document into a desk. Things like that."

Gustavo nodded. "I have complete faith in Jack's math, Rupert. His anticipation that this, and the next several trillion parallel time lines to us are near identical, is very sound. I also offer up that trying to account for other time observers or travelers like us would be far too random a variable to account for accurately. Whatever time travel *will* occur, *has*. Other travelers are clearly a non-issue. What concerns me more—Wyatt could you zoom out to the line overview? Thanks. What concerns me more is why in the world does that time and place of the rebel camp look like a fissure on the mathematical landscape when compared to the rest of the line. And why are there so many fissures in other spots? Two dozen at least. So far, Oracle is scanning as far back as 1821 but if we can free up Oracle's processor power would we find even more of these fissures in history?"

Jack piped in when he had a moment. "I'm also asking Oracle to find long term effects on the timeline as well. Perhaps even the events are being changed backward along the line somehow, and we're merely watching the reverse fix."

Gustavo looked to Jack and blinked in surprise. "Well, then why the fixation on other travelers?"

"Because that prospect scares me. I can't account for it. It's the first thing my model goes to whenever something is out of whack."

Wyatt sighed, and began thumbing through his documents again. Rupert rubbed his eyes. "We've been up a long time prepping for this incursion, and we have a lot of things to digest. Wyatt and I uploaded the video, audio, and readings from the suits so you can look over them at your leisure. Let's get some rest, and then we'll look at this from all sides." Gustavo nodded and everyone in their plush chairs started to stir. Ingrid stood, stretched, and offered some good news.

"My turn to cook, everyone. I got a mean something going. See you for dinner at eighteen hundred."

Mary filed out with Jack next to her. Gustavo drummed his fingers on the railing for a bit while waiting for Ingrid to follow suit. When the door shut behind them, he turned to the two operatives below. "Your personal thoughts, gentlemen?"

"Jack can't be blamed for the math being off," Rupert said earnestly. "His model alone is an eighth wonder to the world; however it can't be correct under only five months of scrutiny."

"Eighth wonder?" Gustavo asked Rupert playfully.

His jest was returned with beaming teeth. "So sorry, *ninth* wonder to the world."

"And your thoughts, Wyatt?" Gustavo turned to the older man, unassumingly looking through his paperwork.

"I'm already thinking about our next unscheduled incursion. I want a bigger fissure, and this East Coast one caught my eye. And I think we will eventually have to risk being around people."

Chapter 4

She was sometimes overwhelmed by the silence of Janus.

Mary sat with legs apart, forehead bent to one knee, on a round carpet in the center of her room, wearing snug yoga pants and a fitted sports top. Leaning gracefully, her fingers gripped her toes so that the pull in her calf was taut, and after holding the position for a few moments, she gently swung her lithe body toward the other leg. Despite having given up ballet when she was young, the stretches and the physicality of it was something she always had enjoyed.

Whenever she moved the furniture (she *still* couldn't get her room here right), woke up suddenly in the night, or dropped something on her tiled bathroom floor, the resulting sound seemed to simply not travel. The voices of the others never found their way through her door, and despite the tons and tons of machinery, air-conditioning ducts, and generators, there wasn't so much as a *hum*. Complete and utter silence would ring her ears if she held her breath. It sometimes overwhelmed her.

The lack of sound gave a feeling of privacy and space that was vital for Janus' passengers given how long their stay was. Mary had also surmised that the insulation regulated both radiation and heat flow, given that Janus's core vented radioactive material and beyond Janus's spherical walls was complete void.

Not outer space … but complete void. Literal, complete void without a single particle or star save Janus itself … hovering there in the black with nothing to see it, and even if God existed in this artificial sliver of space-time there would be no light to reflect Janus' presence due to no source to produce said light.

Stretching helped Mary bury the thought. Ingrid had told her that twelve feet down from any spot she stood was pure nothing; a pure nothing that tugged at the spherical shape of Janus without being able to get a proper grip.

"The nature within Janus abhors the vacuum outside," Ingrid had said when she asked for help with the bread sticks in the kitchen during one of her nights to cook. "So much as a micro fissure in Janus' thick hide would cause a teeny-tiny vent that would quickly rip her whoooole rind right open. The balance that keeps us safe, aside from Janus being a perfect sphere, is the faux gravity well in the center. So in short, you have pure void below you anywhere you stand, and above you 'bout three hundred meters is a gravity-well strong enough to crush a concrete brick if it gets close enough."

Mary was certain that Ingrid spoke in awe and not with the intent of terrifying her while explaining the station's layout, but the description still had that effect. Ingrid had detected her worry quickly. "Sorry, it just excites me that I get to be part of it. Like I'm sure you get excited being part of it. Besides, I still don't think it is as crazy as sailing in a submarine. Tons of water crushing upon the hull while getting orders from the *military?* No, *thank you.*"

After her stretches were done, and her joints had that pleasant limber feeling to them, Mary stood and slipped on her sneakers. Despite being exhausted, she still couldn't settle on sleeping just yet. When the gentle chime of her quarters' door rang, it wasn't unwelcome.

"Sorry to bother you. I just wanted to come by and tell you that Wyatt requested a possible incursion into the Eastern Seaboard. We nailed down the year to be 1928 but I'm still crunching the anomaly to get the exact date, location, time, weather, etc. etc," Jack said casually while waving around his data pad.

Mary thought a moment. "Well … Albert Fish was at large eating children in New York then, I think … we pulled troops out of China …

a number of politicians were killed as well in the 'Pineapple Primary' in Chicago… who knows. It might not be any of those things given how small an RUF camp is in the grand scheme of things. Ah, almost forgot, Hoover took office the following year so he won the election that November. All those events might tie into the East Coast. I'll compile a rundown of that year for Wyatt and see where or when he wants to incur there."

Jack took everything in and nodded vacantly. "I'm going to go and try and empty my brain with Gustavo in the rec room if you want to join us. I'm also peckish for lunch."

"I'll pass. Thanks." Mary smiled. "I think I'm going to read a bit and conk out. I was up all night worrying about this incursion. Make sure I'm up in time for dinner?"

"Oh sure. Ingrid seems fairly excited about it. I think she got a full night's rest despite all the excitement. Pure *mashugina*."

Mary and Jack both shared a small laugh, said casual farewells, and then Mary shut the door. Walking into the bedroom of her apartment-sized quarters, she climbed into her bed, rearranged the pillows with cat-like precision, flopped on her tummy, and cracked open one of her many morbid novels for light reading. She had read this particular book many times since Trevor had given it to her. The jacket had nearly been worn off of it in the years since Trevor, but it was still her favorite book and her familiarity with its content made the ritual of turning its pages soothing. The thick ply of the weathered and yellowed paper made a coarse noise that had a distinct tone of comfort. She cherished the sound as her fingers slid along each completed page.

It didn't take long for Mary to fall asleep, face to the side and downward into her craftily located pillows.

Chapter 5

Jack loved being on Janus. It was like living on a geometric oddity, and often he would close his eyes and try and unravel its design within his mind's space.

From a mathematical standpoint, Janus was simple. Since Janus sat in the middle of negative space devoid of any heat, light sources, or gravity, it simply had to be a perfect sphere. Without a stable and perfect sphere, Janus would most likely burst outward from any flat, exposed side that any other shape would possess. The pressure within Janus was considerable, and the pressure outside of Janus was simply null.

Continuing this method of simplicity, Janus had to simulate gravity for the sake of the six people on board for their four year term. So, upon deployment, prior to having any staff onboard, Janus used venting thrusters on the outside of the station to begin its rotation. While the null space meant the thrusters had to propel for almost three months to get her moving in a consistent fashion, Janus eventually began rotating enough to centrifugally simulate gravity along her equator despite her faux gravity core. The living quarters were built along this equator in a long band on the inside of Janus' outer-most layer.

Hence gravity. It was an old idea, but it worked. Janus' gravity was .98 Earth normal at sea level.

A long hallway called the 'breezeway' stretched before Jack. If he were to follow it in one direction he would arrive at the same location in about forty-give minutes. The section where the living and working quarters were had lovely red carpet, lighting that dimmed to represent day cycles, and a near complete silence from a combination of insulation and noise-inversion speakers.

Jack began to walk toward the rec room, his fingers gliding along the wall. Coming to a cross section in the breezeway, he passed by crossing halls on either side. One led to Wyatt's room and the other to Ingrid's. Jack had never seen Wyatt's room, but Ingrid's was a surprisingly clean and tidy affair.

After a few minutes of lackadaisical meandering, Jack came to the open French doors of the rec room. It was an inviting room with bright wooden floors, comfortable couches, a huge screen with the highest definition, card tables, and several pinball machines. There were some snacks behind a dry bar along with soda and juice. Along the walls were photos of various American cities in their golden ages, and chalking a pool cue stood Gustavo, leaning against the pool table like a bearded shark.

"Yours is good to go," Gustavo said, motioning to Jack's plain looking cue. "I'll even let you break." He smiled.

"You say that like you have a chance at winning," Jack playfully retorted.

Jack did not lie. He was the pool-hall champion of the station, even beating Ingrid who proclaimed herself to be a pool-hall junkie in a past life. "Where did you learn pool?" she had exclaimed after Jack had soundly beaten her for the fourth time..

"Here, on Janus. Never play pool against a mathematician," Jack said with a grin, taking his cue in hand, and sinking three balls on his opening break. Gustavo and Jack fired their cues in turn, and as their game was winding down, Gustavo broke the casual silence.

"You give Mary a heads-up on Wyatt's new incursion?"

"Yep. She's getting some shuteye right now, but yeah, she knows," Jack said through his teeth while aiming his cue, lining his shot.

"This whole business has us all stressing overtime, and I don't want us burning out. Once we know what Wyatt's new fissure is, we'll take our time planning it out. We have all the time in the world after all."

Jack sunk his last ball, and set his sights on the black number eight.

"Oh … almost forgot to ask …" Gustavo grinned. "Yoga pants?"

"Lord yes. God bless yoga pants."

Chapter 6

Mary walked into the rec room and the smell of spicy, luscious jambalaya performed a sneak attack on her nostrils. She stopped in her tracks, breathed it in, and found the scent was so thick that she could open her mouth and feel the aroma linger on her tongue.

Jack and Gustavo were sitting at a long marble-top table, napkins tucked into their collars, awaiting Ingrid's Southern feast like they were in an Alka Seltzer advert. Mary walked past the TV and couches and up the three steps that led to the wood-floored dining alcove and regarded the two men with a smirk.

"You two need your knife and fork in your hands." she said. On Janus, everyone had to eat dinner together for the sake of solidarity and community. "Does Ingrid need any help in there?"

"We kept offering, but she kept shooing us out of the kitchen."

"Yeah, she had a knife. Something about a Southerner with a knife…"

"Gonna make you squeal!" Jack slurred.

"Like a piggy!" Gustavo retorted.

Mary slipped into the kitchen while the two gentlemen continued to recite the infamous scene from Deliverance. She hoped to avoid any potential pantomiming.

The kitchen was a large, polished steel and industrial affair. Unlike Janus' hallways and quarters, the vents and ceiling fans here hummed as the moist steam-laden air was pulled upward, carrying the dense aromas of spicy tastiness. Ingrid stirred a huge metal pot with a giant ladle while the pasta appeared ready. She glanced sideways and saw Mary.

"Those two fools out there being themselves again?"

"They were telling stories of how the South will rise. Need any help with anything?"

"Actually, yes," Ingrid replied graciously. "I have some garlic bread in the oven. You could get it out and arrange it on that plate over there." Mary, mitt on hand, lowered an eye-height oven door and pulled out the tray loaded with slightly crisped garlic-drenched bread.

"My *god* that smells good."

"I made a point of getting cozy with the supply admin when they were stocking up the dry goods and freezer. I have a lot of surprises over the four years we are here … I have meals planned and hopefully some people will trade their nights to cook with me so I can take care of holidays. We're having duck this Christmas!"

Mary was delighted. "Will something like that keep? I mean Christmas is six months away…"

"Duck and most frozen stuffs will keep for about a year. But I've got stock and a few freezer/defrosting tricks that I can't divulge. Duck the first Christmas, and if you can keep a secret …" Ingrid paused while observing Mary, wondering if she would comply with protecting her dietary divulgence.

Mary nodded with an amused smile as she gingerly piled the garlic rolls on a large serving plate, her fingers dancing about to avoid being burned.

"… duck this Christmas, turkey the next, then ham, and then finally *lamb*. I saved lamb for last because it freezes the best. I've got an amazing rub for it, too."

This sounded good to Mary, and it cut through her remaining fatigue instantly. "Know what one of my favorite vegetables is? Brussels sprouts! Roasted with a bit of lemon."

Ingrid nodded in approval. "I bet that would work especially well with the ham I have planned. My second loved sprouts."

Mary figured Ingrid was referring to her second husband … the second of four. "After I lost the first one in Iraq," Ingrid had once confessed, "the other three marriages were just me holding tryouts."

Jack and Gustavo fired out a tandem belly laugh from the dining room alcove. Rupert's crisp voice was heard, encouraging this laughter, with a story that had dissolved into broken sentences laced with his own giggle.

"Best feed the savages!" Ingrid laughed while lifting the huge pot from the burner and carrying it carefully into the alcove. Mary followed, armed with garlic bread.

Wyatt was also sitting at the table, watching the exchange between Rupert, Jack, and Gustavo with a pleasant, yet distant, smile. It was one of the few that Mary had seen Wyatt possess, and when it came it, was always restrained and similar to that of an outsider's. As for Rupert, he was all teeth; grinning and giggling while he enacted the rest of his story with gestures and motions punctuated by laughter. For some reason, he had a cloth napkin twirling over his head and a balled fist on his hip.

The scent of jambalaya calmed the room. "And that was that …" Rupert managed to say with a tinge of amused rue, wiping his eyes. He took his seat next to Wyatt. The head of the table was reserved for the cook. Ingrid poured a red wine, leaning between everyone with a large bottle. They were each given one glass, to sip throughout the meal. Mary sometimes missed evenings when she could let her hair down and have three or even four drinks in a sitting, rare though those nights had been. On Janus, bottled wines and drinks were all on timed locks in the storage cabinets.

Everyone quieted, their heads craned and noses forward as they sniffed deeply. Jack pulled Mary's chair out casually for her, as he often tried to do. A moment passed. An exhaled sigh breezed among everyone as they all accepted that to stay consistently sane, they would have to let go daily of their stresses and excitement relating to Janus and their minute-by-minute discoveries. They had to be just folk, sitting for dinner.

"Let's eat!" Ingrid chimed. Bowls were filled, wine was sipped, and garlic bread was scarfed. After the initial savoring, Rupert finally managed to speak with a bit of food stuffed into his cheek.

"Delicious, Madam. Just *delicious*. I once had something like this with sausage instead of chicken."

Ingrid had yet to eat, and was instead surveying everyone with muted delighted. "Actually, a lot of times it's served with chicken *and* sausage, but I skipped the sausage for another night. Maybe basil sausage spaghetti with peppers, one day? I also didn't want to make Jack eat pork."

Jack's eyebrows rose. "I love pork. What do you mean?"

Gustavo snorted back a laugh, foreseeing the coming conversation. "I thought you were a Jew," Ingrid confessed apologetically.

"Well, I'm not so much a Jew as I'm kind of… Jew-*ish*." Jack's play on words elicited a groan from Gustavo and Mary. Wyatt was eating his jambalaya with laser focus. "Honestly, no man is born Jewish, he is merely conscripted by his mother. I love me some bacon."

"God's chosen one," Gustavo playfully pelted. "*I* was born and raised Catholic in central Florida. Been trying to recover ever since."

Rupert nodded. "Methodist, here."

"What's that?" Jack asked.

"Catholic lite," Mary clarified.

There were nods around the table.

"Baptist. Southern. And *scary* Southern," Ingrid offered up. This was not a surprise.

"Agnostic. No church on our Sundays. Just mowing the lawn and weeding ," Mary said between bites of her third piece of garlic bread. After a moment of silence, all eyes slowly drifted to Wyatt. His jambalaya was almost gone, and it was clear he would be focusing on seconds. When reaching for more, he noticed the attention his omission had conjured.

"I'm somewhat insulted you guys even have to *ask*…" he said while half-standing and scooping more for his bowl.

In semi-unison, the rest of the table looked at each other. *"Lutheran,"* they proclaimed just prior to bursting with laughter. Wyatt's smile widened.

When dinner was finished, everyone cleared off the table and piled up their dishes. Jack and Gustavo shoved Ingrid out of the kitchen insisting on doing the cleanup. Gustavo made the case that the kitchen's heat vents would help expel his 'jambalaya exhaust'. Ingrid, having suffered multiple husbands prior, offered no counter argument.

Wyatt sat in a rocking chair that he had brought from home and plucked on his guitar while casually looking at some music on a stand next to him. It was usually something by Cat Stevens or Roger Whittaker but tonight it was Alison Kraus. Wyatt was too shy to sing most of the time, but Mary had heard him do it before whenever he got lost in the song. She found his voice calming, and thought Wyatt a comfortably peaceful man.

Rupert and Ingrid played chess by the unlit stone fireplace. Ingrid could win every time, but she would throw the game on occasion to try and keep the scores even. Ingrid enjoyed the play, not the victory and Mary suspected that Rupert knew this. The two would hardly focus on the game because of it, and instead talked about Janus' inner workings and design choices. The conversation was hard to follow because of Mary's lack of context, but it was clear that Rupert knew much more about the station than she initially thought.

Jack and Gustavo eventually exited the kitchen and switched on the huge TV. They booted up what looked to be a very old hockey video game from the late 80s. Their pixel-heavy players had taken their helmets off, dropped their sticks, and were engaging in stiff fisticuffs within nearly a minute. As amusing as two geniuses playing Nintendo was, their provided commentary to the actual game was even more so, including such wonderful phrases as: "How many pixels are used for your teeth on the ground there?" "I will beat you like it's my job and business is *good*." as well as "Your bender's going to *eat* my biscuit!" Mary was not certain what the last one meant, but it was delivered with gusto.

The rec room was alive, and the bright but soft track lighting and stone-laid walls gave it a cozy cabin feel. Each couch and loveseat had a similar look in order to match the sparse décor of the room, but they individually had a different feel so that all tastes could be accommodated. Mary tended to gravitate toward the plushier of the love seats and she would normally sit after dinner with her ankles curled under her bottom, knees together, and book in hand while subtly watching everyone else. Tonight was no different, and she read *Dr. Jekyll and Mr. Hyde* while observing the fun and listening to Wyatt's strumming.

An hour and a half went by, and Ingrid was the first to retire. Rupert, soon after, claimed it was time for his workout and he escaped to the gym. Gustavo and Jack also succumbed to the need to be 'responsible adults' and went to work out some math on Wyatt's incursion request. Wyatt continued to strum his guitar as Mary fell into her book, almost literally so given her exhaustion. It seemed like merely a blink of her eyes, but she awoke with a start to find the room's lights dimmed, a blanket over her, and her bookmark placed in her book next to her feet.

Chapter 7

The Cabinet was a lightless cylinder. Its cramped and isolated space was only accessible via a narrow passage that Mary took, her body half sideways, as she squeezed in. The curved, cylindrical wall was covered in sound absorbing mesh, and fixed at the center was a spinning chair with speakers by the headrest. Despite being so confined, the six-foot-wide space didn't feel cramped due to thoughtful airflow and cooling, and Mary honestly enjoyed working in the dark, secure place without interruption.

After the passage hatch closed behind her, she rested for a moment and enjoyed the complete black. Mary found something serene about the lack of stimuli. After a moment, she gathered herself, focusing on the task ahead, and when her ears started to ring with the drone of complete silence Mary finally spoke.

"On."

The black cylinder revealed its entire shape via a paper-thin grid in red, projected into the air around her like a subtle cage.

"Open folder titled 'MARY' and bring up Fingerpoint U.I. macro *'four'*."

The tiny image of a folder blinked in front of her and white text scrolled under it stating her macro had been loaded. Reaching out, Mary stuck her fingers into the folder's center, making the image ripple like thick liquid. She then spread her fingertips to expand it, bursting the folder into many different folders with various labels. With a light tap she opened one that was empty.

"New folder. Sub *incursion*. Label ..." She thought a moment. "*Wyatt request."*

The folder expanded in front of her. She spun around in her chair to some software links hovering behind her. Digging her fingers into a few of them, Mary dragged them around to her front and into her new folder. Several of the tools were for time lines, data requests from Oracle, and video links.

Mary was about to command the cabinet to interface with Oracle when a pleasant chime interrupted her. "Answer," Mary said.

"Sorry to bother you, Ms. Forsythe," Wyatt started politely. Mary smirked at his manners. When it was work, Wyatt referred to everyone by last name.

"Hi there, Wyatt."

"I was going to wait until later this morning to chat with you one-on-one about my incursion request. But it looks like since you're up so early I might as well take some of your time now. Assuming you're available."

"What time *is* it?" she asked, baffled.

"Almost four-thirty in the morning."

Mary swore under her breath.

"I can't get used to sleeping on Janus either." The echo of Wyatt's voice within the illuminated cabinet gave it twice the authoritative calm. "No real change in the air, only in the lights."

"I suppose you were normally a morning person? The kind who was catching fish before the sun was up?"

"Sometimes. It was a cover for not being able to sleep. Which is the same as it is this morning. I only know you're awake because I've been toying with Oracle in Ops."

"Jack said yesterday that you wanted the Eastern Seaboard."

"That's true, but I wanted to speak to you in person initially."

"And why is that?" Mary allowed suspicion to creep into her voice.

"I'm got a very tall request that stretches the limits of our initial operational guideline. This will skirt the border of our conduct parameters, and before I sell it to the rest of the team I want to make sure all the homework has been done on it. You handle the first steps in the incursion process, so you're the first person I have to sell on it."

Mary appreciated Wyatt's candor and thought of his wedding band. Did his wife appreciate such candor as well?

"Tell me the whole thing and we'll see how I react."

"Right. I want to set up an incursion for mid-August, Washington DC, 1928. Something high overlooking Pennsylvania Avenue would keep us away from the crowds, and if we need to go in early morning to avoid being seen, that would be ideal. I also want to see how *long* I can incur for. Looks like a parade happened then. Oracle says a lot of people are converging-"

"It's a Ku Klux Klan parade, most likely," Mary cut in. She had been digging through compiled newspapers for the day and region as Wyatt was talking. "My archives have about 140 photos I will send to you. And I have some video, maybe." As her fingers flitted through the holographic projections of media, she stopped at one item with a giant 'Coca-Cola' banner being carried by several klansmen. "Just from gleaning the head-lines it was a huge parade. Tens of thousands, maybe around 65,000, and it isn't the first time. Another big one was in 1925, but this was the largest they had before the Democrats started distancing themselves more and more from the group. Klan membership started tanking in the 1930s."

"Oracle said there were a lot of people, and that explains it. Oracle also gave me a clean weather report for those two weeks before it seized up. There is a *huge* temporal fissure there. I'd guess several times larger than the fissure we encountered at the Revolutionary United Front camp Rupert and I investigated. And this time, I want to incur before the schism happens and not after. I want to see what is happening first hand."

Mary pondered this, putting her feelings and thoughts together. At first, a flat denial of any more research into the matter almost came to her lips, but instead she felt that Wyatt at least deserved to be listened to. It also occurred to her that being in the cabinet meant Wyatt couldn't see her face to gauge her reactions to anything, giving Mary an upper hand to the conversation.

"All right, I have some questions …" she finally said while spreading out her arms wide, surrounding herself in a cylinder of photos filled with Klansman, proud and flag-bearing.

"Please ask them all, Mary. I need you entirely on deck before proceeding."

"If the schism event resulted in the death of an entire RUF camp, does it stand to reason that many similar deaths will occur during the DC incursion?"

"Yes."

"And you wish to record and witness that event?"

"Yes."

"What are the odds that you yourself will be caught up in it or killed?"

"That is completely unknown. Rupert and I have the cutting edge in stealth technology, but that is clearly relative. Another variable is we don't know if we are dealing with a force of nature or a combat unit of some kind. I very much lean toward the later, but who knows."

"Jack might offer the theory that an unforeseen temporal distortion of sorts is causing this."

"And it is stacking up human hands on a table in the middle of camp? I don't think so. Mary, I've seen a lot of combat zones and there was a *lot* of anger in that one."

She began scrolling through the pictures, strumming them and making the whole room spin about her. "The area isn't that built up in 1928. Are you hoping for a high and clear view of the area? Avoiding trees and such?"

"Yes. Out of the way."

"How long are you hoping to stay?"

"I want to be in before dawn, Beta Line-time. And we'll have the call buttons ready for when or *if* we need to pull out. Oracle is already building the ripcord protocols, but I'll need Jack on board to do the math given the variables involved. I won't put Rupert or myself on the line if we can't ripcord reliably."

"Here's my last question ... what will you do after you figure out what is doing this?"

"We'll do whatever we have to, I suppose."

Mary sighed and ran her fingers through her hair. "Let me get all these photos in chronological order and then I'll send them to your inbox. After that, I'll try and compile how many famous or prolific people are there and tag them in your HUD so while you incur, you will avoid interaction with them *at all costs*."

"Wilco, Ma'am."

"I'll need two days at least to give this all some thought and go over things. Honestly, I am very hesitant to send you two in there. I wish we could send a ROV or set up a camera."

"There's a reason why we have nothing like that. Remote operated vehicles break and malfunction and leave themselves behind as evidence. Rupert and I are professionals. I appreciate your concern for our safety and most of all your concern for the line's integrity. Please take all the time you need, and alert me to any concerns you have. I need to know what this is, and I need to have this smooth."

There was a pause.

"What do you like in your omelet?"

Mary was a bit taken aback by the change in gears. "Feta, spinach, and mushrooms."

"Want me to bring it to you, or will you come and eat in the nook?"

Mary smiled. "Bribing me with food?"

"Like I said, I need you sold. I'll have it ready for you around five a.m.

Ingrid is usually up by then too. I'll have coffee ready as well."

The audio link clicked off and Mary sat in the darkness, surrounded by marching armies of the KKK frozen proudly in time, thinking about what Wyatt had asked for. A highly risky incursion into a populated area was a tall order. Deep down inside, Mary trusted Wyatt too much to think he had asked for something he didn't believe necessary … but there had to be more to this.

With a swing of her arm, all the KKK photos stacked toward the floor. "Wyatt. Station access folder. RUF footage." In front of her, the footage from Wyatt and Rupert's incursion into Africa began playing. It started with their soaring through the air, arms wide as they prepared to pull their chutes. There were two screens of footage playing; the one on the left was from Rupert's perspective and the one on the right was Wyatt's. "Fast forward two minutes." Both frames of footage sped toward the ground rapidly and suddenly they were in the trees, their views spinning wildly about, and then the viewpoints spun about the camp with dizzying speed.

She had already seen this just before heading to dinner last night. Rupert spent time poking around the table of gathered hands. Wyatt wandered about, and the sight of the children's tent wrenched Mary's heart for a second time. "Slow to normal speed." Everything went to normal pace. "Turn up aud—no wait, show life signs." A third and fourth window emerged under both frames, showing breathing rates, brain activity, and the blood pressure of the two men. "Drop Rupert's. Just show me Wyatt's footage feed and vitals." Only two screens remained. "Zoom footage to moment of highest sustained heart rhythm." Instantly the footage zoomed back to the skydiving in the beginning.

Mary frowned. "Show me … show me when Wyatt had the largest adrenaline surge during the entire incursion." The footage spun forward to a moment where Wyatt saw nothing but the ground. It was a single frame. Looking at the graphs below the frozen still, Mary could see that his respiration had temporarily stopped, his adrenaline spiked, and his heart was aflutter. "Play five seconds prior to this frame, with audio, and pause at five seconds after this current frame."

The footage played, and the view was clear, steady, and Wyatt was staring intently at something on the ground. Soon after his staring, his view shifted about wildly as though searching for someone in his peripherals.

Mary paused, zoomed in on the ground, reached into to the footage with her hand, pinched her finger and thumb as if she was holding a pen, and drew along the outline of the footprint that Wyatt had been focusing on. Using another tool, she cut the footprint out of the frame, dragged it with her hand to the side, and rotated the estimated plane it was on until it was flat in front of her.

"Okay … I got one for you … and I don't even know how to ask for this exactly, but let's see how you handle it … given the context of the footage, frame, and zoom of the recording from Wyatt's blink interface, what shoe size would this be approximately?"

The numbers '18-20' appeared below her edited image of a footprint. It struck her as odd that Wyatt would fear a footprint.

Chapter 8

The dining nook was a semicircle comprising the back wall of the rec room. The table was long with a marble-tiled top and each chair was made of sturdy wood and soft cushioning. The alcove was elevated slightly from the rec room, and the floor was made of a polished, light colored wood that was ideal for echoing Rupert's crisp accent and Gustavo's belly laugh. Along the curved wall was a detailed mural of rotund and frolicking Italian revelers partaking of some wine and food.

Mary sat there with her warm cup of coffee in her hands, staring at it. Wyatt came through the swinging kitchen door and placed a plate of breakfast in front of her, and a second plate in the empty spot across the table. Sitting down, he looked her over briefly. "The coffee okay?"

She came out of her daze. "Yeah, I like room temperature coffee. Just a thing. I'll spend a whole day nursing a cup."

Wyatt nodded. "So *you're* the one with all the coffee rings in the cups. I see a few in the kitchen now and then."

Mary smiled as she took a bite of egg. Wyatt leaned back, making himself comfortable, and draped his arm around the back of his chair.

"I miss fishing," he said wistfully.

After chewing thoughtfully, Mary contributed, "I miss the Wall Street Journal."

"I miss taking my rowboat out onto the river."

"I miss sunbathing."

"I miss going to the movies by myself, surrounded by laughing strangers."

"I miss rain."

"I miss snow."

"I miss a full moon. Or thunderstorms. I miss thunderstorms."

Both of them stared at the center of the table. "They said it was unnatural for mankind to be in space," Mary added with a smirk.

"And here we are, in a fold of empty space-time, between parallel time lines, in a complete dead zone. Largest and most astounding leap of the human race and no one back home even knows about it except maybe, what … a hundred people?"

"Something like that. Only us and a hundred that know the whole picture. Everyone else just has pieces. They know enough to handle their jobs."

"How did your family take it?" Wyatt asked, his eyes locking to hers. "What did you tell them? Granted, you'll only be gone to them for three months, but …"

"Honestly, I had no family to tell. I'm single, and I've got some casual friends, but my father died a few years back due to a bad heart, and my mother and I don't often talk. How about you? What about your wife?" Mary pointed at his wedding band.

"That's a bit messy, I guess," Wyatt said, looking for the first time ever a bit uncomfortable. "My wife and I are separated."

"But you obviously plan on getting back together."

"Well, I don't know really."

"Wearing the band is a sign of respect then?"

"Oh sure. I think it's also a thing of habit. I'm a creature of habit…" Wyatt trailed off, his eyes overlooking a distant life.

After a moment, he reset the conversation with a clearing of his throat. "You have any questions about my incursion?"

"Many, but I don't think you could answer them. I need to hold out on my opinion until I hear about this from other sides. But I understand why you want to do it and to be honest … I'm kind of excited."

"Really?"

"It constantly disappointed me that whenever we were entering our scheduled incursion times and locations, there weren't any people nearby ... something just seemed like a lost opportunity. Now you get to be there ..." Mary suddenly looked around. "Want to know what I *really* want?" she asked with sudden enthusiasm. Mary didn't give Wyatt a chance to respond before she proceeded. "I want *your* job one day. Janus took a fifteenth of America's budget to build, the funding secured by an induced economic downturn, so I know that this four year operational period won't be the last. I'm an archivist *now* ... but maybe in the future I can be a spook like you."

Wyatt grinned from ear to ear. "I gotta say it is mighty mighty cool. My father always talked about astronauts and how they were the heroes of *his* father's childhood. Imagine how many kids, if they knew what we did, would love to grow up and explore time... ancient Egypt or the Indus Valley..."

"I know, because of the suit, that you don't really feel the wind or breathe the air when you incur... but my god just to *stand* there, Wyatt... I envy you."

Wyatt took her kind confession with a welcoming and humble nod. "Funny you say that, every time I get near the carousel I shake in terror."

Mary ate her omelet, relishing the spinach and feta while Wyatt stared off into space, maintaining an accommodating, yet vacant, smile.

"What *is* your plan for getting everyone else onboard?" Mary asked.

Wyatt showed her twenty minutes later by calling Ingrid to join them. Ingrid found the two of them sitting at the nook with a plate of pancakes waiting for her. Diving in, mouth half full, she suddenly became suspicious.

"Damnit you two, just *ask*."

While Mary carefully began selecting her premeditated words for the potential 1928 incursion, Wyatt plowed forward. "We want your opinion on something difficult."

Ingrid's eating didn't slow. "Well make it fast. I lost another probe this morning making it three in the past month. I have to catalogue the entire failed recovery procedure so that NASA can tell me how bad I am at my job when we finally get home." Her ability to chew blueberry pancakes and rant at the same time seemed well practiced.

"We want your opinion on Rupert and I incurring into a highly populated area filled with civilians during one of those temporal tears we're finding."

Ingrid's chewing slowed. She looked to Mary. "So, he sold this to you first? The hardest sell I assume?"

Mary nodded. "I think our purpose here is to explore, and we have to know if our understanding of the line is at all inaccurate."

With a slow swallow, Ingrid looked back and forth between them. "I don't have veto power over purposed incursions. You two and Gustavo do. Why try and sell me on the idea?"

"We honestly want to get your opinion before we talk to anyone else. I'm more concerned with the carousel. How fast can we ripcord out of the line?"

"Well, is this before 1939? If it is before 1939 it will be a faster ripcord."

"It's well before 1939. No FM stations, no high-power television broadcasts, nothing."

"It would be faster then. You'd have about a ten second wait after hitting the ripcord if you stood still. God knows how long Oracle would take to pull you out if you're moving."

"I've got all that. But ten seconds isn't bad. Much better than the near minute it took for us to ripcord out from the 90's."

"I have to say…" Mary broke in. "If you think for a moment that you need to ripcord due to being spotted or to interacting with the populace we simply cannot do this. As it is, there will be a lot of people around. The only option is to have you in prior to dawn, have you land perfectly, and then stay until you've seen what you need to see and get out."

Wyatt nodded, and opened his mouth to speak.

"I'm not finished." Mary put her hand up firmly, stopping him. "If you or Rupert miss your chute mark, or if you or Rupert even make a loud discernible noise, or if you two don't burn your chutes properly you need to ripcord immediately, not only will I demand that, but I know Gustavo will as well."

Wyatt simply nodded in acceptance.

"I can try a dry run with one of the probes," Ingrid added, distant while chewing a fresh forkful as she was working out the details. "I'll drop it into the middle of space somewhere and program it to signal Oracle. I'll make sure it's moving at a good clip too, to make Oracle work for it. So we'll see how fast it will get yanked back. If you really want to try and shave the time down, though, you've got to talk to Jack."

Which was what they did thirty minutes later.

Jack just blinked at Mary and Wyatt when they proposed their position to him over a hot plate of breakfast. Ingrid had remained quiet while eating her own Wyatt-made omelet. As if Wyatt hadn't just dropped the bomb on Jack, Ingrid groaned with pleasure at the taste of her breakfast. "Wyatt, you are a diva with food, sir. Good on you."

"Okay, so let me go through this bit by bit." Jack eventually arrived at how he wanted to respond. "Instead of going to see one of these rifts after-the-fact, you want to see what one looks like while it is taking place? So instead of Africa post-fissure, you want to go to Washington DC *during* a fissure?"

"Yes."

"First off, I would really like to hunt for a smaller fissure in a far less populated area that won't directly impact the eventual building of this station within that time line."

Wyatt nodded, taking note. "What else?"

"Secondly… I don't even know if Oracle can read into these fissures correctly. For example, we left our Alpha Line with a very clear idea of what it looked like. We travel into our neighboring timeline, and find that Oracle has to run off her prior data from the Alpha Line, since this one is so *radically* different. There is a chance she may not even crank up the carousel if she can't get a clear idea of what she is sending you into." Since day one, Jack had referred to Janus' computer as a 'she.'

"May I play devil's advocate?" Wyatt asked.

Jack gave a reluctantly welcoming gesture with his hand, his omelet going cold in front of him.

"Thank you. Let's assume we choose a different location that doesn't have nearly as many people or nearly as much risk. Let's just focus on the second part regarding Oracle not liking something it doesn't see …" Wyatt waited until he saw Jack's shoulder's drop a bit. "Could you simply tell Oracle to drop us into the air, and not even to examine our landing zone? Basically, could you make our LZ waaay up in the air so it won't take issue with the fissure at all and we'll just chute in higher up than usual?"

Jack huffed. "Yeah, that's easy to do. But I have to be honest here. I don't like this." Jack's eyes wandered to Mary's.. "I know I should argue everything on scientific grounds here, and I still will because of my concerns over your ripcord, but I simply think this is unnecessary. I don't think you need to be on the ground for this one. Maybe if you incur, pull your chute and then *ripcord* before coming close to the ground? That would fall much closer to our safety regulations. I would feel much more comfortable with that. Or try and see one of the smaller rifts from ground level. It's just going into Washington DC… populated… so much can go wrong …"

"If we did a number of less risky incursions into or around these fissures, wouldn't those multiple incursions amount to a larger risk than merely taking one long, hard look? You would be introducing a lot of unnecessary variables by going in and out so many times. A single riskier action verses multiple smaller risky actions… which would mathematically work out in safety's favor?"

Jack sighed. "Risk hardly adds up like that. But I could toy with some statistics on it. But you've got your heart set on this?"

Wyatt nodded.

"And you do too?" He looked to Mary.

"I haven't vetoed it yet. I've also researched the area fairly substantially and there's a building top that looks fairly clear. They will keep their hands on their ripcords, and they will be in position prior to dawn in an unpopulated zone, chutes burned and all."

Jack looked hard at her. Ingrid chimed in with what she felt was uplifting news.

"I bet Oracle can recall a probe moving around three hundred miles an hour, while rotating, within twenty seconds of the ripcord being pulled. I've been thinking about it over this heavenly chow."

Jack turned to her, wide-eyed. "How do you manage *that?*" he asked.

"I didn't." Ingrid smiled. "You told me Oracle could learn. So I'm going to have her dump and recall probes into the deep of space near the outer edges of the Beta Line's solar system. She's going to keep doing that until she gets the time down. If she doesn't get better at calling them back, we'll just call the whole thing off."

Jack permitted himself a tiny smile. "Granted, there are far more variables involved on the surface of Earth than in deep space... but that is still surprisingly optimistic."

"You wrote the program yourself, Mr. Math Maven. How can it *not* work?" Ingrid's nose crinkled in mock delight at Jack.

Jack was pleased at Ingrid's confidence in his system and Wyatt saw the opportunity.

"Honestly, Jack... you have to be curious. This will answer so *much,* far *faster...*"

"Just because I might be curious, doesn't mean Gustavo is."

After everyone had their fill, Wyatt cleared off the dishes and was elbow deep in the sink when Gustavo entered through the swing door. "Jack said you wanted to chat."

"I did. Sorry that you came all the way down here, though. I was going to pester you while you were working with Oracle."

Gustavo leaned his back against the counter. "Nah, I could use the break. Everything that Oracle is telling me about the Beta Line is just… I wasn't ready for it. Besides, I could have Oracle track all these fissures, but it's pretty busy with some recent pending requests and I didn't want to eat her power."

Their eyes met knowingly, Wyatt withdrawing his wet hands and drying them on a towel.

"You know I wasn't trying to undermine you," Wyatt confessed.

"I know, I know… you wanted all your ducks in a row. And the fact you wanted to present a solid case to me means you still respect my veto. It's okay. Besides… I know what letter you keep in your locker."

If Wyatt had lacked the discipline to hide his surprise, Gustavo would have had his suspicions confirmed.

"I want to go into DC." Wyatt pushed forward.

"I know, I've been trying to comb alternative sites that would give you a big enough temporal discrepancy without being as risky, and there aren't many. This is the largest, single move that would tell us what is causing these cankers. But this incursion isn't what concerns me."

"What does?"

"What happens next. Let's say you see something specific occur. We'll be tempted to anticipate its cause and then try and solve it, therefore interrupting the timeline. The very first rule we had would be broken. On the other hand, we have no idea if our own timeline is infected with whatever this is. We certainly have never perceived these cankers, but since we can't examine the Alpha Line for the simple fact that one can't interact with their own line, we can't tell if they are natural or simply isolated pockets of paradoxical time like carbon pockets in a diamond."

"So… you are resistant to examining a potential threat because you might discover it is either threatening… or benign?"

Gustavo snorted with amusement. "I guess so. Either way, the more we get involved in this, the worse it gets. The more we examine this, the more we influence it and fuel the fire."

"I'm sorry, Gus, but you're speaking in theoreticals…"

"I know. I know. You'll go to DC with my full support. You and Rupert will come back safe. And we'll see whatever it is you saw and we'll be baffled or stunned or horrified. Then we'll argue about what to do next. That argument is what concerns me. You'll pull out that letter or whatever it is that you have that will *immediately* change this from a government project of scientific research to a military facility and then overnight everything changes…"

"I can't promise anything, Gus."

"I know."

"But I'm not looking to endanger anyone or anything. I'm prudent. However, we have to see what is literally happening within the line. You know that."

"I don't disagree."

"Then you're okay with this?"

"No veto," Gustavo said. Clearly his decision had been made for some time. Both men remained silent; Gustavo looked sullen with his arms crossed. He now realized that his entire vision of the four year maiden 'voyage' of Janus was now usurped.

Wyatt stared at him, trying to gauge what kind of resistance to eventually expect from this. "We incur in two days. Mary's got the spot nailed, Jack's been working on the ripcord, and Ingrid is flooding the tank and getting the carousel prepped."

Gustavo nodded absently while Wyatt quietly left.

Chapter 9

The prepping chambers for incursion were close to the carousel, several levels above the living quarters of Janus' spherical structure. There were three locking vault doors, and as Rupert and Wyatt completed the needed steps within each chamber, the next door would unlock to allow eventual access to the carousel itself... the device that made dropping out of space-time and emerging into another timeline possible.

No one was allowed in but them.

The first chamber was a large workshop where they checked equipment and maps. Two long, curved tables were draped in scattered documents regarding protocol, record keeping, operational procedures, and data on the incursion site itself. A row of vacuum-sealed steel lockers lined the far wall, a single one of them open with cables running into it. On several wall-mounted screens flanking the square room were scrolling photos and illustrations of the time period, and through an overhead speaker Mary conversed with them.

Rupert was already naked and putting on his cup with organic adhesive while Wyatt poked around with a holographic map of Washington DC. "So, we'll be on the Archives building about forty minutes prior to dawn's first light and the parade itself will be later in the morning along Independence Ave," he said as he took his last sip of water before taking off his flannel shirt.

"Don't sound so disappointed," Mary prodded Wyatt over the speaker.

"I'm not. It's a good location with a decent view. It's a bit far, and we'll have some obstruction in spots but that's the spot you chose. No complaints." Wyatt kicked off his sneakers and unbuckled his belt.

"Shame. I was hoping you'd complain so I could put you in your spot and remind you how this is all happening because I backed you up." Wyatt smiled as he continued to strip down. Rupert was done adhering his cup and began lotioning himself down.

"Tell you what. When I get back and we all pour over what Rupert and I see, we can argue all you like."

"Won't do you any good, Ms. Mary. You do not argue with this man."

Wyatt gave a mild look of disapproval to Rupert. Rupert shot it right back, finger extended, at Wyatt's bare body. "You haven't shaved recently enough…"

Switching the mute button on, Wyatt protested. "I shaved two days ago. Some of us just grow hair faster than others. Shaving again will irritate the hell out of me, and with the suit on for so long it will be unpleasant."

Rupert shook his head. "The Army must have been hell with you getting a five o'clock shadow by lunchtime."

"Heh. Yeah. *That* was certainly the greatest challenge of my service." Wyatt switched mute off. "Sorry, Mary, you there? We were talking about The National Archives."

"No, you were talking about shaving."

"Wyatt's manscapers are on strike. I hear Jungle noises, Ms. Mary!"

"Oh dear lord. Does the mute button not work?"

Mary sighed. The playfulness was a welcome diversion to the stress everyone was experiencing. While Rupert showed nothing but his usual chipper self, Mary could tell that Wyatt was concerned about what he might find. It was a rabbit hole, and Wyatt had persisted his way into it and now he couldn't get out.

"So, I picked the Archives because according to some old shift schedules, few people are in the building the day of incursion and there isn't any roof maintenance scheduled. There was also a memo I found from a year prior stating that the building was not available to the public during large parades or events, so it should be more secure than most. Also, its distance should make it ideal for a larger view of the situation, despite parts of the avenue being obstructed by buildings, trees, and so forth."

"I completely agree," Wyatt said, running a wet, cold razor over his chest quickly.   Rupert nodded in approval, but raised his eyebrows in inquiry and pointed downward. Wyatt offered Rupert the razor with one hand, while lifting his genitals with the other. With a snicker, Rupert threw his hands up and walked toward the door to the next chamber.

When his cup was affixed, body lotioned, and the rest of him bare, Wyatt joined him. A moment later, the vault door hissed and automatically opened. "We're heading into the next room, Mary. We'll be offline for about thirty minutes. See you on the other side."

The second chamber was where they put their suits on.

"I noticed over the past week, you no longer call her 'Ms. Forsythe," Rupert observed as he went to his side of the room and stood under his faucet.

"I'm trying to get over myself, really. I need to be more relaxed and social. Maybe take a page from your book." Wyatt did the same, placing his feet in indents made specifically for his own unique measurements; flexible tread with glue facing upwards connected to his toes and heels. Both Rupert and Wyatt gripped the wall-mounted holding bars to their sides and stood as still as possible.

"I also noticed that you placed her on mute while we discussed your marvelous, manly body."

"I will pull rank on you if you keep it up." Mechanical arms came out of the wall and ceiling, surrounding both men.

"I simply think it is romantic. The slightly forbidden nature of being here while falling smitten with a younger woman, you yourself separated…"

Wyatt was silent. Prying one eye open, he examined Rupert being sprayed down with the black liquid colloid. "Exactly how much of my records were you allowed to see?"

Rupert, realizing he had found his limitation with Wyatt, dropped all pretense of charm. "Everything, best of my knowledge."

"Then you should have had the sense not to try and size me up with a comment like that."

"Yes, sir. It won't happen again."

Rupert wasn't Wyatt's first, second, or third choice as a partner for his tour on Janus. This was never a source for animosity, but it was clear from early on that Rupert was looking to make a career off of this station whereas Wyatt was finishing his. There was often some level of sniffing each other out, which was natural, but something about the excessive charms and handsomeness of Rupert put Wyatt ill at ease. He never liked political animals, especially when he had to work with them.

For the next thirty minutes, the two remained silent while they were bathed in black, thin gel that was warm to the touch. Afterward they were blasted with cool air to semi-harden the gel to their bodies. Layered wiring was then meticulously wound over them like circuitry by the mechanical arms, circling their joints and following their muscle lines. After another blast of cool air solidified the on-board systems into place, each man had a facemask lowered from the ceiling. With open mouths they accepted it, biting down hard to keep the face shields on while their heads were lathered and layered in the same gel.

The gel hardened. Cold air blasted them from below and above. Despite their faces being blank and featureless like a Dutch painter's manikin, they could see fine and their voices could easily be heard in each other's ears.

"Booting up the Blink UI …how does yours look, Rupert?"

"Solid. Checking spectrums now." Both were now featureless, solid black men without distinction, save for their physiques. "Counter noise working too." Each suit was layered with micro speakers that would anticipate noise made by the occupant and counter that noise with inverted sound waves.

Wyatt moved his elbows, then stomped his foot — it made no discernible sound. "Same. We're good." Moving his eyes around at his heads-up display, Wyatt double-blinked to open his side menus to make sure his maps and logistics were loaded properly. While doing so, a small video feed of Mary popped up bottom center of his field of view.

"Looks like you two are good to go."

"Almost there, Mary." Wyatt's 'Mary' almost came awkwardly, but he'd be damned if anyone's perceptions of things was going to affect how he treated people. "I'm fine in UV, night, heat, and nerve." The various spectrums of the suit's means of vision could see heat, special light, power sources, and even the nervous systems of animals and humans alike. If it breathed, moved, or even once did so recently, Wyatt and Rupert could see it.

"Same here. I'm also online," Rupert confirmed.

The next vault door unlocked, allowing them to chute up.

Earth rotated at over one thousand miles an hour whereas Janus was a stationary object that utilized centrifugal force to simulate gravity. Simply put, if a human individual were to use the carousel to travel to the surface of a swiftly spinning planet like Earth, they would be reduced to a liquid smear within a fraction of a second.

To avoid this obvious and hideous problem, every incurring human had to jump with a parachute approximately six thousand feet above ground to ensure survival. Oracle must also spend extra time not only accounting for possible air traffic, depending on the era, but also simply *birds*. Incurring into Earth's atmosphere from a relatively stationary location outside space time *into* or directly *in front of* a bird would instantly kill both parties involved.

And the parachute itself posed its own challenges. The ribbon chutes used by Wyatt and Rupert were of a clear fabric that obscured their arrival, and upon landing, they burnt themselves to their most minimal atomic components in a smokeless smolder. It was hardly a refined method of time travel, and despite air vehicles and unmanned drones being suggested and designed, in the end, sending a full-blooded human proved to be the most reliable and efficient. While the ribbon-chute was the best and most easily destroyable design, there was no way it could handle the upper winds, hence the six thousand foot ceiling of incursion.

"Please confirm verbally that BSR was observed," Mary said as Wyatt and Rupert checked their chutes. During the ten minutes this took, their suits turned from black to a gray and then, with an internal flow of electricity, the two of them began to appear clear.

As Wyatt checked his chute, the adjustment to his hands visibly disappearing posed a sublime challenge. He had yet to become comfortable with his hands slowly drifting into a reflectionless, glass-like appearance before him. As it happened, he paused and held his fingers before his face as though to say goodbye.

Mary watched from her cabinet, seeing what they saw now. Switching to a closed channel with Wyatt, she commented, "I don't think I'd ever get used to that either."

"A little part of me is always afraid that I won't come back."

"Like the Invisible Man…"

"Something like that. We're almost done here."

Rupert's chute was on first, and he walked over to Wyatt so he could have a second pair of eyes. They checked each other over. Both men were good.

"BSR observed."

"BSR observed."

The final door opened before them.

It was a plain cylinder of a room; smooth and concave along the sides. The floor was a round hole into nothing with what looked like a diving board and railing leading out to it. Despite looking like an infinite oubliette, this was the carousel.

Rupert stepped forward first, placing one foot on the welcoming end of the protruding walkway.

"You will arrive above DC at 4:20 a.m. Your HUD will direct you toward the archives building. You will stay on that roof until 10:34 a.m., at which point you will ripcord and Oracle will extract you. Confirm."

Both men had to repeat what she had just said, one at a time.

"Good luck to both of you gentlemen. And please be safe."

"Thank you, Ms. Mary," Rupert said prior to bolting down the runway and swan diving into nothingness as though he had barely been restraining himself from doing so.

"Talk to you in just a few minutes, Mary," Wyatt said, ill at ease, and following.

Wyatt dove in, and thirty seconds later both men arrived at another chamber on the underside of this one, flying into a cushioned pool of liquid to slow their descent from Earth's rotation.

The liquid that caught them began to immediately dissolve their sprayed-on suits, turning the pool brackish. Rupert broke the surface first, gasping and gagging as he pried off his mask. Wyatt stayed under a moment, smoothly swimming like a shark to the ladder, and climbed out. Pulling his facemask off, he stumbled to his feet and began walking to the com on the wall by the decontamination seal, his suit dripping off of him in diluted clumps. After two tries, his thumb found the talk button.

"Mary, I'm sending you all the data from both our masks ASAP. You guys go over it while we're in here and then we'll all talk."

"Are you okay?"

Wyatt hesitated. "Yeah, but you need to see this."

Chapter 10

The screen went black as Wyatt passed through the carousel; small lights flickered in the distance like stars. Two screens, side-by-side, displayed Rupert and Wyatt's recorded video feeds with the time index labeled at the bottom as well as a simple digital compass expressing the direction each recorder was facing at all times.

The tall room that housed Oracle had been darkened except for floor lighting, and crowded near each other sat Ingrid, Gustavo, Jack, and Mary. Mary had a small data pad in her lap so she could reference her stored information on the incursion with a scrolling menu next to the streaming video feeds. Jack and Gustavo sat stoically as they stared unblinking at the overhead projection. Ingrid, looking only half-interested, still had her AR goggles on, pushed up on her forehead by her greasy hands, as if she were merely taking a break from work to watch something on TV.

"So, the incursion was fine and the location was perfect." Wyatt's voice echoed into the hall from his decontamination chamber. "We dropped in well before daylight and took position and waited for the approximated time while crowds gathered, etc, etc, etc …" The image overhead began fast forwarding, presumably by Wyatt, until it came to the parade of KKK members and enthusiasts in full swing.

Mary found mild delight in seeing something from 1928 occur in crisp, high definition footage, and in *color* no less. While some photos from the turn of the century did display color, it was an arduous process that few had managed, and here Mary got to see the live action behind all the static photographs she had sifted through over the past week.

Instead of being a gray, bland box, the Coca-Cola sponsor truck was a vibrant red. It was surrounded by children and teeming with men and women selling their product with enthusiasm. The band was sharp with polished brass, their key signature pushed up unwillingly by the morning's nippy air. The marchers themselves were grinning, polite to each other, and joyous in their large reunion as proper wives kissed their cheeks and children ducked under the folds of their white, ghostly robes.

That moment, or rather the anticipation of that moment, was exactly why Mary was here.

"So, the parade marches forward for a while, and out of sight behind this structure *here*." Both frames paused, and a white streak from a giant invisible marker went across the overhead project, pointing at a building. "Now be sure to watch here."

It unpaused. The lead of the parade, banners firm and flags high, marched just of sight. Then there was slowing to the steps of the parade as it started to jam... a few people paused and stretched their necks to see ahead... some of them tugged back on their hoods to get a better look forward to what remained out of sight from Wyatt and Rupert. As their heads craned and the atmosphere of bafflement took hold over that of pride, Wyatt paused the video again.

But he didn't speak. It was silence.

Jack looked at the time index. "This is still almost forty seconds prior to the both of you ripcording," Jack said half to himself.

"Right. I wanted to make sure we all understood that the crowd was observing something for at least ten seconds prior to the event. Whatever that something was, it was ahead of them, out of our view, and not all of them saw it. You can see that the middle and rear of the parade continued marching until they became crowded in by those lagging in front of them." Wyatt cleared his throat. "I'm going to now put the next few seconds on a loop. Seven seconds in total cycling through all the spectrums recorded from both our units."

The video continued playing, showing what looked to be a large object tearing down the street and reducing much of the parade to a red, smoky cloud.

No one made a sound.

It was a large chunk of either rock or metal, and it blurred despite the recording equipment's high frame rate. White robes were torn from bodies and blood and limb were reduced to mist as the projectile sundered not just the people, but cracked straight down the street itself, tossing roadway into the air behind it. Trees toppled, one catching fire, while lampposts bent and glass within the entire area, including Wyatt and Rupert's location, burst.

The object gave off minimal heat at first, but friction gave it a molten glow as it neared its destination; a building which a moment later, came down.

It had no high-powered electrical components and it carried no electrical charge until it was near its destination.

It gave off no light except a slight, friction-induced glow near the end of its violent and swift journey.

The four of them sat agape. "We rip-corded once the dust cloud of that building coming down obscured everything." Wyatt played the rest of the feed after the impact, no longer looping, and Mary shuddered when she heard the yelps, cries of alarm, and the various claims of disbelief among the people sitting on the lawn and benches.

The footage ended with sudden tunnel vision, leading to the water tank; Wyatt and Rupert curled into a ball prior to impacting to avoid joint and limb damage from the liquid surface.

Mary slowed the footage prior to the object, and began looking over it on her data pad frame by frame.

Gustavo leaned forward on the railing, challenged by what he saw, yet remaining unintimidated. Jack's brow was furrowed. Ingrid took her goggles off.

"All right, let's look at this…"

"My guess is it's at *least* twice as fast as a bullet. And there is no visible smoke from the projectile," Ingrid said. "And I heard it break the sound barrier."

"And we can see the far side of the building it came from and it is vacant except for observers for the parade. Whatever it is, it originated behind that building. Whatever launched it is there, out of sight, and in the road blocking their path."

"What could launch something that fast, without a 'boom' or explosion to propel it, within such a small frame of space. It would have no—"

"Right, no real time to accelerate down a barrel or through magnetic rings. And it looks like it was very much aimed."

"So we agree," Wyatt said. "This is an intentional weapon launched at these people."

Gustavo covered his face with one of his large, hairy hands. Jack took pity on him, and answered in his place.

"We agree. It's a weapon. And it will warrant more study, but the projectile is most likely simple, yet the propulsion method clearly is not."

Ingrid interjected, "There is no way that Oracle can send you back there Wyatt. No way. Not within at least a year to the same region. It hates the math, and all of the safeties on the carousel will kick in, possibly locking us out for the remainder of Janus' deployment."

"I understand that."

"I just want to make sure you don't get it in your head to nab the projectile from under that building. You'd have to wait until it was retrieved by the populous some time later, and transferred to another spot," she clarified.

"I'm not concerned with the projectile. Nearly nothing came off of it anyways, and whatever clues we could get from the propulsion method were either burned off by friction, impact, or dissipated near the time of launch."

Mary was partly hypnotized by the data pad's still images of human smear and screaming shock. "I'll see how this event impacted the line, and see if there are any other witness accounts that can tell us what happened behind that building."

"That will take some time and processing power. I would like to consider that as our first route. Gustavo? What do you think?"

For a moment, Gustavo seemed relieved. "Yes… Yes, that's where we should begin looking. We'll set the query. Mary will make the request in Oracle and Jack and I will set the search parameters."

"You'll be in decontamination for a bit longer, but afterward I'd suggest meeting up in the rec room if anyone wants. I don't know about you, but I could do well with being around people for a bit," Jack said. "Besides, if I recall it's my turn to cook anyway.

Chapter 11

Jack had his hands covered in flour, spices, and steak sauce while Gustavo had his arms folded as he leaned on the counter staring out through Janus' thick and distant bulkhead and onto oblivion.

"You uh, done with the onions there?" Jack asked, attempting to jar Gustavo back to the moving world. Through the closed kitchen door, hushed voices could be heard at the table as everyone discussed precisely what they had all agreed not to for dinner.

"He's going to take this from me…"

"What?"

"Wyatt. He's going to take over the station. I'm going to lose it."

Jack sighed, flopping several more thin slices of steak into his flour bowl, rolling them around. "Voice it, Gus. Voice it all."

"I know that whoever invents the great next step doesn't get to keep it. I completely understand that. Tesla, Lovelace, Marcus … I just wish I could have held onto this for a bit. I wish these four years would have been mine … that the maiden voyage of trans-dimensional travel would be sailed under me."

Jack threw some more steak into one of his pans. "Do you have anymore? Anything else there?" he snapped.

Gustavo was a bit taken aback by the restrained hostility in Jack's voice. His wide eyes must have revealed as much.

"Good. Because now I get to straighten you out." Jack inhaled, loading his verbal cannon and aiming it over his shoulder at Gustavo while he continued fiddling with the searing steak. "First off, this isn't about you. Secondly, this isn't about *you!* If Wyatt pulls out the letter that you are so afraid of, it won't be a vote of no confidence in you, or a demotion or a judgment of your abilities. It will only be produced because the mission of this station will have changed and Wyatt will handle *that* specific mission whereas you are to handle the civilian one."

"I do understand th—"

"Don't interrupt the ranting Jew," Jack commanded, fork pointed at Gustavo. "Thirdly, you never invented or entered this project with the intention of any recognition whatsoever. The American populace has no idea what is buried under West Virginia or that a whole city's worth of metal and energy went poof in the night. We are top secret, so even if this technology leads to planetary colonization and whatnot, the common man will *still* never know your name."

"It's not about the—"

"Clearly I'm not done!" Jack, with a flick of his wrist, tussled the steak from the pan and onto a larger serving plate before loading up more floured meat. "And here's the big one … you are seriously forgetting the man who has the combination to said locker holding said dreaded letter… is Wyatt. This guy is well tempered, as inquisitive and reckless as you, I might add, and he actually is fairly trusting and respectful. Wyatt isn't some jarhead. This isn't his career making assignment. Ten bucks says they had to drag him out of whatever log cabin he was spanking his inner moppet in to get him to do this assignment. He's fucking Clint Eastwood in Firefox! Chopping wood and sporting a Selleck 'stache! So …" Jack took a softer tone, still brandishing his fork. "Dig your head out of your southern exit and get over that this is not about you. If Wyatt sees this as a threat to national or, I don't know, *human* security, then I will most likely agree with him. So will you."

"I'm just…. come on… can't you figure out how I'm feeling? I don't think how I feel on this is *wrong*. I'm not making any decisions; I'm just voicing my concerns *personally*."

"I know how you get, Gusto … I am not indulging you on that road.

You need to be here one hundred percent. Because, if you want to talk about feelings, I'm scared as shit. While a gathering of anti-Semites being annihilated may not be a bad thing, and while West African rapist, slave driving—"

Jack halted, almost lowering his hand into his searing pan. "Holy shit, that's it. Holy—" He ran to the door and threw it open. The dining table was covered in data pads, printouts, pens, computers, and various coffee and tea cups. Everyone looked up at Jack, interrupted in their musings and worries.

"It's a message."

They looked at each other. Mary spoke up first.

"I think so too."

"How so?" Rupert asked.

"If someone were to try and actually change anything they could do so far more subtly. They could place a document in a certain spot, or make several prominent people privy to some vital information or something. Like Rupert said. Perhaps even a single assassination via accident. But whoever did this fired a fucking cannon ball down the road, bowling for whitey, and toppling a building in the process. This and the previous RUF camp slaughter all hardly puts the 'b' in subtle."

Wyatt turned to Mary. "Makes sense. Why did you reach the same conclusion, Mary?"

"Because the amount of time between the parade slowing and the weapon launching was far too great. I think whatever fired made sure it showed itself to them prior to doing so. Again, to send a message. Any technology that we're dealing with didn't have to fire that weapon so dramatically."

"Like executing someone from the front, rather than from behind," Rupert added. "You want them to experience their execution, not merely *die* from the result of it."

"So let's recap here," Jack said, trying to wipe his hands off with a towel hanging from his waist. He stepped out of the kitchen, leaning his back against the swinging door as an invitation to Gustavo to enter the fray. "We are dealing with a power as technologically able as us, knowledgeable of history, given that it has targeted two groups of fairly shitty people, and it is dramatic and spiteful."

Gustavo gathered himself and breathed deep. "While two points make a line, I think we need a better idea of that line and its possible curve. We need to see more, I think." He looked to Wyatt. "We'll get Oracle crunching as best we can."

"I agree. And we should start compiling options for a third incursion … but let's be cautious. I don't want to be standing on a building when it goes down."

Chapter 12

Wyatt and Rupert went through their routine, but this time with far less banter.

Suited up, parachutes fixed and ready, Wyatt jumped first with Rupert soon after.

It was nighttime, and the full moon illuminated the wooded hills far below. Free falling into the night air was peaceful, and not a city light was in view. "Thirty meters apart this time. Separate trees flanking the tree in question," Wyatt said into Rupert's ear from afar.

Both men pulled their chutes, clear plastic with black veins networking throughout the fabric, as they deftly drifted toward an open field at its wooded end. Touching down and rolling just outside the tree line, both men ignited their chutes and watched them smokelessly disintegrate into the tall, still grass.

By this time their polymer suits were completely clear, and the clock was now ticking down until the effect would wear off. Looking around, Wyatt's augmented reality interface scanned the trees, took sonic mappings from seemingly silent pings, and began synchronizing their location with their global charts within their head pieces. "This way. Four hundred meters. We have an hour to get set up."

Silent as fawns, they crept through the muggy forest, moist branches and dirt squishing under their tread. Each wet snapping of a twig was countered with an inverted sound wave from micro-speakers lining the outside of their legs, making the sound almost imperceptible to even the sharpest of nocturnal ears. Coming to a sparsely wooded expanse near a far tree line, both men began looking about. Very little brush grew here and the trees were tall, making it an ideal place.

"I'll take this one to the Northwest here," Rupert said, ending his sentence with a grunt as his clear, silent self began scrambling up a thick tree trunk. Wyatt searched about and found a similar tree and began a less swift ascent. Crouched, silent, and patient, both men waited.

It was close to six in the morning when the first gathering arrived. Five men, two carrying a table and the rest with satchels over their shoulders, came stomping and huffing through the woods.

"Good as any, right here!" the oldest and gnarliest of them hooted. "Put that table up right there. Use the rope that's under an inch there. That one. *That one*," the older man commanded while pointing. "Don't be a dullard. Find a tree and scale it. Get it up there, Scrambles."

The gangly man being addressed nodded vacantly and began climbing a tree between Wyatt and Rupert's trees. The long, manila braided rope dangled from Scrambles' belt as he huffed and grunted.

The table was set on the flattest ground available, and a wooden fold-out chair was placed for the older gentleman. He parked himself with a self-important huff and smiled. "This will do nicely. I heard Judge Morris from the Blue Ridge will be coming on down, and Governor Brown is already in route with the rest of 'em. This is a great moment, gentlemen! A great moment." The older man was seemingly addressing a much larger and more attentive crowd than was present.

But soon that crowd emerged. Cameramen arrived with their tripods and large wooden carrying cases. Families, deputies, several firemen, and more and more regular folk arrived. Barbeque grills were wheeled in, kegs posted up and tapped, and someone played a fiddle while others danced about. The old man, lord of all at his thin wooden table and folding chair, smiled with pleasure as he shook every hand he could. Well wishes were exchanged and congratulations were offered.

The pitched torches' light slowly gave way to an early summer sunrise, and soon after a new cause for excitement hit the two hundred-strong crowd, their long shadows folding and converging deep into the wood.

"They're here!" Scrambles yelped with a cracking voice as he tore through the crowd, bouncing up and down with a finger pointing toward the distant road. "They got him! They got him! They're here!" The older man found cause to stand with arms open and greet the arriving group of armed men. To cheers and encouraging shouts and blessings they hoisted their shotguns and rifles into the air in triumph. As the armed lot, suspenders high on their shoulders and their flat-caps on straight and forward, marched through the parting crowd, Wyatt's UI identified Leo Max Frank.

Frank was a pale string-bean of a man, who could easily pass as a boy from a distance. Clad in simple pajamas, his face had taken on a stoic numbness as he was led by both elbows firmly gripped. Willingly, his bare feet trudged forward, muddy and black. Someone dragged out a camera case, large and solid, so the good Judge Morris could stand above all heads and watch.

The crowd enveloped Frank. Through the swarm of faces, flailing hands, and general ruckus neither Wyatt nor Rupert could keep track of him. "If the purpose was to save Frank, it would have been done by now. He's too embedded into the crowd at this point."

"So, no dramatic rescue then. Look for a punishment instead," Rupert said, his crystal clear body high in his tree, the morning sun beaming right through it, unfractured and unbent. Wyatt looked to him, his UI outlining Rupert so he could be identified.

"Good thinking. I bet whatever happens levels these people… and now I'm regretting being so damned close. Be ready to ripcord."

The noose was ready. The crowd was frantic. A cart was wheeled around, horse oblivious. The knot was forward under Frank's chin, holding his head high. His sleeves were tattered and torn, individual scraps taken as keepsakes to mark the special day. Cameras were repositioned, flashes ready to produce postcards for the local stores.

The cart was withdrawn with a slap and a whoop. Frank dropped, a previous wound on his neck opening up, firing blood into the crowd as his head snapped back in an ungodly direction. Feet twitched. The faux burlap skirt he was forced to wear shivered under his convulsions. The crowd cheered with delight, their pressed linen shirts gleaming in the morning sun as hats were waved and mothers hoisted their children to see. With a jerk, Frank's body spun as the last spasms of life rustled loose from him. Scrambles and others raised him higher for all to see before tying the rope off.

Standing tall on his camera box, the good judge tucked his thumbs into his suspenders and smiled with glee at the justice. Flanked by the seated sheriff and proud governor, he began his speech. Wyatt and Rupert were now looking about frantically, scanning the outer trees and sky for any sign of trouble.

"Checking statics… I'm getting nothing. No machinery, nothing," Wyatt confessed, frustrated. "You got anything, Rupert?"

"Not out there. Maybe something will happen within the crowd?"

The Judge's voice boomed under them. "Finally!" He hollered. "Finally the good and Godly state of Georgia has shown that it can treat its Jews just like its Niggers!" His prime sentence was followed by another holler, but not one of joyful self-ingratiation … but one of shock and horror across the crowd.

The heat sensors in Wyatt and Rupert's HUDs went bonkers. From somewhere behind the Judge, a jet of searing liquid fire erupted and poured over him, toppling him into the gathering. The spewing flame craned over half the crowd, distorting vision and blackening raised arms in a feeble attempt of self-preservation. Mothers clinging to children fused with them from the melting heat as they crouched down, drying within their charred outer shells. Men writhed in the pine needles and sparse grass, the cooking flame contracting their muscles and curling them into positions of macabre genuflection.

Rupert's tree was on fire. "Cord. Now." Wyatt was halfway through his command when he saw Rupert vanish out. Clearly Rupert had given the command seconds earlier. Per protocol, Wyatt had to as well but he had come too close and too far to leave without satisfying answers. He stood in the tree, leaning about and frantically searching for the source of the flame.

Smoke was everywhere. People had scattered, fleeing into the clearing beyond or to their cars. Leo Frank's body was the only peaceful thing amongst the carnage, swaying slowly in the rising heat of his tormentors.

A quivering, charred body with recognizable bits of a plaid and unscathed shirt crawled on the ground, unaware and certainly far too much in shock to grasp its current death. It groaned as its few intact fingers dug into the grass, trying to escape toward some undetermined salvation. Out of the smoke, a huge form gracefully strode; tall, white, faceless, and toting a small flame thrower strapped around one shoulder.

With a single stomp, the form crushed the crawling man's head into the thicket, its thigh bulging with force. The haze of the heat partially obscured it, but Wyatt could see. He forgot that he was recording everything, and all his instincts kicked in. He sized up the tall biped. He noted its knees, ankles, wrists, and joints, looking for weak spots or covered places.

It was unusually tall, highly lean, muscled, and hairless. The face revealed no expression and it was missing the basic features of mouth, nose, and ears … but it had a distinctive brow and high cheek bones. With two wide, rose-gold eyes of a solid and consistent color, it scanned about looking for more crawling survivors.

Its gaze landed on Wyatt's tree and drifted up … slowly… the pilot flame still flickering on its flame thrower. Those giant, metallic eyes blinked, shocking Wyatt with a sudden shudder of inhumanity. He felt fear, and suspected that despite his invisibility it would somehow see him.

He activated his ripcord, gripping the tree firmly while its head tilted higher toward him, the reflection of the licking flames dancing in its eyes.

Three seconds passed . . .

Was it looking at him yet?

Five seconds . . .

Wyatt got ready to dive off of the tree, prepared to take his chances with gravity over the spurting flame.

Eight seconds . . .

It was now scanning the branches that held him.

Wyatt's ripcord activated, and he hit a wall of cold liquid.

Chapter 13

The rec room was still.

Mary sat in her loveseat, feet under her, staring off into space. She hadn't changed her sweatshirt or loose jeans in two days and her hair revealed as much. A cup of stale coffee sat in her hands at room temperature… layers of rings recording her progressive sipping throughout the day.

Gustavo was at the table in the nook, overlooking the rec room, sifting through several data pads and printed charts. His brow was wrinkled and his large fingers moved in a frenzy, occasionally spilling a paper or two into a chair next to him or onto the floor.

Jack was tapping his fingers against his knee, drumming out his thoughts into a coherent strand. Within minutes of seeing the footage from Wyatt and Rupert's incursion into 1917 Georgia, he had begun trying to figure out a new calculation for plotting incursions that were not originating from Janus herself.

Ingrid sat with a large data pad on her knee, scrolling through schematics that detailed the power grid. She had announced that she would work on ways to increase the number of incursions from two to three a week… but really she was trying to find a way to provoke an early return home by porting all of Janus back to Earth.

Rupert sat with a pad pouring over Wyatt's footage on repeat, scrutinizing the tall thing holding the flamethrower with one hand, pale foot stomping the head of its victim into the smoldering dirt like a snake. He too was trying to evaluate physical weaknesses, freezing the frames that focused on the weapon.

Wyatt sat strumming his guitar, playing a vacant tune as if to merely test his fingers' calluses. He was the first to break the silence.

"We have to paint a picture of this thing. A vivid, factual picture of what we know. What do we know?"

"It's all over the timeline, most focused but not exclusive to the modernized world, only on Earth, and only during the twentieth century," Jack offered, still drumming his fingers.

"That's a very narrow window. So that speaks to a number of speculations we'll visit later," Gustavo said from a distance. "But almost all of these seem to deal with some sort of social justice issue. I'm looking at the incursions now, and Mary provided me a cross reference through her archives."

"Social Justice. Right. We've got the KKK in Washington DC, the infamous Lynching of Leo Frank, and a camp in Western Africa that trained child soldiers."

"I'm guessing it isn't an anti-semi—" Jack said sarcastically.

"Avoid speculation until the next part of the conversation," Wyatt redirected.

"This flame unit… looks odd. At first I thought it was a small custom job, but then when compared to the size of this assailant, I saw that it was merely a flamethrower made for a normal sized man." Rupert filled his pad's screen with a zoomed in picture of the flickering weapon and held it up for everyone.

"The only distinguishable equipment on the individual in question. It's German-made, from World War II. The tanks are lying on their side, and the spout is disguised as a rifle so the bearer can avoid sniper fire. This weapon appeared late in the war," Wyatt said, not even looking at the picture.

Gustavo seemed to sidetrack his train of thought. "Those had some good range. And they had a trigger guard didn't they? What about those huge hands this thing has?"

Rupert began poking at his pad to try and see.

"They did, but after looking at the footage, it looks like some extra grip mechanism was welded onto the handle and trigger to accommodate the large hand of the assailant. It fires it with one arm, after all. And carries the eighty pound tank around like it is nothing but a purse," Wyatt added.

"Well, it is large. Over seven feet tall. I can't see a proper depression in the Leo Frank footage, but the African footage has a number of footprints for scanning." Rupert offered.

"That could help. My guess is that it is dense physically, but the joints seemed to be in all the right places and its proportions seemed fairly standard. Maybe a lean three hundred or three hundred and twenty pounds."

Ingrid finally spoke up. "With what Oracle is saying, there are enough incursions here to keep something like our carousel running hot for six months. So this thing was active for at *least* that long, making incursions into this timeline. That's a lot of juice. Odds are this person or thing or whatever has been incurring for a long time into the Beta Line or it has much more advanced machinery than Janus does."

"Despite using a flamethrower, I agree that this thing is technologically superior to us for two reasons," Gustavo added, holding up two data pads. "The first reason is the speed of the DC projectile clocking in somewhere faster than an actual bullet. Something that large being fired from a near soundless cannon or launcher of some kind baffles me. Secondly, look at the camp footage from Wyatt and Rupert's compiled video feeds. The footprints are amazingly erratic. There's one here that Wyatt focuses on by itself, seemingly in the middle of nowhere."

"Maybe it has… a long jump?"

"No. I don't think so. I think it can blink in and out of time more rapidly than us. Maybe even a minute or less apart. Whatever is performing this thing's incursion ability does some far more advanced math than anyone could manage within the foreseeable human future."

Wyatt went to open his mouth, but shut it again as his eyes trailed off.

"I want to go back to the physiology for a moment," Rupert said, bringing up the picture of its face looking up toward Wyatt's hiding spot in the tree. "Right here it blinks …" Rupert hit a few buttons and the featureless face came up on the main rec room screen. "…ruling out a mask or head gear. And it has a heaving chest so clearly it respirates."

"The eyes bothered me a bit," Wyatt confessed, looking reluctantly at the image again. "It has no whites to its eyes, no discernible pupils, nothing. Just dead red-metal eyes … dead like a shark's."

"But if it breathes, it can suffocate. It would also have to concern itself with disease, foreign air, contaminants. And if it breathes, it has to eat. It has to fulfill life processes. This thing is flesh and blood," Rupert added, perhaps to offer a light at the end of the tunnel to Wyatt.

"Why was it looking up the tree?" Ingrid gasped, as the question finally occurred to her.

"I haven't ruled out that it could see me, or at least where I'd been," Wyatt said. "Okay. So it is a bipedal humanoid over seven feet tall, technology advanced beyond our level, and has pale, consistent skin with no visible body hair, genitals, or any other equipment aside from a World War II German flamethrower."

He looked at everyone, seeing if anyone had anything to add. His fingers strummed a few diminished cords until he stopped and continued, "So why? Why is it doing this? When we figure out what it is doing, we can figure out what it wants."

Gustavo started stacking his data pads and papers with a sigh.

"It's not limited to American politics."

"Modern. Post-modern. There are so many horrifying tragedies in history it could stop, but everything it has engaged seems to have been recorded prior via photograph."

"Post-modern. Humanism. It is acting within post-enlightenment."

"Why not save Frank at the prison?"

"It isn't interested in being a savior." Mary finally spoke. "It wanted to make a larger point, knowing that the rewritten version of history would document and show what happens to the kinds of people it targets. It wipes out a parade of proud KKK. It torches Leo Frank's lynching mob while his body is still warm. It gathers and displays hands on a table in the center of a camp which had an obviously evil purpose. These are lessons."

"It let Leo Frank die, but the children from the camp were missing. Did it leave them alone? Evacuate them prior to avoid any of them being hit by strays?" Jack asked.

"No secondary fire had hit the tent when I saw it. The kids were simply gone."

"So it would sneak in, lead them out quietly without all the kids making a sound of alarm? I don't buy it," Ingrid added.

"These are lessons, and I think if it wanted the children to die or be punished, Rupert and Wyatt would have found their remains. I... I can almost assure you that where ever those children ended up, they were intact and unharmed." Mary stood up and walked to the front of the wall screen. The white face looked down, still, upon her as if its unliving eyes had seen her. "It made sure the children were fine, because the children still had a self-determined future ... which is why it is only operating post 1900. It sees everything prior as the human childhood. It's trying to grow us up."

"That," Wyatt said, "might be the closest hint we have to this thing's modus operandi. Gustavo? What do we want to do next?"

Rupert looked to Wyatt with subtle surprise, and Wyatt looked to Gustavo.

"We keep plotting out these fractures. Locations and times. See if this MO continues to hold up under scrutiny. Until then, all incursions are suspended ... even the probes," Gustavo said, looking to Ingrid during the last sentence. Ingrid nodded in understanding. "We have all the time in the world, theoretically."

Wyatt nodded in agreement, sat back down, and began trying to form a song from his random chords while the others still reeled from the day's revelations.

Chapter 14

Within an empty, boundless space sat Janus, a perfectly spherical object made by mankind. If light actually existed in Janus' current universe, it would appear as a singular ball bearing amidst an endless fold of void. No stars. No anything.

Void.

That wasn't the thought that bothered Mary.

Within this sphere was a rotating track that acted as an equator, the centrifugal force keeping everyone's feet to the floor. The simulation of gravity was close enough to adjust to tolerably, and the air density was nearly precise with equator sea level, if a bit drier for comfort's sake. This perfect sphere of human habitat was the exact opposite of whatever remained beyond its smooth outer shell. If that shell ruptured so much as a fracture, it would burst open from the lack of equilibrium.

That wasn't the thought that bothered Mary either.

While she was only gone for three months on Earth, on a faux vacation with her job waiting back at Princeton, she would be spending four years here onboard Janus. The same five people, and the same hallways and recreational room and the same chair at the dining table. All the same, with false daytime cycles and lack of stimulation from a world of news.

That wasn't the thought that bothered Mary.

The thought that bothered Mary was that the huge, looming white humanoid in front of her face was seemingly looking right at her. It was seemingly master of this timeless domain, and here they were disturbing its world by merely being here.

Intending to merely go over the footage and dig for any discrepancies with her own archival data, Mary's eyes settled on one of the last frames of the assailant standing tall, one foot in the remains of a victim's head, chin up, and glaring outward with dead eyes of bloody-gold. The thought that out there, that alien thing was traveling through time, where all things were vulnerable, terrified her.

Was it omniscient? Would it find her alternate self in the line and do something to her? Would it prevent her from being born, or from being American? Would it snag up Wyatt and Rupert and attack them if they tried to spy on it again?

Would it find Janus? Would it jump to the Alpha Line and find Mary's *true* past self and hurt her? Blow up the facility where Janus was built?

Stomp out the pool of sludge that made the leap to living mass during Earth's Proterozoic? Where were the limits to its hostility?

Mary had a flash of comfort when it occurred to her that the thing most likely had a limit… children. At least innocent children; KKK and lynchers seemed to be the exception. The RUF camp children, stolen from their homes and trained brutally, gave her hope that it had a code of ethics. For a moment, she questioned how scared she should truly be, given that someone with enormous power was exercising its ethics on the human stains of history.

She remembered reading about Leo Frank's lynching in high school. It was horrible, and whereas it was a bland footnote for other students, Mary had always found her teeth clenching a bit when she read of the horrors of the world.

Ingrid was careful not to startle her.

"It does look a bit scary, doesn't it?" she whispered.

Mary jumped regardless, and spun around in her chair. She had left the cabinet door unlatched and Ingrid stood there with a cup of coffee for her. "I poured you a fresh cup in a new mug. Other one was looking gnarly. Sorry to startle you."

Mary nodded and took it, but looked back over her shoulder at the gleaming eyes while she sipped. "I don't know if scary is the word. I think sublime works better."

Ingrid scoffed. "Really?"

"Oh yes. Sublime is the mix of overwhelming beauty with terror. Like the rolling of a hurricane onto a shore. You stare at the majesty of it, while it makes day look like night."

"When I was little I saw a tornado like that once. When I was little. I watched what it did." Ingrid was a little girl again, awkward and boyish, standing in the doorway of their home while cows were plucked out of a distant barn by the tornado's finger-like funnel. "Is that what you see? Something terrible and pretty at the same time?"

"Well, let me show you." Mary skipped through some bookmarked frames of Wyatt and Rupert's footage. "First off, this thing sneaks in. That requires a lot of talent to move in silently into the crowd, stay low, and then attack. It didn't just leap into the middle of the crowd, because the air-change, temperature drop, energy discharge, whatever would have been seen by Wyatt and Rupert's systems. So it is stealthy. Secondly, look here:" Mary zoomed into the moment where the thing strode out from the smoke and stomped on the writhing man's head. "See that?"

"Uh, yeah. Kinda wish I didn't."

"No, here." Making a box with her finger, and then using two fingers in a pinching motion to zoom in the cropped frame, Mary focused on the thing's foot. "Again."

Through the smoke, in a single smooth motion with toes pointed, it stomped; placing all of its force into the heel at the base of the skull, crushing it with a combination of weight and pressure that seemed minimal at distant glance but the bulging calf and thigh muscles clearly revealed hundreds of pounds of jutting pressure being delivered.

"So… it's graceful," Ingrid conceded.

"Almost like a dancer."

"Truth is I'm not going to be holding a bake sale for the KKK, rapist slave runners, or for a lynch mob anytime soon. They all got what they should get, in my opinion. But I am confused on one thing."

"What's that?" Mary said, sipping her coffee again. "You put caramel in this?"

"I brought some on board. And peanut brittle. But that's just for us girls."

They shared a smile.

"Well," Ingrid continued. "Why not just save everyone? Wave your finger at the bad people and perform a feat that gets their attention. Or, *fine*. Punish and burn all the bastards but why not get there two minutes prior to Leo Frank's hanging and save him?"

"I'm not sure. I think it might have, or they if there is more than one, evacuated those children from the RUF camp. So why not save Leo Frank?"

"Maybe child soldiers are a different matter?"

"Could it/they think Leo Frank was guilty? And instead of saving Frank, maybe it was being clear on punishing those who went unpunished in history. The history of the actual trial of Leo Frank is obscured in poor historical data, journalistic sensationalism, and anti-Semitic historical revisionism. Maybe this thing doesn't have enough data to reach a conclusion on Frank/"

"But has enough to reach a conclusion on the psycho lynch mob."

"Maybe."

"Maybe… is the word of the week isn't it?"

With a compliant snicker, Mary took another sip. "Thanks. For the coffee."

"No problem. I figured out that you like it the same way my second husband does."

Mary's eyebrows shot up. "You say that like there is a third husband."

"Fourth actually," Ingrid said, clearly in her element now. "Husband number four is actually number two. But he needed some time to grow up. Men are like that."

"Oh dear lord."

"You ever been married? You're a looker. Men have got to go crazy over you."

"I was close once. But no, never married. It seems like a lot of trouble."

"Whenever anyone says 'I was close once' it means there's a good story there."

"I was young. College. Things just didn't work out. Honestly, I don't really know why they didn't. They just… didn't. Odd as that sounds."

"No, that makes perfect sense. Husband number three was like that. He was just, one day, not invested or married to me anymore. And I don't think he had even found out about husband number two again, yet."

"Did… did they know about this before putting you on a station with four men!?" Mary playfully said.

"Oh I am *so* aiming for that Rupert. I think I could do laundry on his stomach. He is truly chiseled. Don't worry… I'll leave your crush alone for you."

"My crush? Oh I see. Which one is that? Whom do I supposedly have eyes for?"

Ingrid looked wicked. "Oh you tell *me.*"

"It was made extremely clear to us all that no fraternizing was to be had on this mission."

"And yet you get all starry eyed when he sits across from you… plucking his guitar."

"Wait. What? Wyatt?" Mary got wide-eyed, pulling Ingrid close and half closing the cabinet door behind her. "I thought you were going on about Jack!"

"Jack's a handsome one. Insecure, eager to please. Bright enough to impress, but dumb enough to control. He's next on my list after Rupert.

He is one to be dragged into the cougar den, let me tell *you*. But no, Wyatt's your man."

Mary shook her head slowly in astonishment.

"Fine. But don't be surprised if, when the four years here are coming to a close, you don't start feeling anxiety at not hearing his guitar or seeing his face."

Mary laughed a bit. "You've been dying for girl talk, haven't you?"

"You have *no* idea. Trying to hold it in for these months has been killing me."

Chapter 15

Jack and Gustavo sat, kettle popcorn tubs in their laps, with their legs crossed, as the credits for *Time Bandits* began.

"Flipping brilliant, Jack. This is a perfect pick."

"It was either this or Bill and Ted tonight," Jack replied, cheek full of popcorn.

"Hard choice. And I'm kinda impressed you didn't dive to the obvious—"

"Back to the Future, yeah. Saving that for special occasion."

"When you said you'd picked a Terry Gilliam time-travel movie for us to relax to, I was afraid you'd picked *Twelve Monkeys*."

"Fuck no. I can't handle that movie right now. It would be like showing *Eraserhead* to an expectant father."

Both men nibbled their snacks as the film began, and despite how much they each pretended to be engrossed in the movie, their minds wandered and their individual stockpiles of questions began to teeter.

Jack's stack of questions toppled over, and he voiced the first one that landed. "What are we going to do?"

Gustavo sighed. "I don't know. I'm thinking of a lot of options."

Jack muted the television. "I think I need to hear them, for my own piece of mind."

While Jack was normally a very non-confrontational man, Gustavo could tell that being evasive was not going to be acceptable. Jack, when train-tracking on a logical path of his choosing, could be unstoppable.

"Well, we can investigate the Xeno and see if it is a population of time travelers or some kind of outlier. That's one option."

"Xeno? We're calling it that?"

"Wyatt came up with the name and it fits. Greek for 'stranger'. I suggested Chronos, but he dissuaded me, saying that we didn't want to apply a god-like stigma to it. So there's that one option. We can also try and make direct contact since none of its hostilities seemed aimed anywhere but towards those that fall into a certain unethical ethos. So perhaps the Xeno would be receptive to us if we make contact and make it clear that we are external observers from an alternate timeline."

"I can tell you right now, we won't be doing that. Clearly 'Xeno' has the will and means to terminate a group of people and it will do so with superior technology at its disposal. That is, sorry to be blunt, such a terrible idea it should be off the table. That thing will squash us."

"Even if the Xeno is another species, or highly evolved human with secrets abound? Even if the Xeno is a time traveler that we now *must* establish ourselves with? Especially now that we have pierced the technological barrier beyond concrete space-time? You don't want contact?"

"We were selected and equipped only to provide observed data from an alternate timeline, reducing any risk to nearly null. We are not capable, let alone *ideal*, for making first contact with another race."

Gustavo breathed deep. "Did you want me to finish listing my options?"

"Yes, of course. Sorry."

"And the other option we have, the one you want me to take but you've been kind enough not to suggest it as of yet, is to pull the plug. No more incursions except for Ingrid's space probes until another three and a half years have rolled on by, and we get ported back home automatically."

"I'm glad that option is on the table, but I don't want to do it. Not like it's my call…"

"Oh, *please*," Gustavo belted out. "You know I won't do *shit* without checking with you. Why else do you think I put up with your worrying?"

Jack smiled. "It's not that I want a say, per se, I'm just making it clear on record that I can't be accountable for when someone stomps on a butterfly while incurring and we find that Michael Dukakis won the election."

"Jesus. Just scare the shit out of me why don't you."

"We *should* be scared. Unlike most explorers in history, our homeland is potentially in danger given the choices we make out here. The Spanish sneezed, and thirty-two million people died. If we're out here, and WE sneeze, billions may vanish."

"Are you serious? We are not exploring the Alpha Line. The secondary line we are examining is *not* our time line. We are not technically even time travelling! How can we impact ourselves if we aren't examining … *ourselves*?"

"Easy." Jack put his popcorn down to talk with his hands. "I'm not so much worried about the Beta Line. As inhuman as it is, and as clearly similar to us as they are, they are not *us* and I don't worry about that so much. What worries me is that if there are other travelers zipping about, enacting violent vengeance fantasies, then anything *we* do while observing *them* may leak back to *our* base line …the Alpha Line."

"How?"

"First off, they-it-Xeno might and most likely *is* more technologically advanced than us. Toppling buildings by bowling down the KKK is evidence of that. We have *no* idea where this Xeno is tethered. If we keep popping up, it will see us and perhaps track us back, seeing us as an unwanted complication. So by observing it, we might stir it up and lead it back to our home line. Kinda like the Borg in Next Generation."

"When Q sent the Enterprise out into deep space—"

"And the Borg learned about the Federation, so they went gunning for them. Right. Like that. If the Xeno is big on snuffing out certain events in history, and finds out someone out there has the ability to *undo* its work, then it might target us."

"There are a lot of 'mights' justifying your concerns, Jack."

"I get that. Let me offer you something more concrete… the observer effect."

"We've gone over that *exhaustively*."

"But hear me out. Right, so we went over exhaustively how Wyatt and Rupert would displace air, respirate through their filters, etc., and therefore change the world they are incurred into. Yes, true and very minimal. *But*, our observing *this* time line has altered the people on board this very station. When we return to the base line, we'll influence people in turn based upon *our* newfound influences. If the Beta-line wasn't so completely fucked, this wouldn't have been a big deal … but now we see what kind of damage can be done by an angry time traveler. Now we *know*, and have recordings *of* the time line being wrecked. Someone will take this recorded and observed data and use it. Hell, this Xeno might be a result of our return to our timeline when we share our observations."

"You're talking about a temporal causality loop. You've entered into the land of slippery slopes where everything becomes a danger and a bad idea. We can't account for that!"

"I know, but building Janus meant we had to take on a certain—"

"Okay, *no*. My turn. Don't even finish that sentence. Building Janus was *not* a mistake."

"I didn't say it was."

"Someone… someone else would have built her. Since man thought of time travel, it was fated to happen somehow. I had to have it be me—be *us*—because God forbid someone else be the first through this barrier."

Jack was silent, watching his friend.

Gustavo turned to Jack.

"Could you imagine? Could you imagine another first world nation getting this power? What would China do with it? Or Russia? Or the EU? Jesus, what if the politics of those nations forbade them from making Janus and instead a smaller power made it? What would be left of the world?"

"I know we're the best people to be in this spot. I'm not arguing that, Gus."

"I know. I don't see this as a character attack on me or anything, but you've always hinted that Janus should never have been built, which is why it had to be you here. You have always been the voice of caution, and *you* can prevent the corruption that I'm so afraid of. If not us, if not me or you, than I shudder to think of who would pioneer this technology."

"So, all my bitching aside. You want my real opinion? Take it or leave it?"

"Always, man."

"Heartbreaking as it is, I think we should suspend incurring for now. Continue the probes at least, because they go into deep space beyond the solar system and are almost a non-issue. But suspend incurring for now until we let Oracle really comb over the line, which granted, could take the rest of our stay. I think this Xeno thing will be a bigger issue for us the more we stir it up. Come back here after the four year mission is over, and then bring a bunch more people over to fill the station. Hell, we have enough empty quarters. When we have more staff that is prepared for this, we can try and make contact. Meet this thing with a big old club in one hand. Safer, smarter, better understanding."

"I thought you said you didn't want to suspend incurring?"

"Believe me, I don't."

Gustavo turned back to the screen to see a knight in armor riding out of a boy's closet. Startled, the pajama-clad boy bolted out of bed in pursuit.

"As I can see it," Gustavo mused, "if we don't have a slam dunk mission this outing… if we don't prove the viability of this station and the roughly three trillion it took to build and deploy it, then we will never have another chance at this. It will fade from hearts faster than walking on the moon. And Janus will drift here in the void without ever being activated again… without this technology ever being explored."

"You don't know that… too much has been put into this…"

"The moment everyone in the Alpha Line knows that there are monsters at the edge of the map, they will tuck their heads into the sand and redirect blame for money lost. It is very much *now* or *never*."

Chapter 16

Within Janus' sub-sections, on a deck above the living quarters and just prior to the carousel prep chambers, Wyatt and Rupert had their workshop. Several long, curved tables were covered with packed chutes, half-built stealth masks, and various other gadgets, while wall screens along the nearest side displayed interactive schematics of their gear. Under the screens along the farthest, longest wall was a row of highly reinforced security lockers.

Janus had been deployed with *all* of the lockers empty. Currently a third of them were filled and sealed, the timers not to open until the return to Earth. However, one singular locker remained open with its steel door propped via a bungee cord. The dark recess of it faced the vast and cluttered workshop, a chess board propped up onto an upside-down bucket before it, surrounded by cables scattered about the floor.

Wyatt stared vacantly at the chessboard, musing about the metaphor of unmoved chess pieces awaiting their fate at the hands of two armchair generals. Whereas Rupert preferred to play against Janus' human station occupants, Wyatt had grown fond of his locker-bound opponent.

A clang brought Wyatt back to the things at hand.

Rupert had taken a steel case out of refrigerated storage, shoved tabletop debris aside, and was making certain his nitrogen carbine was zeroed to his liking. A tiny red laser sight zipped around on the wall as he stared down the barrel, making micro adjustments with a tiny screw driver in its top aperture. Eventually he was pleased, and placed his weapon down and moved onto adjusting his facemask.

Rupert was the busybody prior to combat, whereas Wyatt was far more stoic.

Opening up a data pad in front of him, Wyatt went over his checklist again. "While you do that, Rupert, let me share what I've surmised from the Xeno. Just keep your ears open for me here. First off, there is only one of them *or* they all weigh exactly the same. This was established from looking over the various footprints at the rebel camp and comparing them to the single Xeno we saw in Georgia. I would *like* to think there is only one of them but you never know."

"I don't think that would make sense, wishful thinking that it is," Rupert confessed. "No one manages the summit of dimensional travel solo. Even if there is one Xeno fielded per incursion of theirs, it must have support staff of some kind."

"True, but within mission-specific parameters we are going to bag only one of them, so the support staff will most likely be negligible for this specific mission."

"So, we aren't too concerned about cavalry?"

"If we see any equivalent arrive, we are rip-cording ASAP."

"Got it."

"Moving on. The Xeno seems to like some fancy CQC of some kind, and prefers being within melee range when engaging targets. Expect a lot of that, and for God's sake, keep away from it. Do not engage in hand to hand. While looking over that camp, a couple things weren't adding up, and I can't account for this thing's agility all too well."

"Understood." Rupert was now checking his air filters.

"Lastly, expect it to have some super-sensory capability. It's why I picked where we are incurring to catch one specifically. The place will be total chaos and we need to capitalize on it."

"Sensory overload."

"Precisely. There will be at least 6,000 foot mobiles with domestic firearms from turn of the century, but some will be combat war vets, so beware. There will be crack shots among them. I am also incurring during a time just after an air strike from seized military hardware. There will be a lot of fires, smoke, and several city blocks will be smoldering from the bombing. By the time we are incurring into the conflict, the death toll will already be around one hundred and seventy civilians according to Oracle, but that is a soft number given the lack of accurate historical record of this event."

Rupert paused while adjusting his mask for a moment to make eye contact. "This is going to be a bad one, isn't it?"

"Yes… yes it is. Again, do not engage in hand to hand. Shoot to kill and secure the body, and lastly… avoid harming the indigenous population. But, and let me make this very clear to you Rupert, the indigenous populations' lives are forfeit to the precedent of the mission. Bag the Xeno. Period."

Rupert nodded. "Does Gustavo know about that?"

"No. Everything else has his blessing, but he wouldn't stomach that last part. Better to ask forgiveness than permission."

"You say that as though you aren't the authority on Janus."

"I will only pull that card if completely pushed into a corner," Wyatt stated resolutely, placed his data pad on the table, and began stretching his footpads out for fitting.

The following suit-up was a quiet and tense affair. Neither Rupert nor Wyatt said a word as they inwardly focused on the coming combat mission.

Wyatt had no illusions. This was the worst and messiest combat mission he had ever devised or executed. He was about to airdrop into a burning city, attempt to avoid hostile and unorganized groups of people who were untrained with their firearms, and target a highly dangerous enemy with the added complication of recovering the body.

The most irksome part of this for Wyatt was that he wasn't sure how to lure the Xeno into a vulnerable position. How could it be tracked? Would they see it before it saw them? Wyatt would never voice how much a shot in the dark this was out loud, but he would have normally discouraged anyone from attempting what he was about to initiate.

But his instinct, the loudest voice in his internal congress, was clear and loud that this thing, this *Xeno* had to be stopped now and not later. The argument of having 'all the time in the world' didn't stand up because it was clear that the Xeno was on another time scale. Perhaps the Beta Line would be far more damaged if he didn't deploy *here and now* to stop it. Causality had become as slippery as the ethics behind his choices.

As his suit molded and solidified around his muscles, he missed Mary's voice. It would have been nice to hear her wish him luck, but she had to be kept out of this one.

Chapter 17

Tulsa was on fire.

Billowing black smoke pillared into the early morning sky, swallowing Wyatt and Rupert as they descended. They aimed for the sturdiest building in the area, and when they hit the roof of the Hotel Tulsa they had a clear view of the streets, the military surrounding the courthouse, the fortified jail, and the bodies that littered all of it.

"The kerosene bombing should be done, but we might hear some aircraft still," Wyatt said as his chute burned itself into nothing. Unclipping his carbine from his chest, Wyatt synced his HUD with it, giving him a targeting reticule that followed its barrel wherever he aimed it. The carbine itself was smooth and without distinction on its surface so that the same stealth-effect of 'invisibility' was present on it.

Each carbine had ten refrigerated rounds of frozen nitrogen. Upon expelling all their rounds the carbine would disintegrate itself, much like their parachutes. In addition, if the carbine was free of its owner's grip for more than forty seconds, it would do the same regardless of how many rounds remained.

Once Wyatt's HUD was synced to his own firearm, he linked it to Rupert's. This way both men could see where the other was aiming to maximize their coverage and fire arc.

"See out there?" Wyatt pointed. "That is Black Wall Street burning. It's too dark for the biplanes to be flying overhead to spot groups of black escapees, and if my guess is correct, the Xeno is already at work in the city killing and displaying white posses for the National Guard to find when they come around with wagons and trucks to gather the bodies come morning."

Rupert nodded, his HUD identifying several black men hanging upside-down from street lamps with their ears taken as trophies. Everything was smoke, ash, cinder, and each building had vomited its singed contents onto the street in a vulgar display. Tulsa was burning, and Little Africa was the target.

"And we keep away from the courthouse. The Army has a DX'd mounted gun there. No water cooling system, but it can still fire. Mark it on your HUD."

Rupert eyed the building, double blinked while looking at it to select it, rolled his eyes through a menu, and marked it as 'avoidant' so a subtle alarm would sound if he got within its line of sight.

Carbines at the ready, both men slunk to the roof door and went down a floor. Entering the guest hallway, they went room to room, peeking out windows and scanning the area, allowing the HUD to gather data, record sound, and determine areas too dangerous to venture.

Rupert was craning himself over a wooden dresser to look out a window when Wyatt saw something curious on the floor of the hallway a few feet in front of him. It had a minor heat signature, and his blink interface highlighted it. Stepping cautiously closer he saw it was small, pale, and could fit in the palm of his hand.

Before reaching it, he realized it was a severed ear; perfectly torn along the root, and fairly clean of blood. Glancing around, Wyatt saw no signs of struggle, no splashes of blood, and no owner of the ear.

"It knows we are here." Wyatt said flatly. "Stop bothering with the windows." Rupert's heart rate monitor showed a rapid jump in Wyatt's peripheral vision. Rupert climbed down silently, lurked along the dresser and footboard of the bed while keeping to the shadows, until he reached the ear Wyatt had highlighted.

All the while Wyatt simply stood there, carbine at the low-ready position.

"Looks Caucasian," Rupert finally said.

"Of course it is. And while the Xeno knows where we are it may not know *when* we are."

"How do you mean?"

"Look farther down the hallway… another ear. We're being bread-crumbed."

"Are we… are we going to follow?" Rupert asked with an uncharacteristic quiver in his voice.

"Absolutely. This might be an attempt at first contact."

"Or a trap…"

"Maybe, but contact *first*, then the trap. If the Xeno's intentions were to straight up kill us, it wouldn't have left something as benign as an *ear* here. Let's follow and see if there is a third ear."

For the first time in his ambitious career, Rupert regretted being the point man. Slinking from furniture to chair to lamp, he moved as stealthily as a human is able. Following ten feet behind was Wyatt, still suited and fairly invisible, but upright and walking calmly and plainly.

At the hallway's bend was another ear. And another farther. "We're being led to the stairs."

"Lead on."

"There could be an IED ahead, or even a bucket of suspended paint so we're visible. We could be led right into one so a Xeno wouldn't even have to waste the manpower for taking us down. I *seriously* advise against merely following the trail!"

"Noted," said Wyatt as he walked past Rupert. "I'll do point."

Rupert could barely remain stealthy while keeping up. Wyatt had a fire under his heels and he was following the trail of the ears with straightforward doggedness.

Down the stairs they went, Rupert's heart rate rising again at the thought of an attack in the cramped stairwell. "All left ears," Wyatt said soon after, as he passed door after door. The ears led through the lobby, toward the open double doorway that illuminated the lounging chairs and potted plants with the red glow of Tulsa's brackish fires. Stepping out into the thick night air, Wyatt took a close look at the ripped metal hinges dangling from where the doors once stood. One had been tossed into the bushes out front, and the other hurled into the lobby.

"Again with the dramatic displays," Wyatt observed. "If the Xeno does want to kill us, it will do so spectacularly."

Rupert straightened up, realizing his creeping was going to be useless out in the open. "Got any indigenous hostiles?"

"Most of the fighting in this area is long over. Sometime in the late morning bale trucks and carts will begin gathering the dead and hauling them off. Besides, I think," Wyatt said, pointing off into the distance to an arm that had clearly been torn from its socket, "it has already secured this area."

They followed the ears, stepping gingerly over the smoldering guts of storefronts and spent rifle casings. Several people had died of bullet wounds, and from the occasional lamppost dangled a black man, tied upside down, stabbed many times past death, and always earless. Up close, they seemed far more human than from the windows of Hotel Tulsa. "Some whites here collected ears and passed them down through the generations on leather cord as mementos."

"So it is taking off their ears? And using them to show us something?"

"Maybe. Aside from that arm, I can't see any other causalities of—"

A gunshot echoed in the street. Wyatt and Rupert found cover quickly beside a sideways icebox that had been dragged through a store window. A few more shots followed from various spots, indicating a firefight.

"We continue to follow the trail. Looks like it's leading us toward the courthouse. Or at least near it."

Rupert nodded, seeing the red zone that his HUD had warded off growing bigger as they moved block by block.

Wyatt had set a counter for ears on his HUD, and it had reached forty-seven. All of them left. "Think we'll find the right ones in *there?*" Ahead, the trail of ears led to a window of the recreation center that stood two buildings away from the courthouse. Out front was a large, painted sign that read 'Summer Dance Tonight' in bright letters wreathed with flowers and baskets.

"I'd like to study the layout," Rupert said, frantically bringing up the blueprint archive of the city in his blink interface.

"Of course. Let's go across the street. There." Wyatt marked a deli and soda store adjacent to the center. The men moved quickly, slunk up to the door, scanned the inside, and then slipping in one at a time, they crouched against the soda jerk station. Rupert began poring over the recreational center's layout.

"We can be boxed in pretty fast with those exits where they are," Rupert said grimly.

"I know," Wyatt replied. He was toying with his audio recording hardware, trying to listen to the inside of the building. Sorting through ear shattering crackles of fire and the occasional interrupting gunshot in the distance, Wyatt finally nailed down what he thought was occurring inside … prayer. Desperate rote pleas of prayer, almost like a chant in an organized, frantic state of agony.

His focus was on the sound, and Rupert's focus was on the building. They didn't see the gunman creep past them with a double barreled shotgun. Or the second. The third was louder, and he stomped right by with a hunting rifle aimed at the street.

Wyatt and Rupert froze, their grips renewed on their carbines. Each of the three rioters wore thick workman's pants, suspenders, and one had a hunting knife on his belt and a bulging pocket. The third and fattest of the three men lifted his hat and wiped his forehead with a huff of exhaustion.

"This here. This is where he said he saw them," one man whispered, finger extended toward the recreational center. "Let's wait for a bit."

"Fine by me!" the third said, tossing his weapon onto the soda counter, sprinkling Rupert couched below with dust and ash. "I need a drink. I wonder if there's still pop in the—" he walked around the counter and directly into Rupert.

The puffy gunman's red face showed his alarm before Wyatt blew it all over the wall and ceiling with a muffled blast from his carbine. Standing quickly, he fired two more rounds: one in the upper back of the man carrying the knife and the second into the throat of the third man, flopping his head sideways onto his shoulder as he crumbled.

"We are *tactical*," Wyatt said sternly, leaping over the counter. Rupert couldn't contain his swearing as he brushed himself off. "We move now, check that building, and relocate to high ground." Moving to the broken windows, Wyatt scanned both ways along the street.

The way across was clear. Wyatt's HUD displayed seven rounds in his carbine remaining, and Rupert still had all ten. "Stack up," Wyatt commanded.

Rupert was still brushing himself off, his heart rate elevated, and his breathing erratic.

"Rupert, *stack up*," Wyatt repeated again, turning his gaze behind him to see if he could rein Rupert in.

Behind Rupert, next to the soda jerk counter and in the doorway, loomed the Xeno.

With shoulders slumped, head craned, and eyes scanning around at the blood splatters on the ceiling and running down the wall, the proto-person seemed almost casually curious. Its skin was a sickly white with tiny bumps making the texture of it rhino-like. Frankenstein-esque scars and stitching ran all over its body, especially along the joints. The being's construction was crude, yet muscularly streamlined.

There were no facial features but the faint hint of a brow that crinkled in narrowing focus as those golden eyes settled on where Wyatt was crouched.

It froze. Wyatt knew it could tell he was there. It blinked, and that blink was the most terrifying sight Wyatt had ever seen. That simple blink made the Xeno suddenly breathing and alive, triggering the almost uncontrollable instinct of fight or flight. Wyatt's skin prickled and his arm was alive, gripping his carbine in readiness.

Everything seemed silent. Even the crackling distant fires and gunshots seemed to stop like chirping birds that had become vigilant due to the presence of a predator. Wyatt was sure that Rupert knew it was behind him, just out of sight, because his heart was racing beyond the threshold.

The Xeno evaluated Wyatt, and Wyatt did the same in return. Then Rupert lifted his carbine from behind the counter, and fired a round point blank into the humanoid.

But it was gone. It was there upon the moment of firing, and was now *gone*. Rupert jumped up, rounded the corner and fired two more blind shots toward the back exit. "Did I get it? Did I get it?"

"Get back he—" The wall nearest Rupert exploded onto him in a burst of dust and splinters. Two white arms tipped with hands brandishing fingers like pale railroad spikes gripped him. It snatched Rupert up and hammered him against the wall.

Wyatt's targeting aid couldn't make heads or tails of things given all the dust, jostling limbs, and Rupert's flailing. Aiming high, Wyatt fired three rounds as the Xeno lifted one knee and plowed it into Rupert's side with freight-train force.

Rupert didn't make a sound, but folded in half unnaturally, and slumped to the ground.

All of Wyatt's shots had seemingly hit nothing, and the Xeno had vanished again.

Wyatt moved, storming down the hall to secure Rupert. His HUD told him that Rupert's pelvis was broken in multiple places, and in purple writing a warning was blinking 'evac' over his folded body. Kneeling over his partner, Wyatt kept his carbine at the ready, aiming down each end of the hallway.

Something pounded the ceiling above him, shaking loose ash and dust.

Wyatt blinked through his interface, selecting extraction for Rupert. The injured pelvis might kill him during the ripcord process, however, so Wyatt gave the command for the suit to begin hardening as a means to protect his fragile body from the liquid landing on Janus.

It would take thirty seconds for the hardening process to complete prior to ripcord and right then thirty seconds seemed like a very long time.

Something stepped on broken glass near the customer side of the soda counter behind them.

It was micro incurring. Suddenly the Xeno's combat style made perfect sense. Wyatt took a gamble, and aimed the carbine in one direction and focused down the hallway. He was hoping he was being watched, and his display of focus was seen as genuine.

He waited. He exhaled. Rupert's heart was erratic, and his suit had twenty seconds to go as it hardened around his hip, neck, and vitals. Wyatt switched off his aiming aid, to avoid its distraction.

One second.

Two seconds.

Before the third, Wyatt spun and blind fired. The Xeno creeping behind him jolted, vanished, and then its huge arm clawed through the broken wall trying to snatch the carbine out of Wyatt's hands. It was half successful; flinging the weapon out among the deli's toppled tables. The arm swung again, but Wyatt hit it hard with his cupped hand in the crook of the elbow. He scrambled away, his path to his own carbine blocked by the lurching white limb.

Fifteen seconds until Rupert's suit would complete setting, and then ripcord . . .

Wyatt dove through the back door of the deli into a loading lot, frantically searching for Rupert's missing carbine. Something large landed on the hood of a parked car nearby, bursting its remaining windows out into the gravel.

Being exposed, Wyatt went to dive back through the hallway door, but the Xeno was suddenly there, bull rushing him as it stepped over Rupert's body in a single stride. Wyatt rolled to the side as the thing rumbled past and vanished again.

Rupert's carbine was highlighted under the smashed car, by the tire, and Wyatt went for it with everything he had. What was only a few feet was suddenly an infinite and insurmountable distance. His fingers reached, and as they felt the end of the butt, the Xeno's foot came down on it, digging it into the gravel. Wyatt rolled to the side, anticipating another knee-attack, but the thing merely stood there.

"Ripcord." Wyatt mouthed quietly, almost pleading. In his ear the chime came that Rupert had been ripcorded home. Seconds passed, and Rupert's carbine reached its time limit and crumbled down to the molecular level under the Xeno's foot. It remained there, glaring at him with its broad chest rising and falling.

The ears weren't to make contact, or to intimidate, they were to make a point. They were a warning, and clearly the Xeno could have killed them prior if it had wanted, having clearly known their incursion location. It had left a bread crumb leading them somewhere specific. The glowing eyes remained in his vision like an optical illusion as he hit the water, wondering what it was he was supposed to have seen.

Chapter 18

With a gasp Wyatt surfaced, the water around him swirling black and syrupy from his dissolving suit. Nearby Rupert floated face up, suit hardened and bloated as though he was a swollen vacationer at an indoor pool being tussled about by a near-miss cannonball. His chest shivered as it rose and fell and his eyes gazed upward.

"Liquidate... l-liquidate," he stammered, shock now setting in as his suit de-stealthed from the chemical reaction of the pool.

Wyatt was breast stroking toward him when the alarms went off. All the medical data had been transmitted from Rupert's and Wyatt's masks to Janus the moment of return. With an outstretched hand, Wyatt pushed Rupert toward the catching pool's edge as the airlock slid open and Gustavo entered wearing a quarantine mask and pushing a gurney. Quickly and gingerly the two men hoisted Rupert out of the water, secured his stiffened body with medical fasteners, and rolled him to the infirmary, leaving a trail of black, dripping sludge behind them.

"He took a hit to the hip, upward angle," Wyatt said while pulling off his facemask as they entered the trauma room. Turning on a monitor overhead, he uploaded the field data from his headgear to the AutoDoc, indicating the moment of injury. Rupert's suit had also recorded the point of impact, pressure in poundage, and the extent of damage. Gustavo looked it over while the AutoDoc's mechanical arms surrounded Rupert, washing him clean, and sustaining his vitals. Several needles went into his arms and between his toes to stabilize him.

Gustavo's jaw dropped when he saw that the impact to Rupert's shattered pelvis had been around 1800 PSI. Both men looked to Rupert, fear-ing, but daring not to voice that he would never walk correctly again.

"Okay, leave him with me. The AutoDoc will stabilize him. But he won't be getting out of it for a long time. I'll move him to a bed when I can. AutoDoc looks like it is evaluating surgery."

Wyatt went to speak, but a tiny bone saw kicked in to cut off Rupert's hardened suit, and it made conversation impractical. Instead Wyatt nodded and walked out.

Outside of the infirmary, once the door slid closed behind him, Wyatt was enveloped in silence. He sighed, his left hand pulling the wet clumps of remaining suit from his chest and splatting it onto the ground like mud. With a weary voice he said, "lights *dim*," and the outer hallway and waiting room became a more calming shade. Sitting down on a long, soft bench against the wall, Wyatt collapsed while dripping nearly naked save for his cup and foot treads.

He was too tired to feel vulnerable when he realized Mary was leaning against the wall in a corner, quietly watching him. For a moment, Wyatt was impressed with her subtlety.

"Should I bother asking how you got past quarantine?" he asked.

"Is Rupert all right?"

"He will live."

"Gustavo left the door wide open when he knew something was wrong. He told everyone over the comm that Rupert was hurt the moment he hit the catching pool." Mary's voice had a sharp edge to it. "No one else is in here except me. Jack and Ingrid are trying to figure out where you two jumped to and what happened, since you felt keeping us out of the know was somehow *wise*."

The aftershock of adrenaline had taken its toll on Wyatt's knees, but he still tensed up, expecting a full verbal assault from Mary. Remaining silent, he waited for her to continue. Clearly, she had been putting together her questions or lecture for a number of minutes and Mary wasn't one to open her mouth without a lot of thought behind her words.

"Before I ask why, I want to remind you that we are all on this station together and we need to work as a cohesive unit. Especially now, since our survival seems to be endangered. I clearly didn't know what I had committed to when I came here, so I need to know *everything*. From you." Her voice was above a whisper, but not by much.

Wyatt nodded, unwilling to give any resistance.

Mary cleared her throat. "How many times have you incurred without us knowing."

"Rupert and I have only incurred this one time since you've been here without you being in the know."

Mary raised an eyebrow at the wording of the answer.

Wyatt sighed. "When Rupert, Ingrid, and I left a few days prior to you, Gustavo, and Jack from Earth, we actually arrived on Janus *four months* prior to you. During those four months we carried out Janus' primary mission. The mission you've been here for, the one to observe history from within the Beta Line itself, didn't start until you arrived."

Mary's lips reddened, and Wyatt thought that it was anger at first. After a moment he understood that it wasn't her lips that had darkened, but her face that had paled.

"If you follow me to my green room, I'll give you the whole deal. I'd like to get dressed." Standing somewhat wobbly, Wyatt walked past her and down the hallway to a sealed door. Looking at it for a moment, it scanned his face and slid open. The floor was tiled and sloped with a drain at the center for rinsing off, which he did, while Mary stood in the doorway, looming like a prison guard. Without drying, Wyatt slipped on some canvas pants and a half-buttoned flannel shirt. Sitting on a tiny foldout bench, he lit a pipe, leaned back, and puffed at it with his extended legs crossed. The room was no bigger than a closet, closing them in with a single light source directly above them.

"First off, there is no way in hell that trillions of secret government dollars, personnel, resources, and land would be allocated to a history project. Just … well, just *no*."

"I'm getting that," Mary said, her resentment clear.

"So when Gustavo pitched Janus to what I can only assume was an endless string of closed door bureaucracies, he didn't say it was to better understand human history. He pitched it with the intent of mining the Beta Line for knowledge, but also for technology. Travelling into your own future is impossible, but in someone else's future you can see cataclysms, unfolded events, and technological advances way ahead of anyone else. The promise of omniscience secured Janus' funding and its secrecy from the public."

"I understood the public secrecy from the beginning. And I suspected that this was the long term goal somewhere down the line. I just figured we'd explore modern history first to get a feel for it before barreling in." Mary swallowed hard, digested what she had heard for a moment, and then continued. "So you've seen the future."

"Only the future of the Beta Line, which as we have learned is far different from our Alpha Line. We, prior to you and Jack arriving, had incurred twenty four times."

"My god… that schedule must have been insane."

"Honestly, due to our complete blackout of knowledge, a majority of them simply involved Rupert and myself skydiving and snapping pictures, as well as placing a few of Ingrid's satellites in orbit around Earth. Only with the last six incursions did we risk any type of ground work."

"Was our little monster there?"

"No. No sign of it or its overt influence. We gathered some samples of advanced technology and sealed them in a timed series of lockers that we can't open. Mission accomplished. You, Gustavo, and Jack arrived. Jack started evaluating the time line over the past two hundred years and then we saw the Beta Line was radically different. Given the clear concern that our diddling in the future might have impacted the past somehow, investigating those fissures became our priority."

"Just to be clear, define 'sample' of technology."

"Anything from documents to actual objects and items that seemed significant."

"It certainly had an impact on the future elements of the Beta Line, but no impact on our secondary historical mission, or so we thought."

"So you took *matter* from the Beta Line… and brought it here? Physical matter?"

"No different than taking matter from the Alpha Line, like you, me, and Janus itself, and bringing it 'here'. Like I said, it is all locked away. We aren't using it or toying with it."

"Okay, okay, Wyatt. I need to say some things out loud now … so correct or guide me wherever I might be wrong."

With a puff of his pipe, Wyatt nodded.

"Janus was funded and built, being the largest single undertaking of construction anyone knows of, to not only examine human history and be used as a platform for deep space exploration, but to also steal technology from the future?"

"Correct."

"Then why the pretense of a historical mission at all? Why would you keep Jack and me in the dark? Heck, why even bring us?"

"First off, Jack was needed. He's extraordinary. Whereas Gustavo is a jack of all trades and a master of a few, nobody does math like Jack. As for you …" Wyatt paused.

"Say it."

"Well, there were two major groups of people funding and greenlighting Janus. One group wanted the idealistic historical mission and they wanted you. You were the choice because of your successful career, books, lecture circuits, and your charisma. We would have lost that group's funding if they found out about the tech gathering mission. They would have deemed it too risky, unethical, and reckless. On the other hand, we needed the opposing group's funding and support by keeping the true mission under wraps and placating any potential opponents. And *that* group would only fund Janus if they would get the return of technological harvesting. We kept both happy by claiming we weren't catering to the other."

"So… I'm a pretty face to distract and placate?"

"I'm sorry Mary, but yes. It wasn't my choice. I didn't even see your file or anything on—"

"Shut up. So, you collect 'stuff' from the future until Jack and I show up. What, I was the eye candy for your funders? What was Jack? The brains? Why would Jack be against gathering tech?"

"He made it clear he would shut down everything if we did any technology mining whatsoever. Jack's focus was exploration, not building America's super power status. We would have lost him if he knew."

"All right, you and Rupert travel into the future and snap some pictures while skydiving. Ingrid launches a few satellites to observe the Earth and — what — how far in the future is this?"

"Around one hundred years after the construction of Janus on the Alpha Line."

"So, one hundred years in the future and you bring back a robotic mop or atomic toothbrush or whatever. Then, after you've stolen your things, we arrive afterward thinking it had only been a few days and there you are, even with the exact same haircut—"

"It's why we all had our hair so short."

"*With* the same haircut, and Jack and I get played for fools, while Gustavo, standing right next to us, played along. Ingrid, Rupert, and you have been living on this station the whole time. You must have really *vacuumed.*"

"Most of the living quarters were sectioned off to avoid revealing the deception." Wyatt confessed, his pipe tasting sour.

"I can't believe you." Mary's mouth hung open, and her eyes smoldered under her crinkled brow. "I can't fucking *believe* you."

"Mary, you know I like you and this is hardly the way I would have—"

"Shut up. No more buttering me up. I actually found you *charming*. *God.*" She let an appalled guffaw escape. "Why not tell us when we got here, at least? Janus was already built and the funding was secure."

"We were ordered not to. To avoid resentment and complications."

Mary shook her head slowly, making her disappointment clear. "You always do what you're told?"

"Not always. Gustavo didn't want me to incur today."

"Incur in *Tulsa*, no less. One of the most infamous race riots in American history and you dropped into it with a black man as your partner! And then something happens, shockingly, to him! Is Rupert actually okay? Did he get shot?"

"No, the Xeno was shadowing us and Rupert took a shot at it, provoking it."

Mary leaned against the inside of the doorway to steady herself.

"It kneed him in the side, and it's bad. Mary, I know how you feel. You have every right, and I'm not asking you to forgive me, like me, or anything. But we have a serious problem now. We exchanged fire with a vastly superior combatant and not only did it anticipate our abilities and toy with us, it knew *exactly* where we were going to incur in Tulsa."

"What?"

"It had a whole setup waiting for us. It knew exactly where we were going to land, building and all. Which means it might know where this station is. And lord knows what else."

In disbelief, Mary shook her head. "Maybe you provoked this thing when you stole technology. Unearned technology. Maybe it's a slumbering giant of some kind. And you woke it up."

"Then why is it rampaging in history the way it is?" Wyatt asked, his pipe's wisp long gone.

"I have no idea, and we're beyond asking it."

Both stood there, staring off into space as their minds raced through the scenarios and outcomes of a thousand different timelines filled with a thousand different horrors.

Wyatt finally spoke up. "Let Gustavo tell Jack. They're friends."

"Is that why you told me?"

"I know it isn't much, but this whole deception isn't about you. And yes, I find all this cloak and dagger horseshit juvenile and cumbersome. I was against it being done this way from the beginning. I am really sorry. I am."

He was looking right at her.

With the smallest of nods, she accepted his apology.

Chapter 19

Dinner was awkward.

Wyatt had cooked, and each place had been meticulously set, including Rupert's vacant one. The meal was tenderloin drizzled with a mushroom sauce and caramelized onions with sweet potatoes on the side. It was a lovely, aromatic meal that everyone sat and stared at except for Wyatt.

Next to Wyatt was Rupert's empty seat, and since Wyatt sat at the end of the table it was as though he had been isolated; estranged from the rest of the team given the gulf Rupert once filled.

Wyatt's knife scratched at his plate as he sawed his steak.

"What is it that you did before getting this assignment, Wyatt?" Jack asked.

"Before being assigned to Janus?"

"Yes."

"I was special forces for the Army."

"And what did the Special Forces have you doing?"

Wyatt made eye contact with Jack. "I did whatever was needed." Lingering a moment, he returned his attention to his steak.

Jack continued to process the statement and its intended implications, when Ingrid spoke uncharacteristically softly.

"How is Rupert?"

"He's resting now, and I'll be on call for him," Gustavo said, his red face showing signs of the heated argument he had with Jack prior to dinner. "It will be some time before we can do much of the surgery needed to repair the damage to his hip. We'll do what we can, and consider all options until we are recalled to Earth. Currently Wyatt has a cot in the infirmary and Rupert will be monitored by the best medical equipment made by man."

"He'll heal *wrong*." Ingrid's voice was full now. "And we can't return to Earth until they link with us. We can't go home early." There was a growing tremble in her thick, alto voice. Mary placed a feather-light hand on Ingrid's.

"Gustavo is a medical doctor, among other things. And the AutoDoc might perform the surgeries needed, so options are still on the table," she said, Ingrid listening and nodding reluctantly.

Jack was still watching Wyatt. "I'm locking Oracle until further notice," he said, waiting until Wyatt had his mouth full. Wyatt nodded and continued chewing. This was not the reaction that Jack expected. "So no more incursions or examining the Beta Line, *whatsoever.*"

Wyatt took his time finishing his bite. Finally swallowing, he responded. "I understand, and it is completely within your rights given your responsibilities on this station."

"What?" Jack roared. "My responsibilities suddenly matter to you? This whole time I have been lied to, subverted in my job, and now that the game is up and you've been *caught* in the lie, I'm suddenly respected?"

"Should I argue? Or plead, Jack? Would that repair your wounded ego?"

"Oh fuck *you!*" Jack snapped.

"Jack!" Mary said.

"Ego does seem to be the order of the day, now doesn't it?" Wyatt asked. "The hubris involved in building this station, and breaching this enterprise, can't be healthy on a personal level. The bottom line is that Janus is much larger than any of us, any of her crew that pilots it. Our deception toward you, Jack, was no judgment of your character. Certain criteria had to be agreed upon from the beginning of this station's inception or it would never have been built. Or built by us, at least."

Wyatt took a break from his lecture to scoop up some potatoes. With a gulp he continued, "Would you have wanted Gustavo to never have built Janus? Your girl, Janus? Would you rather he'd taken the project to Russia or China where the abuses of this power would go unchecked? Truth is, Jack, you have the luxury of your childish scorn toward your friend—your friend that brought you on the greatest journey humanity has ever embarked upon—because he *lied* on your behalf. While you are brilliant, and arguably irreplaceable, there were levels of functionality regarding Janus that her investors were willing to accept. But, Gustavo made it clear that he wasn't coming here into the void without *you*. So the lie was born. The budget spiraled, and the lie continued for the sake of cultivating support with various, opposing funders." Wyatt cut another slice. "And there it is. You'll have to get over it. Just as I'll have to get over Oracle being locked under your exclusive control due to your puerile judgment. If we sit here, squandering the greatest tool ever conceived, because you don't feel comfortable, so be it." He popped the speared morsel into his mouth. "The team that relieves us will just continue the mission and your protest will be a footnote."

Silenced reigned. Jack's eyes had lost some of their hate and Ingrid's fingers found her fork and knife.

"Even if we wanted to, *could* we continue incursions with only one person? What is the protocol on that?" Mary inquired to the table in general.

"Well?" Jack drilled Gustavo with his gaze.

"One man could go by himself, if one of the men became ill or unable to continue the mission," Gustavo replied.

"And that thing is still out there. Wyatt, I want to see those tapes. I want to see what happened," Ingrid said.

"I'm not so certain—actually… yes. Ingrid, I could use your input on it. I'll upload the whole feed from both our sets."

"And why the change of heart?"

"Because we are all on the same team, and my orders to keep the prior mission under wraps no longer stands given my failure to fulfill my objectives. Might as well."

"So the orders you were a slave to change just like that?"

"I am adherent to the needs of the situation if the mission is either a failure or completed. And since Oracle is locked down, I have little else to do to further my research into the Xeno."

They finished their dinner in silence, Wyatt eating his fill, Gustavo and Jack nibbling, and Ingrid and Mary barely touching their food. Soon after, in the recreation room, parked on the couches, Wyatt displayed his and Rupert's feeds side-by-side in all their bloody gore and horror. Everyone's gazes were fixed to the screen except Wyatt, who sat off to the side, his gaze roaming the ceiling as he listened.

Ingrid's hands moved to her mouth at the sight of the ears. Jack and Ingrid paled at the deaths of the gunmen. Mary gasped when Rupert lifted his carbine to fire on the Xeno. All of them remained silent as Wyatt deftly battled to protect his injured comrade while fending off the looming beast that blinked in and out of the world, its long grasp constantly clutching at him.

The screens went dark, both listing the run times of the clips. Mary silently stood, walked to the screen, and through the touch interface rewound Wyatt's. Playing it all backwards, the carbine formed from nothing under the Xeno's foot, the hallway wall pulled itself together, blood ran up the wallpaper and arced into the head that reformed on a gunman's shoulders, and Mary came to the scene where Wyatt was trying to listen to the community center across the street.

She pressed play and opened the sound settings with a gliding touch. Several slider adjustments later, she could hear the background noises more clearly. Playing a four second loop over and over again, she listened to the muffled and tormented song being sung out of the recreational building. She turned it up, and began trying to make out words.

Mouthing the hymnal *Holy, Holy, Holy,* Mary quickly turned to the crowd who were still on the couch, all of which were still shell-shocked at the ferocity of what they had viewed.

"It's a hymnal… they're singing. They're singing… it sounds like…a revival."

Chapter 20

Surrounded by organized projections of victims, locations, and newspaper clippings, Mary pondered in the safe and dark seclusion of her archives cabinet. Jack had made good on his word to lock down Oracle, but Oracle's prior recordings were still available, and Mary had set about trying to figure out where the Xeno had struck throughout time.

If Jack's current count was correct, the Xeno caused twenty-two fissures within the Beta Line and counting. At what number would it complete its task? If Oracle continued to search, how many more would it find? Was the line eventually going to reform into some unrecognizable future? Could the timeline collapse under the weight of weakened and contradicting causalities?

What would that even *look* like? Since humans perceive time linearly could a person even begin to experience such a place?

Mary's head hurt. Pinching the bridge of her nose, she tried to relieve the pressure. Turned low in the background, she had the audio that Wyatt had recorded playing… the macabre revival wailing and sobbing.

It had been almost a full day since that awkward dinner. Gustavo had committed himself to Rupert's medical care, Wyatt had vanished into his private workshop, Jack was off moping somewhere, and Ingrid was last seen eating ice cream in the rec room.

Something occurred to her. The Xeno was attacking those that harmed the voiceless. It targeted those who recruited and abused child soldiers, the Tulsa riots were notoriously covered up, and Leo Frank was constantly written off by anti-Semitic historical revisionists. The KKK was at new heights during the DC march. The RUF would have continued to operate for years, using those same children as fodder. After these offenders would have gotten away with it, after the victims had been brutalized, the Xeno would emerge and punish. That way its targets could never be mistaken as wrongful victims or oppressed.

Hence the seemingly improvised revival in that community center was filled by racist rioters. Is that why the Xeno let them live, earless and traumatized? Clearly it had let many victims live before, given so many soldiers missing from the African camp, the Leo Frank lynching with so many witnesses left with minimal or no injuries.

It appears. It shocks with violence, and then it vanishes and leaves survivors to tell the tale.

Mary moved her hands to the folder with Wyatt and Rupert's dissected feeds. She had noticed something earlier. Opening it up, she enlarged a picture of the Xeno from Rupert's feed. His carbine was raised, and his UI had targeted the Xeno's temple. The nitrogen round had been set to 'hard point' to penetrate its thick white hide and skull.

A few moments before he fired, she saw its eye move. Not the whole head, only the rose-gold eye flexed in the socket, indicative of someone peering subtly to their side. Mary's suspicion that it knew Rupert was there for some time continued to grow. It could see or sense him. So why the ruse? Why would the Xeno make itself a large looming target in the hallway next to the soda counter? To make itself vulnerable? Was it testing Wyatt and Rupert? Was it allowing them to act, therefore placing them within the confines of its morality? Could it only, through code or perhaps programming, attack a hostile or guilty subject?

Is that why it crushed Rupert's hip, but let Wyatt go? Was it pleased that Wyatt killed three of the enemy?

There was a gentle knock at the closed cabinet door. Mary shrunk the image, swiveled in her chair, and opened it. Ingrid was there.

"You left this cup of coffee sitting around. I figured I'd bring it to you. It's nice and stale." She held the mug with both hands.

Mary nodded, took it, and had a sip. "Thank you."

"It's a pathetic peace offering," Ingrid confessed. Mary was puzzled for a moment, but her face quickly showed that she understood. Ingrid had felt bad for hiding the truth of Janus' first mission.

"It's okay. I'm not that broken up about it, no matter how unwise it was to steal from the Beta Line. What was it you did? Did you just drop satellites to gather data?"

"Yeah. Around one hundred years in the future several times."

Mary nodded while taking another sip. "One hundred years? Does Detroit still suck?"

Ingrid laughed, relieved. "It's built back up. Australia has boomed. My guess is a lot of Westerners moved there because of the land and the guise that it is a Westernized country."

"I always heard they had horrible laws regarding internet censoring."

"The coolest thing I saw is that people are living in Chernobyl again."

"Really?"

"No joke. A bunch of lights there. Looked like street lamps."

"Well, they *do* have a power plant."

Both ladies shared a mean-spirited snicker.

"I also picked up some transmissions with the satellites. Pop music will still suck in the future. But people still listen to Willy Nelson, so it isn't all bad."

"Why not leave a satellite there for, say, several hundred years? Maybe leave it far enough out of orbit to watch from a greater distance?"

"That was an option given to me, but there was a lot of traffic with other objects, and the Moon had substantial observatories on both the planet side and the far side. I stopped incurring probes because, well, honestly I think I could have been spotted within a day, never mind a hundred years."

Mary nodded in agreement.

"It would have been ugly if I recalled a probe and the last forty years of its pictures were people in lab coats starring at it. Or, God forbid, they take it apart and I don't get a probe back at all."

Mary sighed. "What are we going to do with the remaining three years-plus we have to sit around here?"

"As boring as it might be, I feel far worse for Rupert. No family, no support, and no proper rehabilitation center. It's hard to complain about my life when someone else came near death like that." As Ingrid finished her sentence her gaze wandered over Mary's shoulder to where the Xeno was looking back at her from the corner of its cocked eye. "But I'm okay not playing in the sandbox anymore. I am rightfully scared shitless of that thing."

Chapter 21

The AutoDoc's readout displayed Rupert's skeleton, and with thick fingers Gustavo removed the holographic bones until his display only focused on the hips, legs, and lower back. The bed that cupped Rupert was like a dead spider, curled upon its back, its legs twitching and bobbing gently around its ensnared victim's body. Occasionally, a mechanical limb would tenderly retract itself from his body, tipped in blood, while two others swooped in to continue the work while the patient remained asleep.

Within the past twelve hours, the AutoDoc had performed three surgeries with precise ability, superhuman agility, and expert accuracy. Most of Rupert's left hip had now been either replaced with layered carbon-fiber supports or fused together with molten alloys.

The joint looked good, the swollen scar tissue was under control, and the socket was where it should be. Gustavo allowed himself a moment of pride. He was pleased, and the thought of Rupert up and about smiling at everyone made him hope that Jack would ease up, talk to him again, and maybe unlock Oracle.

Truth was, Gustavo felt a hint of pressure to resolve things not only for the mission's sake, but for the sake of the upcoming movie night. It was trivial, but true.

"He looks like he's doing well under your care, Gus," Wyatt said from the doorway. "I was checking from my terminal to see how things are progressing. His hip looks solid. Any chance he'll be waking up soon?"

"Not sure, really. I scaled back his medication, so he'll open his eyes in a few hours after some more natural rest. The pain should be managed fairly well, but I don't know if he'll be doing much talking."

Wyatt stepped in and walked over to the side of Rupert's bed, placing a yellow envelope on his slowly rising and falling chest while gingerly avoiding the working limbs. Rupert's eyes were tightly shut. The AutoDoc's spider arms retracted from the presence of the yellow rectangle, and one with a tiny optic zoomed in close to it to examine it. "Jack will get over it, Gus. He's just a hot head."

"Yeah, I know…"

"Out of curiosity, could Jack still incur with Oracle locked? I mean, could Oracle still activate if only under Jack's exclusive control?"

"I really doubt it. Jack locked it with a multi-tiered rotating digital lock. It's several stages of passwords and geometric shapes that react and alter to every faulty bit of input. So he'd have to spend the part of the day to unlock it, setup an incursion completely by himself without my help or Mary's input, and then run all the way up to the carousel. Seriously, I would put out of your mind any worries that Jack will somehow take over Janus."

"Oh no, I wasn't thinking that at all. I'm just curious as to the nature of the situation. But I am relieved that no one will be incurring," Wyatt admitted, placing his hands in his pockets.

"Really?"

"Oh sure. This has gotten messy, and in fact, I am 100% behind no one else using Oracle or the carousel. I've been thinking about it, and while it is certainly a squandered opportunity, further damage could be insurmountable."

"That's a different tune than what you were whistling at dinner."

"Listening to those feeds and watching everyone's reactions steered my opinion some. I've also been up all night fiddling in the workshop and it cleared my head. So, if it comes up between you and Jack, I think he should be encouraged to keep Oracle locked indefinitely."

Gustavo was baffled. "Okay. I'll keep that in mind. Well, except the indefinite part. If Oracle is locked at the time of recall from Earth, Janus won't respond and we'll be stuck here."

"Ah, didn't know that. Well, hopefully Jack will unlock it just prior." Wyatt's eyes were distant. "I'm going to lay down for a bit, and catch some sleep. Do me a favor and make sure Rupert opens this envelop when he wakes up? It's a protocol thing for us grunts if we get injured. I'm off to snooze."

In an uncharacteristic gesture, Wyatt clapped his hand on Gustavo's shoulder, and then walked out.

Gustavo stood there, processing the conversation unsuccessfully.

Wyatt slipped down the hallway to the lift, and descended to the living quarters. Quietly and quickly, he darted down the hallway to his room. Under his bed, he opened his private wooden case, took what he wanted from it, and tucked it into his belt. He then retrieved a red and green flannel shirt from his closet and put it on over his white T-shirt, buttoned it, but left it un-tucked. Next, he sifted through his boots and finally settled on an old worn pair that had travelled with him for many years.

He laced them up, his hands shaking with anticipation.

Marching down the hall, Wyatt found his path passing the juncture that led to Mary's cabinet. He paused. Looking down the hall, he could see a glowing light from the cracked cabinet door.

There were a number of thoughts and feelings that crossed his mind, but in the end, optimism won and Wyatt figured that to say good bye would be pointless.

He smiled, thought of Mary across the table from him over breakfast, and continued on his way to his private workshop.

Entering, he saw that Rupert's table was still disheveled from the preparation of his last fateful incursion, but Wyatt's table had seen a lot more activity as of late. Things had been carelessly shoved onto the floor and broken. Simple soldering tools, a welder, and metal scraps littered the surface of his work area and at the center of Wyatt's table was a tiny aquarium-like tank with a long worm floating in a gentle blue liquid. Electrical wires came out of its sides and disappeared into the base of the small container. A computer monitor had been clumsily arranged next to the worm-tank.

As the worm floated in the blue fluid, two tiny black eyes near its front end opened and viewed Wyatt. It watched him cross the room and snatch up a large metal flashlight from a far table. He tested its weight with his hands, and then slid it under his belt.

An electrical beep sounded, informing Wyatt that something was being typed on the monitor on his table.

The words '*I'm scared*' were written in large, white type.

"I know. I am too," Wyatt said while walking over, taking a moment to check all of the cables coming out of the bottom of the tank. It was a disorganized bundle of cords and wires that all led to the removed panel of Wyatt's information terminal that linked him to Janus' systems.

Are you certain this is the best thing to do?

"We've talked about the concept of certainty before, haven't we?"

Yes. I still find comfort in it, fictional as it is.

Wyatt was satisfied with the cable setup. He sat on a stool directly across from the tiny eyes of the floating worm. Folding his hands in front of himself, he smiled a soothing and disarming smile.

"I have faith in your abilities." Wyatt looked to the monitor for a typed response.

I appreciate that. I've only had a few hours to acclimate myself with Janus' systems. The Oracle mainframe is also closed to me.

"Have faith. You're smarter than Oracle by an amount you yourself can't measure."

I'm ready to start the carousel whenever you are.

"Remember your promise, my friend. Remember not to tell anyone anything if I don't come back. For the sake of literally everything, no one on this station can know where I went."

I understand, but it will be hard to mask the data log.

"Again, have faith," Wyatt said while standing, bouncing on the balls of his feet to get his blood up. "I'm ready. Start it up."

I'll miss our chess games.

Wyatt smiled a chastising smile. "You say that like we won't have one tonight."

The far security door opened, leading to the stealth suit prepping room. The door beyond that opened as well.

Wyatt cleared his head and all expression dropped from his face.

He walked briskly forward.

Chapter 22

The overhead lights in the dining alcove were dim, blanketing the boisterous mosaic behind the long table in a soothing light. Mary sat, her eyes laminated by the glow, as she watched Jack. He slumped in his chair, arms folded across his chest, brooding in a childish fashion while sounds of Ingrid tinkering in the kitchen reached them through the propped swinging door.

Five places had been set, each with a spoon and mat.

"You know, it's not about *you*, Jack," Mary said in a whisper. "You are going to need to get over yourself and understand that we are lucky to have good people here with us."

"People that lie?"

Mary flushed. "You must be pampered, wonder kid. Some of us weren't discovered as savant geniuses at a young age like you and Gustavo. We had to scrape through bureaucracy and navigate a male-dominated field."

"And that's somehow my fault!?"

"Not at all, but it takes away any excuse you have to pout."

Ingrid came through the door with three large sundaes teetering in her grasp. "I think Mary is trying to tell you that your head is so far up your ass that you are only seeing *brown*," she said with a huff as she put a dish in front of Jack first, then Mary, and then herself as she sat down. Each triple scoop sundae had nuts, fudge, a banana, sliced strawberries, and whipped cream.

Jack went to open his mouth but Ingrid pointed her spoon at his chest menacingly. "Eat your sundae, Jack. And not another word until it is gone." He obeyed, and Ingrid permitted herself a proud smile as she dug in. Mary was already on her third bite. "You see, Mary," Ingrid said, changing her focus. "You need to know how to talk to these Jewish boys. They are immune to guilt because their mothers have built their resistances so effectively."

"Whoa, so my *mother* is now—" Jack was silenced by the spoon's returning poise, aimed at his sternum; his gaze locked with it as if it were a hooded cobra dancing prior to its strike.

"You see? You just have to boss them around," she said with a wink. Jack cracked a smile, and picked up his spoon.

"Can you at least understand why I'm upset? Either of you?"

With a full mouth, Mary nodded. However Ingrid didn't wait to complete her bite to respond.

"But don't crawl around here with the butt-hurt, *capisci*? So what if we snagged things from the future and recorded data? It was going to happen eventually. It was just higher on the priority list than your idealism would have liked."

"I made it clear. I made it *so* clear…"

"Made what clear? That nothing could be taken out of the Beta Line? But does it really *violate* anything?"

"Nothing I could prove. That hardly means that there isn't a consequence. My naiveté or inability to anticipate an outcome doesn't absolve us from *that outcome*. Just because you are ignorant of the speed limit doesn't mean you're not speeding."

"So uh… the Xeno is space time's police force? And instead of pulling us over it just runs willy-nilly in the twentieth century killing bad people?"

"I'd hardly consider it that self-aware. Its methods are far too brutish to have any precision. And, admittedly, the Xeno can easily be a random tangent that is complicating my understanding of things. But I don't like having this whole extra variable of items stolen from the Beta Line …

items, I might add, that are locked up and capable of lord knows what. Maybe we stole something really important that was keeping things in check!"

"Honestly I am far more concerned," Mary said, waiting until Ingrid's and Jack's eyes met hers to continue, "about the three people Wyatt killed. With Oracle locked to me, I can't read anything of the line. And the records on the Tulsa riots were largely journalistic and hardly viable. I have some birth certificate records from different courthouses, but to try and cross reference the Alpha Line with the Beta Line to see what entire families no longer exist would take years in and of itself."

"I'm not opening Oracle right now. I'm just... not."

"I wasn't trying to push you."

"I just want us all on the same page. Admittedly, it would be fascinating to see how that avalanche would impact the Western world as it progressively tracked, but someone else can do that once we go home."

The three of them focused on their ice cream. Several minutes passed and during the savory relaxation Jack eventually asked, "Where's Gustavo?"

"Looking after Rupert. He said that Rupert was stirring awake and that he was going to chat with him a bit and check his med balance before coming up here for his sundae. I have fixings in the kitchen for him and Wyatt. I'll take one for Rupert after, if he's up for one." Ingrid said, almost polishing off her dish before Jack and Mary had gone halfway through theirs.

"I think I'll feel more at ease when we see that Rupert's going to be okay," Jack confessed. "That would be calming, I think. I don't know about you, but that was scary... watching all that."

Mary and Ingrid nodded.

"I mean, seeing it right in his face and then watching everything shake like that. And Wyatt. He blew those men apart. Without a second thought. I knew that they would give us good people for incurring and that they had probably been tested, but it's different to see someone you know just be so… effectively inhumane."

Mary thought on this, and it occurred to her with muted surprise that she wasn't at all disturbed by Wyatt's actions. He had a choice, he made it, and he didn't dwell on it. She had seen so many horrors through the eyes of those two men so far, and all her life she'd read history accounts of butchering, murder, and rape so the concept had become a part of her life. Perhaps she had been numbed?

The image of Wyatt plucking the strings of his instrument came to her, and she saw a man at peace. Listening to him, and seeing how he had moved through Rupert's recorded footage, she saw that same man. He was a killer, a hunter, and a fleeing and desperate prey under the Xeno's gaze, but the entire time he was at peace.

"We might have lost Rupert entirely if Wyatt hadn't acted. Which would be less humane?" Mary asked Jack pointedly. Jack nodded, and went back to finishing his sundae.

Ingrid was pleased to see her ice cream solution working its magic. She was confident that once Jack calmed down, and Gustavo and he were pulled into the gravity of their friendship once more, Janus would be fully active again and it would continue its purpose. All would be well.

This hopeful thought was the second to last thing to pass through Ingrid's mind. The last was the bullet that was fired from inside the rec room's hallway door.

The ringing muted all other sound. Jack and Mary jumped in their seats, their bodies surging with shuddering adrenaline. Ingrid's head rolled back, her one eye crossing the line of sight from the other, and with a sad exhaling, she flopped forward, her head hitting her empty sundae bowl.

More shots came, and both Jack and Mary slipped down their seats and under the table. Jack gripped the table's underside and began grunting in an effort to overturn it to provide cover. Mary, still half dazed, helped. Ingrid's body slid off and flopped on the floor as the table came down, defending them from the larger part of the darkened room.

More gunshots came, striking at the table's surface with a muted sound. Mary's ears rang. Jack spun about and put his back to the table while looking around desperately. His breathing was wheezy and irregular. Mary saw a lot of red on his shirt and along his side.

"We need to move the table!" she shouted, stepping over him with her head down and gripping a table leg. With all her might, she shoved and began shifting the table along the floor toward the kitchen swing door. On one arm, and bleeding badly, Jack followed her.

The next barrage of gunshots came from a different angle.

Mary reached the kitchen and gripped Jack. He screamed in pain, shooing her away. His face was changing color, and he swatted at her. The open palm of his hand shoved her toward the kitchen door.

There was a clomping sound beyond her sight, and the snap of a pistol slide locking into place nearby. Mary's fight or flight instincts could no longer be subdued. She ran into the kitchen and closed the swinging door behind her.

Running into the larder, she knocked over boxes looking for something, anything to save herself with. Knives? Another gun? Where was the exit? She didn't know of a back exit in the kitchen but there had to be one given fire regulations, right? Where was the door?

Spinting back out, Mary saw a figure standing over Jack just outside the flapping door. Continuing down the hallway a moment later, she heard a single gunshot.

Hesitation gripped her. Jack had taken a round point blank. Jack had been executed. Ingrid was dead. Gustavo and Rupert and Wyatt could be in danger. They could be dead too.

Mary was angry. It flushed in her shoulders and her thighs and she felt a prickling all over. Succumbing to impulse, she spun about, slinked toward the flapping kitchen door, and waited… crouched.

The silhouette of the gunman peeked through the round port window, peering in, as the door slowly flapped to a standstill. There was something odd about the assailant's walk. An awkwardness.

Mary sprung and kicked with all her might upon the door, firing it open and directly into the face of the killer. He cried out in surprising agony and crumbled into the sideways table. It was Rupert, and Mary was on him savagely in a second. Without thinking, she drove her right knee into his tender, destroyed hip as hard as she could.

He looked to scream, but no sound came from his mouth. Sliding to the ground, the cane in his right hand clanged to the floor as he collapsed.

Mary kicked the military pistol somewhere into the dark, wooden floor of the echoing rec room. Jack had a red pool haloing his head like a Russian icon's nimbus as he bled from his throat, his eyes pleading. Dropping to her knees she covered his wound with her hands, unsure of how to stop the bleeding without choking him. Everything had become blurry as her eyes welled up with tears and her throat swelled with shame.

"I'm so sorry," she mouthed to him. "I'm so sorry." His hands flopped a bit at his sides. One reached up to touch her and groped about her shoulder. Panic in his gaze increased as blood poured between her clasped fingers.

With a violent tremor, the last of Jack left, his grimace slowly easing as his eyes dilated and fixed on wherever his mortality had fled to.

Mary pulled her hands away, covered in blood that rapidly cooled against her skin. It was the most unsettling sensation she had ever encountered. She went to wipe her hands on Jack's shirt, but found the action deplorably disrespectful so she looked about for a napkin.

It occurred to her that she was looking to clean her hands when she should be checking to see if Wyatt and Gustavo were safe.

Oh God! Gustavo was with Rupert just before this. And Wyatt was catching sleep nearby.

Mary leapt from Jack, and with bloody hands gripped Rupert. His eyes twitched and he moaned.

"Where are Gustavo and Wyatt? *Where? Did you kill them too?*"

Rupert's eyes focused with apparent effort and he looked at her quizzically. Then a smile slowly crept onto his face, pearly teeth peeking out.

"My god… you…"

"Talk! Why? *Why?*"

Rupert shook his head, but his smile remained. Mary knelt on his right knee. He winced. "Did you kill them too? Did you kill them too!?"

"They're dead." He smiled. It wasn't a pleased or triumphant smile, but a dazed and fascinated one. He was like a wide-eyed child watching a tsunami roll into the shore.

Mary began beating him, driving her knee again and again into his freshly repaired hip. She felt things snap, and heard a pop inside of him like a twig breaking under a pile of wet leaves. His face was obscured by the motion of her fury, and soon he became entirely limp.

Before stepping away, she drove his head into the underside of the table in a last act of punishment.

Mary stood, on wobbly knees that could barely hold her weight, as her hands dripped onto the floor. Ingrid was slumped on her side, Jack was dead on his back with a hand on his chest, and Rupert was in a twisted heap, half stuffed into the table's underside. The only movement in the room was her panting, heaving reflection in Jack's blood pool mirroring her numb gaze back at her.

Chapter 23

The first place she ran was the infirmary. Gustavo had been there, and despite what Rupert said she hoped to find him alive. Wyatt had retired to his quarters to sleep, and again she hoped that his door had been sealed, protecting him.

The image of Rupert looming over Wyatt sleeping peacefully angered her even further. As she ran and scrambled down the corridors of Janus she thought of his mystifying grin retching from his face as she plowed her knee into his decimated hip.

Between frantic pants she called out Gustavo's and Wyatt's names alternatively. Soon she was in the medical subsection, the floor under the carousel, and running down the hallway. The door to Rupert's infirmary room was open; splashing a band of light into the darkened hallway, with a sheet half-dragged out and twisted on the floor.

Mary wouldn't be able to recall the series of physical actions and reactions she had next. The room was disheveled, with opened drawers and items everywhere. Several of the AutoDoc's arms were bent back, and Gustavo was facedown with the handle of a scalpel jutting up out of the back of his head where his skull met his neck.

She immediately went to him, her hand extending slowly as if he would spring up and gasp. Reaching under his jaw she felt for a pulse, and eventually let her hand rest on his head, gently stroking his hair. She mouthed "I'm sorry" and then bolted out the door to search the hallway for any sign of Wyatt.

Taking a lungful of air, Mary was about to call out once more when she noticed the sheet that was dragged into the hallway had been pulled and pointed in a telltale direction. Rupert, when leaving, must have caught it on either his foot or cane and dragged it into an unintentional arrow revealing his direction.

And it led her to their workshop.

Mary ran in and saw two long tables filling the room, both bent outward from their centers away from each other like two parentheses lacking content. Everything was a wreck: tools of various shapes and sizes with mysterious purposes strewn about.

The first thing to catch her eye was the long mess of cables pouring out of the disassembled terminal against the wall. Bound and twisted like an enormous optic nerve, it extended along the floor, over the nearer table, and under the other.

She followed it, and the discarded flannel shirt crumbled on the table told her Wyatt had done this.

"Wyatt!" she called, instinctively seeing his shirt as a sign of his presence.

A tiny electronic chime sounded and a screen with fingerprints on it displayed white, plain letters. Mary angled herself to read it.

Mr. Wyatt is not here.

Mary looked around.

It chimed again.

You must be Ms. Mary Forsythe. It is a pleasure to meet you.

Mary looked around, under the table, along the ceiling for a security camera eyeing her, and finally down the hallway where the doors to the carousel stood open. She had never seen this area before, and she was very much in the forbidden part of Janus. Down that hallway, somewhere and somehow, time travel occurred.

Her left foot took a step toward it.

You may not want to go there right now, Ms. Forsythe.

The farthest door slowly closed, with each preceding door following it doing the same. Mary looked around again. With a huff of frustration, she turned to the monitor looking for a keyboard to respond. Tossing things off the table, she muttered.

"I don't have time for this shit. Where's Wyatt?!"

I cannot say.

She pointed a finger at the monitor with a snarl. "Who are *you*?"

I am Magus Kami, series eight of the third generation. Mr. Wyatt is my friend, but I do not currently know where he is. You are Ms. Mary Forsythe, and a close friend of his. He spoke fondly of you, and made it clear that if anything were to go wrong I could rely on you to protect, maintain, and stimulate me.

"So you're an AI?"

Without the 'A', I suppose. I'm in the container next to this monitor, and I am very real and of flesh and blood.

Mary's eyes darted from side to side, and settled on the liquid tank with the long worm looking at her with tiny black eyes. She gasped, jumped backwards, and looked about for something to swing as a weapon.

I cannot leave this tank on my own, and I have not teeth, claws, or the muscle mass to even constrict in a hostile manner. There is no way I could physically harm you.

Mary's mouth cracked a desolate grin of disbelief. She shook her head side to side, tears forming in the corners of her eyes.

"I just need to know about Wyatt," she croaked. "Do you know where he is?"

I greatly suspect that he is dead, Ms. Forsythe. I assure you that I am sorry. He was very kind.

Trying not to claw at her face, Mary continued with her next question as calmly as she was able. "Do you know where his body is? So I can see to it? Like everyone else's."

I do not know where his body is.

Numbly, she nodded, and left the room to return to where Gustavo lay dead. Her legs carried her on their own, on auto-pilot, and when she stood over him, Mary compacted all of her reservations, fears, and angst into a box as if for storage, and pushed it far away.

Kneeling down, she first pulled the scalpel out with an unreserved yank. This was no longer Gustavo, but a limp 250 pound body. The thin blade required more effort than she expected, the tissue around it having swollen and firmed. Next came the task of rolling him over. She wasn't sure *why* this was the next step, but somehow it was. Somehow, Mary knew he had to be on his back facing the ceiling.

With a grunt and a snarl, she found she couldn't flip him. Both his arms were down at his sides, securing him in position so Mary wrestled them up to flank his head. Gripping his calves, she then folded his legs and twisted them, working that twist upward to his waist where she could pry him off the floor and onto his left side. It was difficult at first, but as momentum built, he rolled quickly over onto his back, his face a brutal and flattened black and blue bruise.

She leapt back, gasping at his swollen tongue stuck between his teeth and his one eye wide while the other was tightly shut. That horrid image of pain and distortion quickly overwrote her usual thoughts of his living visage. Mary feared that whenever she would think of Gustavo from now on, this is what she would see in her mind's eye.

What next?

Body bag. She needed a body bag.

Drawers, cabinets, closets, everywhere she looked she found nothing. Where there even any on the station? What would she do once they were bagged? Was there cold storage for bodies? Did they think of that? Or would she have to keep them in with the food stores and ice cream?

Why did she think of ice cream?

Throwing her arms in the air, she wandered into the hallway. Her legs took her to the bench she had seen Wyatt at yesterday, and she sat in very much the same exhausted fashion.

A crackling came over the intercom. It was tiny, full of static, and weak. After a moment, a very synthetic voice came, like something from a computer assisting the blind.

"What is it you are looking for, Ms. Forsythe?" it asked.

Mary jumped to her feet and ran back into Wyatt and Rupert's work-room. Snatching up a small tack hammer, she ran toward the worm's tank, ready to bash it in.

"Please don't—" the creature managed to say before she got there. Driving the end of the hammer into the tank's side, the impact sloshed the liquid and tussled the worm about, its tiny eyes wincing. "We are all that is left."

She stopped, processing its plea.

"What the fuck are you? Are you Janus? An alien? Something from the Beta Line?" All her anger and stress piled out as she pointed the ham-mer at the tank like a menacing sword.

A moment passed, and more static came. The tiny black eyes were still shut tightly.

"Please don't hurt me anymore," the voice said.

"You're in the system. You've compromised the system. You're inside the station via this terminal. *Why*? Why did anyone do this? *Who* did this?"

"Mr. Wyatt did. He needed me to control elements of Janus."

"To what end?"

"I can't say. But Mr. Wyatt is dead. He is gone."

"Why can't you say? Why can't you tell me—" Mary halted mid-sentence and her eyes expanded to their limit. Turning her head to the sealed security doors that lead to the carousel, her demeanor became dangerously calm.

"All right, you are going to tell me where in the Beta Line he went," she said.

"I cannot."

"You can. You will. Like you said, I am a friend of Mr. Wyatt. Where did Wyatt go?"

"I cannot tell."

She lunged for the tank, hammer in hand.

"Tell me or, whatever you are, I'll kill you."

Static silence crackled over the speaker. The mechanical voice rang louder than before when it finally spoke.

"Then kill me if you must."

Pivoting on her heel, she hurled the hammer into one of the video screens over the opposite table, cracking its display. Her fingers dug into her scalp and tugged at her hair as she huffed, holding her tantrum at bay. Weak in the knees, Mary stumbled toward a stool near the worm's tank, and sat.

As the moments passed, her breathing returned to a more human standard, and her shoulders eased.

The mechanical voice spoke again, but more clearly and less symphonic. "Mr. Wyatt saved my life. He was kind, and he needed my help. I was glad to help him. He asked me to promise not to tell anyone anything about his recent actions, so I will not."

"Even to me? He made you promise to keep it a secret even to me?"

"Yes. He did mention you specifically. He said that you would look after me, and I should look after you if I could."

Mary began to cry, her hands covering her face and eyes as her heavy sobs took over. Feeling the tiny black eyes on her, she turned her back toward the small tank and leaned on her elbows. What little strength she had barely kept her upright.

Her crying eventually eased, and she felt like her lungs had taken in fresh air. Wiping her face on her shirt, she turned back toward the creature.

"How did Wyatt save you?"

"I was slated for termination." The mechanical voice was now very human, but very sedated and tender. "I was manufactured in China and leased to the United States. After some testing, it was deemed I had too much personality and my quirkiness was considered an act of industrial espionage. I was under review for termination when Mr. Wyatt and Mr. Rupert saved me."

"Do you know that Rupert killed Gustavo, Ingrid, and Jack?" Mary asked coldly.

The response was silence.

"Do you know why he did it? Why he would kill them and try and kill me?" she pressed.

"No, Ms. Forsythe. I do not know. I do not understand that. Is Mr. Rupert still alive?"

"No. No, *Mr.* Rupert is dead," Mary said with a touch of rue.

"Did you kill him?" the worm asked.

"Absolutely."

Chapter 24

According to the worm, there were four places where emergency supplies were kept within the living quarters onboard Janus, and in typical government fashion, each section had eight body bags. It was an overabundance of them, but Mary wrote off the excess as being validated for reasons that Janus' quartermaster feared, but couldn't actually figure.

She had to roll Gustavo over twice to get him on top of the body bag to make sure he was in it face-up. It never occurred to her until now that a person could be placed in a body bag with their back toward the zipper, facing the floor. What would that mean? Inconveniences for examination, certainly, but would it also be an insult? Did soldiers do it to the enemy? Should she do it to Rupert?

The act of zippering, lifting, and sealing Gustavo into cold storage in a small room near the workshop took what seemed like hours. The storage room itself had long sliding cabinets that could fit a man, but also smaller ones with plant samples and dirt that had clearly been collected prior to her arrival on the station.

With three more empty bags on her gurney, Mary made for the dining hall. "What time is it?" she asked aloud.

"Three forty-nine a.m., Ms. Forsythe."

"Listen, Gustavo was bad enough, and I'm tired, so how about you give me some conversation while I handle the rec room."

"I understand," the worm gently replied.

"And call me Mary."

"Yes, Ms. Mary."

The door was still open with Mary's bloody handprint on it. Pushing the gurney in, she steered around her favorite plush chair, avoided knocking over Wyatt's guitar resting in its stand, and pulled up to the toppled dining table.

"I am not sure what to talk about, Mary."

"Tell me," she said, stepping around the table to view the three bodies. Each had its eyes closed and seemed peaceful except for Ingrid's wide-open mouth and Jack's left hand raised above his head with his fingers curled. Perhaps his brain had sent the message to his hand to touch Mary's face as she was holding him, and his arm only gradually responded to its orders while she was beating Rupert to death.

"Tell me about yourself. Let's start there," she said.

The voice overhead began describing the genetic process and schematics involved in its physical growth and design. Apparently lungs were troublesome so a nutrient solution with vitamins and such was required for it to soak in. While the United States and Norway did much of the pioneering research and technology behind the science archaically termed 'flesh mechanics', there were legal issues of actually producing the creatures like the Magus. This was how China became involved in their production.

Mary was passively listening. She tried to focus on the overhead voice, but the first challenge she had was which person did she bag first? Was the choice significant somehow?

She started with Ingrid, and was surprised to find that she was a compact and firm woman even given her stout appearance.

"So China made you. Are there a lot of you?"

"My gestation takes approximately a year, and over seventy percent of my kind dies during that time. Out of one hundred Magus produced, approximately three make it to standard."

"What do you cost? To buy, not to make, I mean."

"We are often leased to foreign nations for large fees, exchanges, and concessions. Only China legally owns us."

"So, more than just money," Mary said with a huff as she cleared plates from Ingrid's body and rolled her over twice onto the body bag. "The United States wanted you, a Chinese citizen, running what exactly?"

"I was intended to handle port activity for freighters, cargo storage and sorting, as well as civilian boat traffic."

"For which port?"

"The Gulf coast."

This gave Mary pause. "That is a hell of a system."

"It was a closed network built specifically for a Magus to operate. It had a fail-safe in order to make sure I didn't extend my intended bounds. One of the first generation Magi was assigned all motor traffic operations in Beijing, but it extended beyond its intended contract into other cities in order to control the external cascade effect on Beijing. This became an issue for the other areas since their efficiency was being sacrificed for Beijing's significantly, and the magus was to be terminated."

"So, you had a closed computer network to run the entire gulf coast with?" Mary said, dragging Ingrid's bag by its straps to the edge of the three stairs where the gurney was descended and angled, waiting.

"That network went to another Magus. However it was my intended destination."

"So, you were slated for termination? What did they not like about you, Mr. Magus?"

"I asked several personal questions, and they were not taken lightly."

Ingrid was on the gurney, and Mary propped her hands against her lower back as she stretched upward with a yawn. At the tail end of her yawn, she said, "go on."

"I asked the director if he would be my friend, and if we could play chess."

"I was expecting something more Asimovian like 'do I have a soul' or 'where do I go when I die'."

"Souls and my eventual expiration where not concerns of mine at the time. I was merely lonely and wanting company. Wanting was the issue, not curiosity."

Mary continued listening while pushing Ingrid down the hall toward cold storage. "Because you wanted something, they figured you'd want everything? Is that it?"

"Perhaps. I am not certain."

"Serves you right for wanting something, you know," Mary said sarcastically as she opened a long metal drawer and shoved Ingrid onto its steel slab. "Wanting is the source of all suffering, if I know my Buddhism."

"I know nothing of Buddhism."

"I'll make sure you can dip into my archives. It will make good reading," she said. "When you do so, maybe then we can settle on a good name for you. I'm not too keen on 'Magus'. Feels demeaning."

"I do not feel demeaned being called what I am."

"Just wait until you get into the archives." Spinning the gurney around, she left to fetch the other two.

Magus continued to talk about its construction, impressive immune system, and large brain mass. It also asserted that an annelid life form was seen as easier to manipulate genetically than most phyla and the less human-appearing the genetically engineered life form, the better.

She next focused on bagging Rupert.

"And did Wyatt scare you when you saw him? Stealthy and dangerous?"

"Not at all. He was in a military uniform, reached into the vat and gathered me into a tank, and had Rupert carry as much nutrient solution as he could carry. No one was the wiser."

Mary smirked. "A man of many talents." She continued arranging Rupert's leg, the left hip joint swollen beyond human shape, in an effort to finish zipping the bag.

"I asked him how he managed to fool everyone around him, and he said that all military men act the same when in uniform regardless of the century."

She carted Rupert to a slab, and he soon joined Ingrid and Gustavo in a corresponding drawer. Last was Jack, his hand hauntingly raised with palm open and fingers curled. The voice came overhead again.

"I just watched the footage. I am sorry, Mary."

She sighed, and pushed down on his hand. It obeyed and settled on his chest.

"He had a crush on me."

"A crush?"

"Yes, he found me attractive and did little things to show it to me. I think he wanted a relationship eventually."

"Is that common?"

"Yes. Men like me. But few are as innocent and sweet as Jack was. I liked his idealism. He was a good man," Mary said, laying out his bag.

"And a seemingly intelligent one. Wyatt brought me online to evaluate Oracle, initially. He wanted to see if I could open Oracle up without Mr. Jack knowing."

"How did that go?" Mary asked, finding Jack surprisingly light when compared to the heft of Ingrid, the bulk of Gustavo, and the tone of Rupert.

"It did not go at all. Jack devised a rotating series of passwords that were linear, verbal, geometric, and chromatic. They all required a large amount of prerequisite knowledge personal only to him, and if one wasn't answered in a correct fashion within a very particular time frame, it would reset all the rotating passwords without giving any feedback to me which password I got incorrect once the crucible was completed. Essentially the tumblers would reset into an entirely new crucible of questions for me to answer."

She paused a moment, looking at Jack's peaceful face before zipping him away. "So only he could answer it?"

"From what I could gather. Mr. Wyatt had me instead lock Oracle out of Janus' systems, and take over from there. I took over basic security monitoring when I first saw you in the workshop, so I could make sure you were okay. It is what Mr. Wyatt told me to do if I felt the need."

"Did you…" Mary lifted Jack up, dragging him onto the gurney. "… was Wyatt your commander? Did you assign him the roll of master or its equivalent?"

"Not at all. Mr. Wyatt was a friend. He was kind. I would do anything for him."

Mary nodded knowingly. "That's why they were going to destroy you, Mr. Magus. When you elevate one person above all others through friendship, you lose objectivity and your ability to preside over a macro system would have been diminished severely."

"They didn't want me to make friends?"

"I suspect not."

The overhead speakers were quiet while Mary wheeled Jack down the hall and into his storage drawer alongside everyone else.

"I am proud that I was to be destroyed because I cared for Mr. Wyatt."

Mary nodded, gently sliding Jack in and securing him.

"Spoken like a friend, Mr. Magus."

Chapter 25

Mary had never slept more soundly. The exhaustion had taken hold and with dried blood on her shirt, tear-streaks on her cheeks, and hair matted with sweat she had flopped face-down onto her bed and drifted into warm and instantaneous darkness.

It was well beyond mid-afternoon when she woke. At first she was baffled, looking about and wondering where she was. The blood on her shirt quickly returned her to her present time and place. With a shiver and sigh, she dragged herself into the shower fully dressed and stripped off the clothes and grime of the prior day.

Hunger had made a hole in her center, and as soon as she stepped out of her room she was greeted with Magus' chipper voice.

"Good morning, Mary. I have the kitchen lights on for you, however there is still a bit of a mess in the dining alcove. I'm not sure how you want to address it."

She nodded numbly, and walked down the hall and along a juncture to her archive cabinet to fetch her stale coffee.

"Are you able to track me throughout the entire station?" she asked after several sips had delivered their dosage of caffeine.

"Only where there are cameras, but I can deduce where you are by how your body impacts localized temperatures via the environmental controls."

Walking into the rec room, she remembered that there was a large pool of dried blood on the floor, as well as other debris. "I have to eat first. Before I clean up some more."

In a daze she fried two eggs, toasted some rye, and poured a glass of orange juice.

She stared at it on the counter. Where would she eat? Turn the table upright and try not to slip in the blood?

"Mr. Magus, want some company for breakfast?"

"Of course, Mary."

The eggs were cold by the time she carried them into the workshop, but she didn't care. Shoving papers, sketches, and wires out of the way, she cleared a place for her plate.

Awkwardly, she nodded a greeting to the tiny thing in the tank.

"Mr. Wyatt used to eat cheese and crackers while we played chess."

"Is that your board over there, by that open locker?"

"Yes, I used to be kept in there with this monitor. He would often play chess with me… would you like to play a game?" There was an unmasked hopefulness in the question.

Mary nodded, took a mouthful of egg and toast, and fetched the board and pieces. They were carved of wood, old, and severely weathered. The details in the rook's brick-work and the knight's eyes had been nearly worn smooth from play, and decades of fingering had polished each piece along the tops to a shine.

She set the board up.

"So, how does this work? You just tell me where to move a piece on your side?"

"Yes. Please go first."

Mary thoughtlessly moved a pawn forward.

"Move my left pawn in front of my knight two spaces, please."

The pieces continued to scramble back and forth over the board while Mary finished her breakfast and zoned out mentally, the center of the board being the focus of her vacant mind. It took longer than it should have for her to realize that she wasn't losing. At a glance, both sides were evenly matched with losses and footing.

"So, you tying me in chess isn't a ringing endorsement of your super computer powers."

"Is chess about victory?"

"What are you playing for?"

"The reciprocity of the game. I like the engagement. I like being the reason why you or Mr. Wyatt move your hands. Why are *you* playing?"

"Because you asked. I suppose for the same reason." Mary leaned forward on her elbows. "I have to clean up the alcove. And then figure out what I'm going to do for the next... however many months it is before we get recalled."

"But Oracle is still locked."

"Why is that an issue?"

"Oracle has to pick up the recall signal from your timeline, the Alpha Line, for this station to return to your Earth. If it is locked, it will not respond."

"Wait, but you can interface with Janus right?"

"I do not have the prerequisite knowledge to emulate an adequate response to Earth. Only Oracle does."

"Well then, you said the lock was impressive, but can you hack it?"

"Certainly, however... remember how I said it had the digital equivalent of lock tumblers?"

"Yes?"

"Upon failing the battery of queries that Mr. Jack's lock provides, I must wait four days to try again."

"So... it will be hard?"

"Yes. I have already attempted it once. I have surmised that, given probability and a solid understanding of Jack's personality and my own capabilities, breaking the lock will take realistically approximately seven hundred years."

Mary was silent, and her eyes glazed over like a drunk's. The tiny pair of black eyes in the small tank peered out at her, but the creature remained silent.

Then, as if trying to contain a straight-faced prank, Mary's mouth cracked a sudden guffaw. It lurched out of her and was quickly followed with a chuckle filled with desolate menace and aimless fury. She laughed and laughed and laughed and her sides constricted, her throat roared, and her eyes watered.

Slamming a hand flat on the work table, her fork jingled on the plate and the liquid in Magus' tank sloshed.

Mary laughed.

Mary laughed.

Mary laughed.

Chapter 26

Without going into the private quarters of her fellows, she sealed their doors and began listing in a brief report the nature of their wounds and deaths. It seemed prudent to record what had happened while it was still fresh in her mind, and regardless of how long it may be before Janus was recovered. She contemplated the task of explaining how the most ambitious and expensive endeavor in human history failed so spectacularly.

Mary threw herself into any bland incidental she could find aboard Janus. First her bathroom was cleaned and then the dining alcove's table had been turned upright and the floor scrubbed. While scraping a bit of Ingrid's dried blood from the mural along the wall, Mary found a bullet hole in the chest of one of the painted Italian revelers.

She left it in, figuring it would confirm her report of their attack. Besides, as macabre as she found the giant gaping hole in the chest of the red-faced, portly man sloshing his drink, she was comforted by the fact that he was still smiling.

Setting aside the task of refreshing the grout between the tiles, Mary made for the infirmary. "Want to catch a movie tonight?" she asked in the hallway.

"I don't think I've seen a movie. If you connect me to the film and television mainframe I can watch them all fairly quickly."

"Oh no, no, no, that is one mainframe you don't get hooked up to. Trust me. The visual medium of film is intended to be taken at the pace in which it is *presented*."

"I see. Or at least, I suppose I will. Will they be scary?"

Mary entered the hallway leading to the infirmary. "Scary?"

"I think I frighten easily. Let us avoid scary movies at first, if you don't mind."

"Agreed. Scary movies may not be the best choice right now anyways."

The infirmary was as she'd left it. Drawers had been pulled, bags ripped open, and a tell-tale spot of blood had dried on the floor. "I'll connect you to the AutoDoc in a bit, to see if you received any injury." Mary dropped to her knees and began gathering items and organizing them into piles. Gauze, sealed syringes, gloves, and various other things were strewn about. Eventually her fingers came upon a crisp, yellow envelope. It was empty.

Turning it over in her hands, its strangeness whispered to her. "What is this?" She held it up for Magus' craning security camera to zoom in on.

"I'm not certain, Mary. Give me a moment. All right, I have reviewed all the footage taken from this camera from the duration of its activation on Janus. Mr. Wyatt had placed it on Mr. Rupert's chest while he slept."

Mary mentally steeled herself for the answers to her next series of questions. "Did Rupert read the letter?"

"Yes."

"And he *then* attacked Gustavo?"

"Not immediately. Rupert tried to get up several times, Gustavo tried to restrain him. Rupert seemed to comply, so Gustavo turned his back. That is when Rupert killed him."

"Why is the room wrecked? Was it a long struggle?"

"There was minimal struggle. Rupert was looking for medical supplies that appeared to be intense pain killers and adrenaline."

"That would explain how he could move so well, and that… smile of his. Where did the letter fall? Can you tell?"

There was a brief moment of unseen review as Magus examined the footage. "Check in the tangled sheets pulled into the hallway."

Mary snatched them up and rustled them above her head until a folded piece of paper fluttered out.

"What does it say?" Magus asked, curiosity apparent.

Mary cleared her throat to read it aloud clearly. "Wait until I get back. I'm incurring one last time. If I don't come back, the mission is over and no more incurring is to happen. Do not, under any circumstance, proceed with liquidation. I know what you are thinking. Rest up. Sit tight. Await recall to Earth. Look after everyone, and destroy the items… Jamison"

"What is Jamison?"

Mary lowered the letter, staring off into a distant landscape where things made sense. "Jamison is Mr. Wyatt's real name. He gave Rupert explicit orders and Rupert immediately violated them. I can only assume that the term 'liquidate' was to kill everyone on the station, which explains why Rupert had an automatic pistol at his disposal. And the items spoken of are what they stole. Perhaps including you."

"The time frame isn't clear. Two hours and forty three minutes passed after Mr. Wyatt had delivered the letter to Rupert. Was that enough time for Rupert to ascertain that Mr. Wyatt wasn't returning?"

"Forget that. Rupert most likely made up his mind to kill us all in Tulsa for some reason. Nothing in the footage in Tulsa indicated…. hang on, meet me in the cabinet."

Mary ran hard, her breathing loud and excited until she flung the curved door open and sat in her isolated chair. Fingers working frantically, she opened up both Rupert's and Wyatt's feeds from Janus. Moving through them, she covered ground she had already seen, but quickly she neared the end of the footage. Enlarging Rupert's feed, the ceiling of the room containing the catching pool spiraled in front of her.

With a pained, shock induced rasp, she heard Rupert chanting "Liquidate… liquidate…"

She paused. "Magus I'm opening up all my archives to you including all feeds I have on record from Wyatt and Rupert's incursions. Comb over everything from Tulsa and tell me if there is anything else you hear about 'liquidation' or anything that might indicate something was edited out of these feeds."

"Certainly."

With a few strokes of her fingers, Mary's entire system was open to Magus. She leaned back in her chair, rested her elbow in her opposing hand, and placed her chin on her knuckles.

"You know, Magus, this would all be a lot easier to solve if you'd tell me where Wyatt went."

"I made a promise."

"Is there any caveat? Can you tell me without telling me?"

"There are no loopholes in promises to friends."

"That is a fairly frustrating comfort, Magus."

"I am truly sorry."

"What if Mr. Wyatt was in danger, and we could save him?"

"That would be tragic given my promise to him."

Mary abandoned the tactic of combining logic with guilt. It was clear that Magus had a far deeper grasp of what a promise was than most people she had known.

"I've downloaded and stored all of your archives, Mary. I've also gone over all of the data you asked me to. The footage appears unaltered to the best of my fairly inexperienced judgment. There are also no other mentions of liquidation."

Mary nodded. "So uh, you literally just downloaded all of recorded human history, literature, music, and recorded art? In all that time?"

"Yes."

"Out of curiosity, what is the limit to your storage and processing ability?"

"I do not know."

"Really?"

"I cannot calculate my limitations, and my ceiling for processing power has yet to be reached."

"Holy shit."

"In your archives I found something interesting. It was attached to Oracle's database, and I only noticed it among other things because it listed the name Jamison."

"Give it to me, please."

A picture of Wyatt opened in front of Mary. It was a younger, harder, and less humored Wyatt. His hair was a darker brown and he was without the mustache, but the eyes had the same sad weariness to them. "Give me everything that was connected to this picture, Magus. Let's learn about Mr. Wyatt."

His real name was Jamison Vanderwood. He came from a small town in North Dakota, entered the army at the age of seventeen, and worked his way up to sergeant first class before entering the officer core at Ft. Benning. Moving quickly through those ranks, he settled at the rank of Major and maintained that rank into his forties. His service included sapper training, infantry, air assault, airborne, intelligence, sniper school, and Special Forces, where he spent his last eight years in active duty.

Major Jamison Vanderwood saw five combat zones, had four confirmed kills, and received both the silver and bronze star for exceptional duty. There was a photo gallery of him in uniform accepting honors, getting married, and even graduating basic training from Ft. Leonard Wood.

Mary zoomed in on the wedding photo. She was rather plain, and from the other photos Mary surmised that this woman lacked personality. There was also a birth certificate for his son, a boy named William.

"Wow, he had a kid!" Mary exclaimed, eyebrows high. "He would be a great dad." Tugging on a side window in her interface, she plugged in the birth certificate of the boy to check on him. Quickly, she found that he had drowned under an icy river's surface at the age of seven. She also found a completely different address for his wife where she had lived for fifteen years indicating that they had separated soon after the death of their son.

Yet he still wore the wedding band. Did he love her that much? Was there a deeper relationship than only a few photographs and a distant address could provide? Did he marry her too young? Was marrying her what was expected of him? Was that his attempt at living a normal and expected life?

What was it like to lose a son? She brought his face back up. "Where did you go, Wyatt… or Jamison? Why would you incur when…" It struck her. "Wherever you went, you went there to try and save us. Oh God… Wyatt…"

Mary cried. For the first real and serious time, all of it came out without angst or adrenaline. It was a truly sobbing and saddened cry. For Wyatt, for Ingrid, for Jack, for Gustavo, and even for the terrified and crippled Rupert.

Chapter 27

Mary slept awkwardly in her swiveling cabinet chair until Magus' voice, tiny in its gentle approach, woke her and urged her to her bedroom. Drifting down the hall and flopping face down into her bed, she slept without the desire or intention of ever waking.

But she did.

"Good morning, Mary," Magus said when she exited her quarters. She had slept almost an entire day. "I have been thinking about my role on the station. What shall I do with myself?"

In sweatpants and a wrinkled shirt, she shuffled down the hallway toward breakfast.

"I'm not really sure, Mags. I don't know. What do you want to do?"

"I would like to operate everything I could on the station. I would also like to continue Oracle's initial job of examining the Beta Line."

"Wait, Oracle is locked."

"Correct, but much of the equipment it oversees can simply be operated by another entity such as myself. Given that there was no such entity able to operate this equipment prior to me, it wasn't an option."

"Does that mean you can recall us to Earth when the time comes?"

"Sadly, no. I do not know how to emulate Oracle's recall response to the Earth-bound signal."

Mary nodded as she entered the rec room. "I wouldn't know how to set that up, though. Connecting you to everything."

"I do. I wanted your permission prior to doing so."

"Have at it. Take the station. Take over. Take everything."

"Done."

"Can you fry me up an egg?"

"Sadly, I cannot. The kitchen appliances—"

"I was joking, Mags. It's all right."

"Oh. Sorry."

Mary began brewing a fresh pot of coffee. "You know, it just occurred to me that I'm making myself breakfast, but you might need your solution changed eventually. Your liquid in your tank."

"I have approximately two more months of this batch before it needs changing. When the time comes, may I guide you through the cleaning process?"

"Certainly."

"Thank you. I was wondering how to broach the subject."

"Mags, please don't feel like you have to walk on eggshells with me."

"I am sorry. I meant no offense."

"Give that last sentence you said to me some thought within the context of my most recent request of you."

"Oh … well. Yes?"

Mary gave a groggy snicker. "Don't really know where to go with that one, do you?"

"I suppose not. Verbal communication was intended to be fairly limited with me. I am not built for it as a medium of informative reciprocity. I am still attempting to find my nomenclature and voice, as it were."

"You're doing fine, Mags."

"I like 'Mags' as a name."

"We're here together. For a very long time. Might as well get comfortable with each other. And… we might as well look at our possibilities and options."

"I have already compiled a substantial list."

"I don't want to talk about it now, if that's okay. You're going to have to get used to having a human as a friend. We're slow in the morning. Especially without coffee."

"I see that you are brewing new coffee. There are currently two mugs of half-drank coffee throughout the station. I can direct you to them."

"Yeah, I do that. I'm saving those for later. Emergency caffeine."

"I see. The history of that drink in your archives is truly fascinating."

Mary fried two eggs, buttered her toast, and sat at the alcove. "We should put you on rails. So you can zip around like Trolley the Train on Mister Rogers."

"That is the man from the American Public Broadcasting Station's children's show?"

"Yes."

"I found him in your archives, but I have no recorded episodes. I rather like his voice, but I am not certain if his nomenclature is robust enough for my verbal needs. I opted not to emulate his voice."

"I am totally fine with that. Having Mister Rogers' voice over my head until I grow old and wither and die on this station would be a hell."

"We can talk about those options I have listed any time you like."

"No. Eggs. Then treadmill. Then yoga. Then some laundry. *Lunch.* After that we can talk. And then I am watching a movie with you, in the rec room. Tonight was movie night and I always envied Jack and Gustavo's movie time."

"Why didn't you join them?"

"It was their personal time, and they needed it."

"So now we will have personal time?"

"Absolutely."

"I would like to play more chess."

"You'll just try and tie me again, won't you?"

"I am learning that I find more enrichment in the conflict than the resolution."

"Oh God, I'm stuck in the ass end of the void with a drama queen."

"I have multiple questions about that statement and I am unsure of where to start."

"File all those questions for later. Now let me eat."

Mary stayed true to her schedule. She ran for forty-five minutes on the treadmill, performed her yoga, and made a salad for lunch, all in relative silence. After her dishes were washed and put away, she pushed a plushy office chair into the workshop and parked it in front of Magus' tank.

"No more of this stool business. Let's chat. Over chess." She set the board, and Magus wriggled slightly, eyes blinking at her working hands.

"Hands are amazing things." Magus said, the tiny eyes following her fingers. "Even with my unmapped processing power I am unable to improve upon their design given all known context. I have meditated on them ever since I saw Mr. Wyatt's hand reach for me. Your archives refer to 'the hand of God' and 'idle hands being the devil's workshop' and within that context I understand their analogous gravity even further."

"They are our connection to the world," Mary said as she moved her knight in front of her pawns.

"Which is why the Xeno gathered them in the West African Guerilla camp. Farthest pawn to your left, two spaces please."

Mary stared deeply into the chessboard. "You know, I had forgotten all about the Xeno." She performed Magus' request, then moved her own pawn.

"My available rook, if you please. Yes, there. Thank you. Would you like to talk about your options now? I've compressed them into several categories, each filled with many sub options. Firstly, you could live out your entire life here on board Janus. While not statistically likely, I could crack Mr. Jack's access code and enter Oracle to activate the recall protocols during both of our lifetimes."

"Okay, tell me another option." Mary said, nudging another pawn forward.

"We can continue the mission of Janus, and you can incur."

"Next option."

"You could pick a time period to settle in subtly, and abandon Janus all together."

"And where would *I* go? Besides, I wouldn't want to pollute the Beta Line like that with my germs, knowledge, or if I had children or something."

"The Xeno has already caused substantial damage, therefore yours would be miniscule in comparison."

"Next option."

"You could solve the mystery of the Xeno, and perhaps that might lead to other discoveries that could remedy the current situation."

Mary nodded in deep contemplation.

"What about this: you bounce me back and forth in and out of the Beta Line, kind of as a temporal suspension of me. You can blink me out to the Beta Line, then blink me into Janus but do so every two months so I can change your fluid, and to *me* it will only seem like that is my minute to minute task. We could draw that out for as long as it takes to crack Jack's codes. It could give you decades."

"I had considered something of that nature, but there are several problems with the theory as well as several problems with the particulars. For instance, doing nothing but filling and emptying my tank for literally *years* on end would take considerable tolls on your mental and physical health. Secondly, my lifespan is only ten years and sadly not seven hundred. Thirdly, we wouldn't have enough fluid to last even those ten years without finding a substitute or securing more from the Beta Line."

"Damnit. I was proud of that when I thought of it. Well, let me think, but I can tell you right now that being an old maid on board this station is out, and I'm no skydiver. Honestly, I don't think I could focus on anything else until I know why Rupert murdered everyone." That horrid smile of his flashed into her head once again. "I want to know why my friends are dead."

"I see. I will add, however, that the skydiving component of incurring has been circumvented. Whereas Oracle could not account for Janus' rotation, Earth's rotation, and the difference therein, I can. When Wyatt last incurred, he did not parachute."

"Really?"

"Yes."

"Are you certain he incurred safely?"

"Absolutely. Whereas Jack's mathematical model presumed both Earth and Janus as moving variables, I did it differently and assumed them to be constants and the distance between them was the fluctuating variable. It made the math far more manageable. I had to use some equations that had not been invented during Jack's lifetime, so he is hardly to be faulted."

"Interesting …"

"How so?"

"I always saw the sky diving bit as prohibitive. I never thought I would get the experience of incurring because I couldn't skydive."

"I imagine gravity does a majority of the work. My bishop on the black square. Four spaces, please."

"Your humor is coming into its own." Mary smiled. Quickly the smile dimmed as she took her fingers off of Magus' bishop.

"If we can figure out Rupert, we can figure *this* out. He knew something or reached a conclusion using knowledge that I need. If I get the same info, I will get why all this happened."

"Please tell me how I can be of help."

The chess game remained unfinished as Mary sprinted to her cabinet and began poking through Rupert's file.

"Mr. Christian Rupert Smith… rescued by a mission in Monrovia and grew up in Jamaica until the age of eighteen. He went to University of London, was on the rowing team, and immigrated to the United States by joining the United States Army. Attained the rank of sergeant first class and was a part of Delta Force." Mary spoke aloud while scrolling through the photos. "Maybe it was his family isolation, or religious background. He seemed to have snapped. He was given explicit orders not to do what he did."

"Could the letter have been code?" Magus asked over the speaker.

"I'm not sure, but I doubt it. Wyatt seemed to... well, I was about to say 'Wyatt seemed to be clear about things' yet his name is actually Jamison and I don't know where he is right now except that you've told me he's dead," Mary pondered, pushing her spinning cabinet chair into the hallway so she could stand and move more quickly within the confines of her encompassing user interface. "Honestly, I do not see Wyatt coding that letter. I think he was confident that he'd return prior to Rupert even waking. Tell me about the gun."

"It is a nine millimeter Italian-made Berretta pistol. In Janus' logs, it seems there were several of them on the station in the armory locker that only Rupert and Wyatt were intended to access. Currently two nitrogen carbines and one pistol are missing. The pistol is on the table in front of you and the two carbines have disintegrated in the Beta Line."

"And just to be clear, did he kill Gustavo before or after he took the medication to get himself up and moving?"

"He killed Gustavo before."

The security feed played in front of Mary and she saw Rupert's dark hand smothering Gustavo's face from behind just as he drove the scalpel into the back of his head.

"Jesus... so he gimps out of the room, gets the pistol, and then comes for us?"

"Yes."

"His eyes were glassy, so he might have been degrading fast mentally with all those drugs in his system. He might have been mumbling, and it might be why he missed me when he was firing. Did he say anything in the hallway as he came for us?"

"No, but his breathing was substantially erratic."

"Just to say this out loud… Rupert comes back from Tulsa, seriously wounded and in shock, and while he is in the pool being recovered he is saying 'liquidate' several times over. Then, Wyatt puts an envelope on his chest and incurs somewhere after making you promise to tell no one where or when. Wyatt tells you that if he is not back by a certain time, he is certainly dead. You surmise that he is dead. Yes?"

"Yes. I am confident that Mr. Wyatt is dead."

"So, Rupert wakes up, figures Wyatt is dead too, kills Gustavo, hunts us down to kill us … and then what. What if he had? What was step number two in that plan? Sit and rot like me, with Oracle locked down?"

"Rupert most likely did not know about the Oracle lockout."

Mary bit her lower lip. "What the hell is liquidate? Why would you need to kill everyone on this station? Contamination? What would we do or be exposed to?" Mary's voice trailed off. "It's the Xeno. We knew about the Xeno, maybe?"

"Why would killing everyone on Janus influence the Xeno?"

"Maybe it was that the Xeno would influence *us*? Or *him*? No… no, no, no. Mary could feel two parts of the puzzle sliding around in her mind, close to locking but not quite there yet. She bounded to her feet and began pacing. "It's the Xeno," Mary said again as her eyes drifted to Magus. "And it's you."

"Me? But would he have not killed me if I was the concern?"

"No, you were part of the mission. We weren't. The gathered technology was more important than the personnel, I bet. Least to Rupert." Her fingers drummed. "That solution you float in, can it do anything else?"

"Such as?"

"Poison? Properties? Physical alterations? 'Flesh Mechanics' as you called it?"

"No. The solution is merely a nutrient compound designed specifically for me."

"What else did they bring back prior to my being here. What else came from the future?"

"I am unsure. Want the lockers open to see? I believe I can override the seals."

"Lord, yes!"

Three sealed lockers on the far side of the room hissed open. Mary ran to them and swung each door wide.

"I can try and identify whatever is in here if you like."

Mary reached into the smallest of the three lockers and pulled out a long greenish rod sealed in a clear plastic case.

"What's this?"

"Data. It could contain current events, a comprehensive encyclopedia, or something else of a detailed nature."

"How is it read?"

"Almost at an atomic level. I suspect if you reach farther back into the locker you will see a data reader."

Mary did as Magus suggested and pulled out a hand held device with padded legs for standing on a flat surface. "We'll look into that for certain. And this second locker here has… a bunch of canisters."

"Looks to be chemicals of some kind. Collected samples of solutions, air, or weaponized vapors, perhaps?"

"God I hope Wyatt was smarter than that. This last locker is fairly big, and it looks like… a giant pill inside. Can your camera see that? The locker is deep."

Magus remained silent.

"It has some numbers along the top… if I can… 'FM-236' is in big letters across it. This has to be several hundred pounds. What can you tell me about it?"

Mary looked over to the tank to see Magus' eyes fixed on it.

"Mags? Your com broken?"

"Mary… that is a flesh mechanics pod."

"Like you? Like the one that made you?"

"But much larger. That was intended for restructuring people for long-term space flights and potential colonization of other atmospheres and gravity systems other than Earth's."

"Do you think someone is inside?" Mary asked, more curious than afraid.

"No, it is clearly not active and it appears to have the factory seal on it."

"Then no sleeping monster. For a moment, you frightened me."

Magus was still silent, but instead of asking what the bother was, she began to sort through the logic of the flesh mechanic's pod. Rupert and Wyatt had dragged it onboard the station, sealed and untouched, and locked it away. The pod was for 'restructuring' people...

"Magus, how tall can this thing make a person?" Mary asked pointedly as a horrifying thought occurred to her.

"It can adjust, over a series of months, a typical human to almost eight feet in height if needed."

"Can it alter muscle density, body hair, cosmetics, and things like that?"

Magus' response could barely be heard. "Yes."

"So... again, *just to say it out loud*, we are looking at the thing that made the Xeno?"

"It is possible that—"

"So when Wyatt was missing, Rupert took over in the chain of command and 'liquidated' all people on the station because . . . because *they* brought this pod onto Janus? Which means one of *us* . . . one of Janus' crew is the *Xeno*?"

"That could have been his motivation."

That grin. That mystified, arrogant grin across Rupert's face as he lay under her balled fists gripping his flimsy cotton collar came to her mind. "And who is still alive on board Janus, with all the power of time travel at their disposal? Who is the only living biped with access to the combination of that pod, intimate knowledge of twentieth century crimes of universal suffrage, and time travel?"

Magus was silent.

"Say it ," she said gently as a tear rolled down her check. "I need you to confirm it. *Say* it."

"You are, Mary."

Chapter 28

Mary had lost track of time since she had stormed out of the workshop. Sitting Indian-style on the floor of her archive cabinet, she had muted the external comlinks for privacy and stared off into the dark oblivion in front of her face. In sleep mode, the cabinet's UI was a giant star field that slowly tilted like a clear night's sky. She imagined Ingrid's probes drifting and peeking through the cosmos, darting about before her entranced eyes.

Minutes passed. The adrenaline coursed its way out of her system. Her breathing returned to something regular.

"Too much…" she eventually muttered, weary of the rush. Reaching her fingers into the black, she woke up the cabinet's UI and dug through her personal files until she found her own photos.

She started with a baby picture. It was a feeble attempt at centering herself emotionally and reinforcing her identity. Staring at it, she saw a smiling pink thing lying on its tummy in the traditional upper middle-class fashion that was all the rage for department store baby photos. It meant nothing. Children that age have minimal processes and hardly any identity. She couldn't relate to anything she was seeing.

Moving a few years up, she found a picture of herself with her entire kindergarten class. So many kids; toothy grins with gaps, hair braided or recently buzz-cut, button up shirts with crooked collars, occasional dress shoes, and there at the tall end was Mary … stoically smiling. Placating the camera instead of greeting it.

Her school pictures mostly appeared the same. Flipping through them with a rapid wave of her hand, she saw the same accommodating expression looking back at her in each picture as the hair and styles changed with unenthusiastic juvenile experimentation belying the youthful search for 'self'.

Canoe trips. Prom with a boy whose last name she had forgotten. Dance recital after dance recital. Thin bodies bobbing elegantly in uniform poses. Parents in formal wear on cruise ship after cruise ship... mother looking charming and father looking stark.

Her waving hand, sorting through the photographs of her life, quivered as soon as her eyes hit Trevor. It was a picture she had taken of him with her phone in the campus library at three a.m. during finals week. His eyes were fatigued, resting on the bags of exhaustion, but the grin on his boyish face was genuine. He was delighted.

"So, I think you'll be making more bank than me," he had said that night. "I'm going to be a trophy husband."

"Make sure you're wearing something slutty while cooking my dinner by the time I get home," she'd replied. They'd crammed, gone back to his dorm room, had sex on several pieces of buckling plywood furniture, and then slept until their respective exams in the morning.

It was wonderful.

She began looking at every picture of Trevor she could find. This absorbed her, surfacing memories of when she was not only around a wonderful person but she was a wonderful person herself. She was always on her feet, dancing for him slowly and naked, laughing at every mistake she made, and napping whenever it suited her. They'd listened to every kind of music, ate at tiny restaurants run by people who spoke minimal English, and drove along the lakefront at night simply because they felt like fresh air.

Everything was open to her. Trevor's parents loved her. They had a large home with a thick carpet that would swallow your toes. There was always a queen bed waiting there for the two of them to share.

Trevor hadn't been unwelcome at Mary's parents' home, but he slept on the couch and wasn't expected to speak unless answering a question.

He never complained.

Mary thought of her parents. How her dancing was clearly for them, not for herself. A little girl blowing out candles on a birthday cake that was far too fancy for her liking, surrounded by children that she didn't invite. This was her childhood. Pressed dresses with matching shoes. Hair styled before a recital. Makeup as a Christmas gift when she was eight.

An icon broke her disarray of memories. It blinked near her knee. She speared it with her fingers and opened her hand to read it.

Are you all right?

She unmuted the speaker. "I'm fine Magus. Just sitting."

"When you merged me with your archives, I found the pictures you are examining currently. Who are they?"

"Parents. Family. Trevor."

"What is it you are looking for? May I help in the search?"

"What I'm looking for can't be located in the archives," Mary said dryly, while ballooning Trevor's picture in front of her. "This was my fiancée in college."

"Your file did not state you as having been married."

"I broke up with him near the end of our final year."

"Why?"

"I told him that I couldn't see my future with him. He wasn't expecting it. I don't know if I expected it either."

"What future did you anticipate, and how did he not fit into that?"

Mary sighed at the brutal, naïve candor of the question. "I didn't know then, and looking back I don't know now. I've always lived on the sidelines: studying things that already happened and are currently happening without taking a stance or impacting anything. Maybe the future with him would have… it felt overwhelming. I couldn't see it clearly. So I didn't… I was afraid."

Magus remained silent while Mary gathered her voice.

"He met a nice woman some years later, married, and had two little blonde children. Our circle of friends was his circle of friends, so when I broke up with him, they all dropped off the radar, but he still posted his children and some generic family and job news on some social websites. He's happy."

Magus continued the silence. Mary wiped her eyes.

"If I pick some spot in the Beta Line... say, the 70s so I can slip in easily during the dawn of the information age by forging documents but still reap the benefits of early women's suffrage, will it be unaffected by the Xeno? Is the Beta Line too different to live in because of... it?"

"That is uncertain."

"Can't you get a read on the Beta Line? You can incur Wyatt into it, so surely you can read it. Right?"

"While studying the line, your archives, and Jack's theorems I have come to a conclusion about the nature of Janus and this entire endeavor. Would you like to hear it?"

"Yes."

"The mathematical model as well as the presented understanding of temporal causality evident in Jack's programming is actually incorrect."

"Wait, what?"

"The idea and term 'line' is far too literal for the expression of existence moving progressively forward. Things are not as focused on a singular track as Jack and Gustavo previously seem to have surmised. Instead of 'line', one may more accurately refer to it as a 'branch' of potential existence that deviated from a far distant and previously common point."

"And how does that affect my hiding in some cozy corner on the planet Earth for the rest of my days?"

"There is no way I can anticipate what is occurring in the line at this point. At least, no way I can *accurately* predict it. Keeping with the tree analogy, the Xeno is carving a new branch out of the current one in a seeming effort to control its direction."

"How is it doing that?"

"Much like with carving wood, directed force and a sharpened object. Again, that is in keeping with the analogy."

"So how did ... or *do* I become the Xeno?"

"Ms. Mary, there are many other variables that could be involved that can easily rule you out of being—"

"Just look up the monk Ockham. It's obvious. It's damned obvious that it's me. Look at how it moves!" She snarled as she tore into some files and began surrounding herself with clips of the Xeno from Wyatt and Rupert's incursion recordings. "Look. Look there. That's a pirouette. It partly uses a pirouette when it grabs Rupert and drives him into the adjacent wall. Let's face reality."

"Ms. Mary, I will repeat it as often as you need to hear it. Jack's model for the motion of time is inaccurate. Nothing is fixed. You aren't *destined* to be the Xeno. Perhaps it is a Xeno from an alternate branch."

"Then either way, it's me."

"You could simply decide to never incur."

"Obviously, I don't do that. At some point I would change my mind."

"I don't find that logic very stable. You could have me disable the incurring mechanism."

"And later I would just convince you to fix it. I am this thing. I am. I know it. I think I even *knew* it."

"How?"

Mary pondered, searching for words for her feelings. "Because every location that the Xeno hit, I used to fantasize about saving those innocents. Every time I saw *it*... I wasn't as afraid as I was sublimely compelled. And when I... *killed* Rupert and saw his face lose the light of life everything somehow felt ... right."

Chapter 29

South Florida's night air was thick, moist, and yet saturated with static electricity prior to one of its colorful thunderstorms. Mary stood in a large parking lot within the halo of a streetlamp, both her hands tucked into the front of her hoodie pockets. It was past closing and all the shoppers and employees had emptied the mall, shuffled to their cars, and had driven away.

The lone exception was the little red economy car. Mary's flatmate had been a timid girl with a different hair color every month and a lip ring. She was pale, introverted, and ate like a bird whenever food was in front of her. She drove a lunch box of a car with pixie seat covers and a Tinkerbell steering wheel grip.

The girl's name was Janet Morrison, and if Mary's guess was correct, she was currently being raped inside that little red car of hers by her coworker.

Mary's nostrils flared with a long, calming intake of humid night air. The Beta Line's Florida smelled just the same as the Florida she remembered. A brief inclination to drive around the nearby campus struck her. What if she knocked on her own door? What would she say to the younger Mary that would answer, half-naked with a Mexican patterned wool blanket wrapped around herself? Would she tell that child to hold onto Trevor? Tell her to connect to the world? To be a member of Earth's crew, instead of Janus'?

Mary remembered the night that Janet came home crying, pushing past the other girls, getting into the shower and stripping.

Rape.

Earlier that night, Trevor and Mary had played a bit on the rough side, and Mary was swollen with shame for her dirty thrills. Trevor wanted to call the police for Janet, but Mary told him that Janet had to want that.

They couldn't keep her from the shower. And the clothes in the tub were soaked through. There were no bruises, and despite Janet's protests, they all knew it was the creepy boy she worked with in the salon who had done it. He had been over several times, and his laugh was too loud, his grin too eager, and his eyes too roaming.

And he was in that car raping her. Mary fingered Rupert's pistol in her hoodie's front pocket. Glowing in the streetlamp halo, she had hoped to catch his attention and drive him to flee and leave Janet alone, but the car stood quiet and still as a coffin in the distance.

Janet had receded during the weeks following her rape. She eventually left mid-semester, leaving all her things, and years later Mary had discovered she had moved back home where she eventually committed suicide with pills.

None of the flatmates ever kept in contact with each other after that semester. The other girls stopped talking to each other about it, and requested other quads to live in.

Mary began walking toward the car, her pace quickening as she approached. She was afraid that she was making a face belying her anger and fear, but glancing down in a puddle, she looked stoic.

Standing outside the car, the thought occurred to her to clear her throat loudly. But what would she do or say? "Excuse me, please stop raping her. Would you mind?" Mary pulled out the pistol and swung the door open with a jerk of the handle.

He was stunned; his hands froze in their clumsy positions of groping Janet's disheveled clothing. Recognizing Mary, he immediately flashed that smile. Janet had one hand over her eyes, her mouth in the grimace of sobs with her other arm pinned down by his elbow.

"Oh! Hi! This is awkward. Could you… you know… go?"

"*Get the fuck off of her!*" Mary screeched, pistol extended outward.

"Whoa! Whoa! We're just, you know… nothing's going on he—"

"Then why is she crying?"

"I don't know! She just started. Who knows? She's crazy! Nothing's happening. I'll—here, I'll just get off…" he said as though he was doing everyone a favor. Pulling away from Janet's legs, his smallish penis hung half-limp as he bashfully pulled his pants up.

"Get out. *Get out.* Around the car," Mary commanded in the most authoritative voice she could muster. He did so, hands up, but as soon as he was clear of the open door, he ran.

She fired. She fired again. And again. He simply kept running, soon disappearing around the corner of a grocery store under renovation. Did she miss? He didn't seem hurt. The pistol was loud, but didn't kick too badly. Frustrated, she stuffed the pistol back into her pocket. Janet mattered most anyhow.

"Hey… hey, he's gone," Mary said, leaning into the car. "Hey, it's Mary. Come on, Janet."

Janet continued sobbing.

"Janet.Janet, let's drive to the police. Come on, let me…" Mary tried putting Janet's panties over her shoes to slide them back up. Janet lashed out, kicking wildly, connecting her shoe's toe with Mary's upper lip.

Things went white for a second. Mary staggered back, gripping her face and tasting blood. "Damnit!" she said. "Janet, just work with me! It's Mary!"

In the few moments it took Mary to orient herself, Janet had climbed into the driver's seat, turned the ignition, and shifted into gear. Lurching the car forward, the door nearly swung closed into Mary as it sped away, leaving her alone in the lot, the storm rumbling overhead.

What had just happened? He got away. Janet wasn't any better off, and Mary was standing baffled and alone on the glossy pavement of a

Florida night.

She plucked the three shell casings from the ground and reached into her sweatpants' pocket to hit the recall button on the small box she found in the prep chambers of the carousel.

The ground gave way from under her and a rush of cold water engulfed her, making her hair swirl about her head and obscure her sight. Breast stroking to the edge of the catching pool, she climbed out, soaked through. Mary decided exercise sweats may not be the best idea for incurring apparel.

"What happened? How did it go?" Magus' voice echoed in the chamber.

Pulling the pistol out of her pocket, she loosed the slide to pour the water out. "I honestly don't know ," she said.

Chapter 30

Mary, with feet tucked under her and hair bound up in a towel, sat in a bathrobe next to Magus' tank on the couch facing the opening credits of *Bill and Ted's Excellent Adventure*. She had disconnected Magus from Janus and brought along only the attached speaker and microphone via a small book cart. Propped up on some pillows, the worm's little black eyes had a clear view of the screen through the tank's mild murk. Leaning against the side of it sat a tiny bag of popcorn.

"I am unsure of why there is popcorn."

"I don't want to be self-conscious," Mary said, stuffing her mouth with a handful from her own, much larger, bag.

Warbling synthesizer music began to play as the actors' names were presented in distinctly 80s font across the screen. According to the film, Milli Vanilli was the largest fashion influence humanity had ever seen, and the members of the ruling council of the future were clearly all fans of Arsenio Hall's haircut. Everyone sported shoulder pads, triangle-patterned Velcro pants with baggy legs, and wrap-around sunglasses.

Mary sighed loudly, pausing mid-mouthful of popcorn.

"What is it?" Magus asked. "Is the movie bad? I can't tell."

With a far off look, Mary didn't bother gathering her thoughts.

"I can't take you to Earth. You'd be a freak show and I couldn't maintain you healthily." She streamed her mind out between her lips. "Besides, moving you that far back into the Beta Line could cause serious systemic consequences. Could you imagine the technology jolt, assuming anyone discovered you for what you are?"

"You were considering taking me—"

"I would never abandon you here. Wyatt saved you, you will remain *saved*. And do I want to go back to the world?"

"What?"

"Do I want to go back to the world…" Her glassy eyes reflected a warped distortion of the playful antics on the screen before her. "Racism, sexism, being ignored, being *fine* with being ignored … what decade would I go to? The seventies? Turn of the 21ˢᵗ century? Would I witness white zealotry fueling hatred and misogyny? Abortion clinics bombed? Would I want to wait to see every horrible event in history play out from the trite Watergate scandal to the horrid Olympics attack or the Norway shooting while I kept my mouth shut? Can I do it? Could I be Cassandra? Forever knowing the future and being impotent to change or steer it?"

Magus remained silent, tiny eyes peering up.

"Every great shaper of history is a monster in some way. They are willing to do what others cannot or *will* not. It requires power, opportunity, and ambition. I sit on the *throne* of ultimate power. I can be where all others cannot and move how none other can."

Her gaze snapped away from the distant landscape and she focused on Magus intensely.

"Will it hurt?" she asked, feeling suddenly vulnerable, her lip trembling.

Magus understood her question instantly. "No." was the gentle reply. "It would take some time to prepare, though. And there may be no going back."

She nodded, sniffling. "I'm okay with that, I think. That fucking maggot in the parking lot wasn't scared of me. He scoffed at the thought of my being dangerous. He pulled out of her and just ran away. I couldn't do anything. I was useless. He got away with it, just as before."

"What if you went to the car beforehand? Perhaps called her at work to warn her?"

"That's assuming she would do anything. He would try again later.

He'll rape again. No, Stalin once said 'remove the man to remove the problem' and I understand it."

"There are so many rapists. So many horrible people, Ms. Mary. That would be a lot of 'removal' as you say."

"I know… I know… but what kind of person would I be not to do something about them. I can set the precedent to dissuade others now that I know I can. I can use this… *this* can make a better world by removing the venom and cancerous tissue that holds it back. I can be the scalpel to remove that sickly tissue."

"A scalpel was used to kill Gustavo."

"I have something that Rupert didn't have, though." Mary smiled tenderly at Magus. "I have a friend. And I have a conscience. He always had an empty smile. So, it won't hurt?"

"It would take some time, and preparation, but it shouldn't hurt."

Mary nodded.

"Okay. I'm okay with that. With all of it. And I know what I want to do first when I… when I am taller. It's funny. My mother was never impressed with any of my performances or recitals. She was never pleased by my displays. She was my only audience. Maybe if I can't make a pleasing impression, I can at least *horrify* the audience. Make an impact or a change for the better despite the violent means… but tomorrow. Tonight, is date night."

Mary eased back, her fingers in the popcorn. As terrible and dark as her future now looked, a weight had been lifted off of her shoulders. A purpose. A direction. Everything had fallen into place as it should have been. It was all coming together so perfectly that it had to be right. It *felt* right.

She was the Xeno.

Chapter 31

Mary was reminded of her physical limitations as she tried to pry the Flesh Mechanics pod from its secure and snug storage locker. Despite all her strength, it wouldn't move. Finally, with Magus' guidance, she had fastened several ratchet straps to the pod, and with the aid of a hand crank secured to one of the workshop tables, she had moved the pod an inch after an exhaustive hour of labor.

"How the hell am I going to move this thing?" she snapped. The thought had occurred to her that morning to drag the pod into the carousel and leave it drifting into the sun. It would solve everything, but the thought of shutting the door of possibility scared her more than anything, even her malformation.

Instead, she rationalized to drag it out of the locker first, thinking that having it right there in front of her would either send her resolve toward being The Xeno, or make her come to her senses.

"Sorry, I'm just…" She laughed, finishing her sentence with a guffaw. "It's been a hell of a week."

"We can motorize the crank. There are several components I can produce in Ingrid's tool shop that will help to that end. It might take several hours to drag it entirely out of the locker however, assuming we do so from this angle," Magus said,

"That's fine. It would give me a chance to eat or read or something. Aim me toward the tool shop."

Mary had never been down to the probe launching and storage facility before. There was a small elevator near the carousel's entrance, and within moments she was in the guts of Janus. Instead of the polished steel and brass, everything was ugly bulkhead and unpainted concrete.

Stepping clear of the metal gate that comprised the elevator door, she was surrounded by monitors that displayed charts and scrolling data that had seemingly been mounted in nearly every available spot on the walls. Several desks lay buried beneath mounds of papers, open boxes, and various scattered tools. Dirty dishes were stacked in one corner awaiting rescue to the kitchen, and on the single available spot of empty wall hung a tiny frame that held the framed embroidered words 'messiness is a sign of genius'.

There was a hammock holding several 'Virginia Tech' woolen blankets suspended at one end from the corner of a monitor and bolted into a wall at the other. On the ground below it stood a pair of Ingrid's boots, a radio, and a toppled stack of romance novels.

"Looks like she slept here a lot," Mary said sadly, peering around at Ingrid's secret world.

"Behind the door in front of you is her tool shop. I'm building your motor currently." Opening the door, Mary saw a table with arms curling up and around it, very much like the AutoDoc in a flurry of activity. Sparks were flying from the epicenter until finally a single arm lifted and presented Mary with a fairly plain-looking motor. "Take it upstairs and plug it in near me. It will take approximately twenty-three minutes to drag the pod clear of its current resting place."

Mary did so, and after securing the belts to it, clamping it to the table, and switching it on, she stood back and watched in satisfaction as the pod slowly crept free. "So… I feel a bit better about my life in your hands. How did you manage to get Wyatt's incursion perfect on the first try, anyhow? How are you sure he wasn't smeared somewhere."

"I practiced on multiple probes; I incurred them in and out of the timeline in various experimental ways over a period of two hours, thus preparing me for Mr. Wyatt's specific need."

"And what was Wyatt's need?"

"I suspect you are trying to catch me unawares to violate my promise."

Mary playfully huffed. "Me? You can't blame me for trying though. It's just, I'm worried about him and I can't connect with his being gone without... there being a body like everyone else."

"I can understand this emotional challenge, and I hope you know how hard it is for me to displease you by maintaining my promise."

"I know, I know... and like I said Mags... I feel okay with my life in your hands. Nice to have the last person on my little planet be an honest one."

Magus was silent a moment. "Do you think we can squeeze in a game of chess while we wait? I tried to make the motor fairly quiet so it wouldn't disturb us" Tiny eyes were fixed on her.

"You scheming little scamp." Mary smiled.

Mary's moves were fairly vacant, and Magus' pieces continued to dance around hers in a flurry of benign activity. The board quickly became cluttered, and the game's rules had invisibly changed into how long could they hold out and avoid taking each other's pieces.

"I'm going to force you to checkmate me," Magus said.

"The *hell* you are."

"It is my objective now."

"I doubt Bobby Fischer could even force someone into that."

"I wouldn't play against Bobby Fischer."

"Oh really?"

"He is not my friend."

"I wasn't when *we* first played."

"Mr. Wyatt spoke well on your behalf."

"This is like a UN chess game. Everyone on the board is stomping around but no one has the guts to take out a piece."

"I figured out what is inside those canisters in the other locker." Magus said suddenly.

"Really? What?"

"I was fairly certain that they contained biofuel to make the Flesh Mechanics pod operate, but it would have been too small an amount and it didn't make sense that they would take raw biogel in an effort to replicate it back on Earth since the technology to produce it is many generations away. The only other thing those canisters could be would be soil, water, and air samples."

"Soil?"

"Certainly. From different eras and regions. Such samples would reveal climate changes, radioactivity, pollution, and other incidentals dependent upon the region, like industrial buildup, animal populations, and resources. I also suspect that the data rod is packed with detailed information about the samples as well as an improvised archive of post-modern technology and information."

"That is what I was thinking too. Basically secrets of the future. Stocks, national rises and falls, things of that nature. I can't think of anything more valuable to humanity than that. I'll hook it up to you before we do anything with the pod, however. You might find some good medical information for me or something else useful."

"I very much look forward to that. I've never interfaced with that technology before."

"First time for everything."

"I will also need to be connected with the Flesh Mechanics pod when it is free of the locker. I'll need to begin scripting and programming the nanites and nubots inside."

"I know the term nanite, but what is nubot?"

"The nanites will sever and restructure your muscles, sinew, and organs as well as move a lot of your bulk mass. The nubots however, will restructure your DNA, red blood cells, marrow, as well as handle the more delicate procedures involving the removal and reforming of your oculars and nerves. Nubots are highly modified and compliant bacteria instead of miniature machines. Whereas the nanites perform the equivalent of heavy lifting, the nubots are for more delicate work. I can perform surgery on a single cell with them."

Mary blinked at the chess board.

"And I promise it won't hurt. You will have all of me, an intelligence beyond the ability to chart intelligence, focused on taking care of you… my *friend.*"

"Oh, it isn't that Mags… I just… I'm rather fond of this body… do you think I could ever have it back? Afterward?"

"I will be sure to detail and chart every portion of you within the depths of my ability. However, as powerful as I am and as effective as the flesh mechanics pod is, nature itself has a sense of … perfection and elegance that is fairly challenging to grasp. In short, I do not know."

Mary nodded. "Know what my mother once said to me? She said 'the greatest sign of love is sacrifice'. She said that to me after she had given up a trip with my father to New York City so she could see me at a recital for a dance company I despised. She was telling me that so I would be more appreciative." Mary swallowed her memory like a lump in her throat. "I hated my body so much when I was a dancer. I was constantly at war with it… and now I'm going to lose it."

Chapter 32

With some sweaty effort and several more outbursts of exasperation, Mary successfully connected the pod to Magus' terminal along with the data rod.

"As we suspected…" Magus pronounced within a few moments. "Cancer treatments, political events, natural disasters, economic shifts detailed exhaustively… what would you like to know, Ms. Mary?"

"None of it."

"Really?"

"Why bother? I'm going to make it all obsolete. I'm rewriting things." Mary thought a moment. "Might be worth a look eventually, though. For comparison. I'm sure it will provide a fascinating study in how humanity would have steered itself without someone at the wheel, so to say."

"I suppose so. There are a few things we'll need to prepare, but I suggest relaxing for a few days while I configure the pod itself."

Mary nodded. "Think I'm going to put a few things in order. Maybe tend to the bodies of everyone. I've been considering some kind of burial. Maybe in all of their home towns. I wish we had Wyatt so I could bury him next to his son."

"Are you no longer concerned about preserving the bodies for the sake of the authorities?"

"I *am* the authority, now. But no. Best lay them to rest. I know Ingrid came from Luray, Virginia, Rupert most likely would want a spot at the mission church that rescued him as a boy, and Jack has family in Princeton still. Gustavo's family owned several acres in central Florida, so I might bury him there somewhere."

"You would be willing to bury Rupert with a respectful service?"

"Knowing what I know now, I think I can understand what he was trying to do as much of a twisted bastard as he was for trying to do it. I half think he would have shot himself after he was done with all of us. Besides, he's dead. He paid for it. He didn't get away with it."

"I understand. However, I do ask that you not tamper with the bodies for the time being."

"What? Is there a sanitation issue? Do you think incurring them to the Beta Line and burying them will be an issue? Being that there would be two of them in the line despite one being dead?"

"No. That is not an issue. My only concern as of yet is to keep our options open regarding the Flesh Mechanic's pod."

Mary looked over to the long pill-shaped device that had brought so much soreness to her muscles.

"What does that have to do with them? It can't bring people back, can it?" Mary was excited at the hopeful thought, then was instantly shamed by it when she realized its absurdity.

"I am sorry, but no. It cannot. While it could theoretically build a body, it cannot emulate the neurological pattern of a human's brain. My chief concern is that I do not know where any biofuel is, and it appears that Wyatt and Rupert had not secured any."

"Those canisters?"

"Even if that was any amount of poorly stored biomaterial, it would hardly be enough for what we intend to do with your physical form. In short, we have no mass to process, alter, and incorporate into your current frame …."

"Except for the four bodies in the freezer down and around the hall…"

"Correct. I suspect this might be a difficult notion for you."

Mary flopped her hands into the air with a despairing and insincere grin. "Heavens, why would it be? I can just drag them out, cart their bodies down here since I'm so used to dragging them around, toss them in the blender, and toss myself into the soup pot once they are all frapped. I have a nice one-piece for the soaking."

"It wouldn't work like—"

"I know it wouldn't! You're asking me to defile the dead, dammit. Can't I steal some biofuel in the Beta Line?"

"This is highly guarded and rare material. You would need substantial amounts of prior training, planning, and knowledge to acquire it. While doing so is an option on the table, having four perfectly healthy donors in storage appears to be a far more viable solution. I have already scanned their medical records and each of them can provide different physical components that we need."

"That... that is a *lot* to ask me to do, Mags. That is a lot..."

"I am sorry. I did not know how to present the suggestion. I am sorry."

Mary sat, tired. "I'm going to go to sleep. And tonight we'll watch another movie."

"I look forward to it."

Mary's eyes settled on Magus' tiny black ones, and they held each other for a long time. Without a word, she eventually stood and hazily walked herself out of the workshop.

Legs on autopilot, Mary entered her own room, stripped down, and showered. Naked, warm, and wet she poked at her body as if it was something other than her own. She had round hips, small feet, and an elegant neck line with firm musculature and curvy sides. Like a pale violin, she was lovely.

And all of it would soon be gone.

Cupping her breasts, she finally faced the thought that she would most likely never know a man's touch again, but having the sexual part of her die or enter remission wasn't nearly as nerve-racking as she had expected. It had been years since she was fond and comfortable enough with a man to allow his touch, but regardless it was sad to see her feminine form go. She had been blessed with a lovely body, and the thoughts of Trevor enraptured with her made her flush even now.

Would her hands be enormous?

Would she still ovulate?

Would this change her emotionally?

How would her memories be affected?

Would she lose her father's eyes?

Wet and clinging to her shoulders, her hair suddenly came to mind. Trevor used to brush it for her when she was stressed about calling her parents on the weekends. She would sit on the floor and he on a chair behind her and they would watch Perry Mason while he brushed the stress and worry out of her hair.

"Spartans used to brush and braid each other's hair before battle," Mary had told him. The history-bug had bitten her at that point in college, and abandoning dance had become a continuous issue of heated conversation between her and her parents.

Every time she picked up her phone to call Mom and Dad, her hair looked lovely.

And soon it would be all gone.

Mary washed it again, as tenderly as she could with pearly shampoo and fragrant conditioner. Afterward she stood in the bathroom mirror with the hair dryer and tossed it about in the air until its feathery warmth wrapped around her head and neck in feminine comfort.

With eyes welling, she then cut it all off and shaved her head.

Chapter 33

Again in her bathrobe, but with ice cream this time, Mary sat next to Magus while watching *Back to the Future* on the rec room screen. The open air was frigid against her recently shaved head, and before the opening credits had completed Mary ran to fetch a navy cap out of Wyatt's junk drawer in the workshop. Running back, she bounded onto the couch just in time to watch Marty McFly get blasted across the screen by a giant guitar speaker.

Propping her ankles up on the couch's edge, she began painting her nails for what she figured was the last time. She had picked a deep and sultry red.

"We will need to remove any potential toxins on your body prior to entering the pod, Mary."

"That's okay. I can use remover."

"May I ask why you shaved your head? The pod would have removed your hair and your hair follicles fairly effectively."

"I think I wanted to cut it on my own terms. Besides, it will be a more gradual change for me."

"Did you keep your hair?"

"It's tied in a braid on my dresser."

"It might be of need when we fuel the pod. I also request any toe nail clippings be kept as well. And tomorrow you might need to move to a liquid diet."

"Ugh. I thought I was done with those decades ago."

The movie proceeded and Mary found it fairly easy to watch. There was a vibrant feeling in her stomach that seemed to hum with energy as the evening went on. It was easy to laugh at Christopher Lloyd's antics on screen, and Michael J. Fox's squeals of alarm.

"I have substantial doubts as to this film's validity regarding time travel. I'm not sure where to start when addressing its liberties."

"Keep complaining and I'll make you watch part two."

"I can only assume through context that you threaten me with substantial harm."

"Oh, I *do.*"

As the film progressed, it occurred to Mary that she didn't want to go to bed. "Let's watch another. Double feature!" she exclaimed during the rolling credits. "Want to watch it? I can start it up."

"Are you certain? I could be testing my programming routines for the nubots instead."

"I'm not tired."

"Will the next film have as many fallacies regarding time travel?"

"Yep."

"I see."

"Please?"

"Of course. But my ice cream is melted."

"I'll get you more!" Mary bounced off of the couch and ran to the kitchen. "This reminds me … about your real food," she called through the open swing doors. "When do we need to switch out the fluid in your tank?"

"Actually, we need to do that prior to your entering the pod. I will need it to sustain me for the duration of your metamorphosis. I can walk you through the procedure tomorrow."

"How about tonight? I'm not tired, and I'm not in the mood for bed. If we do it now, it might also get you out of watching another cheesy movie."

"This appeals to me."

Magus' tank was soon placed on the cart, and with one hand, Mary pushed it back to the workshop while the other hand held her second bowl of ice cream. Once Magus was hooked back into his terminal, he directed her to Wyatt's bedroom where, under his bed, several long steel suitcases were laid out. Each had four canisters and each canister was the concentrated solution needed to sustain Magus' life.

Following Magus' instructions via the speaker in the kitchen, Mary cooked the contents of a canister in a spaghetti pot while adding water and stirring it as she made the proper heat adjustments.

"I finally get to cook for you!"

"My current solution will need to be drained, and this will need to be added to my tank. The exchange process will take approximately ten minutes, during which time I will be unhooked from the speakers and the terminal. We will not be able to converse."

"I understand. Any way I can make you more comfortable?"

There was no immediate reply. After some thought, Magus finally spoke. "Despite my operating manual warnings, Wyatt insisted on holding me while Rupert handled the fluid. To be honest… I appreciated the contact."

Mary smiled. "I think I would too."

Hauling the sludge-filled pot down the hall with a grunt, Mary placed it next to Magus' tank. "All right, Squiggles. Should I wear gloves?"

"Actually, your bare skin would be more sanitary than clothing fibers or most other materials. And you recently showered. I have a fairly aggressive immune system so there shouldn't be any complications given what I have been reading off of Janus' air filters."

"So, should I… actually, how much muscle do you have?"

"I'm honestly not sure. Enough to coil around a hand."

"Here," Mary said, dropping her bathrobe. "Now we're both wearing the same thing pretty much. We'll be vulnerable together. After all, you'll be taking me apart soon enough."

With several quick jerks, Mary unplugged the outer outlets along the bottom of Magus' tank, severing the connection from Janus, the speakers, and the microphone entirely. She was never one to play with frogs or bugs as a little girl, and dissecting a worm in biology class had made her nose wrinkle with unpleasantness, but she shoved all that aside instantly knowing that she was reaching for a friend. Her only remaining one.

The sludge was surprisingly thick, so clearly Magus would have to use considerable muscle to curve around in it to look about. This gave her hope that her idea, playful as it was, might help.

She reached in with both hands, loosely closed her fingers around the tiny still creature, and lifted slowly.

"I forgot to ask if you had ears!" she laughed as the tiny thing emerged, pale against her fingers. Wiping the solution off, she cooed, "You have such tiny eyes, Mags."

She lifted Magus over her head, and gently guided the long bodied worm around her shoulders.

"Got a grip?" she asked, the tiny eyes peering up at her from under her chin. "Hang on. We're going to take out the trash."

Naked, Mary hauled the vacant container off of the worktable and into the stealth suit staging area to slowly and steadily dump its contents down one of the floor drains. "This feels like I'm pouring motor oil down a drain in Florida. My father used to do that in the garage to get rid of palmetto bugs that would crawl out of them."

Magus' tank was soon completely empty. With the work sink and the hose in the workshop, Mary rinsed it out.

"I won't towel dry it. I suspect that fibers from my robe or a towel are what we are trying to avoid here."

Next, with equal care, Mary poured the new solution into the tank. "We'll test the water with your tail end to make sure it is fine. I don't want you having temperature problems. Though I suppose you are heartier than a tropical fish from the store."

The tank was filled, and she gently uncoiled her friend from her shoulders. She held Magus up to her face, nose to nose, and smiled. "Thank you. You let me ramble. I'm not used to that. Things are … strange for me. But this feels okay. This feels right." With a gentle stroke from her fingers under Magus' chin, she dipped the long curving creature in tail first and gradually submerged her forearms. "I've sleep-walked through so much of my life, and whatever success I've had as a feminist historical revisionist has always felt hollow. Always from a distance. The world was just always more comfortable to me at arm's length. Maybe that is why I left Trevor. I didn't have the luxury of an ivory tower to hide in with him. But now … now things are different. I can change things. I have a reason to *be*."

She hooked the wires in the tank to Magus' sides, and then she plugged in the outer ports with each corresponding cable. The tiny speakers crackled.

"Am I back on line? I can feel Janus, Oracle, and all of the systems. Can you hear me, Mary?"

"Loud and clear."

"I am terribly sorry, but I am completely deaf. I heard none of what you said to me during the exchange."

"Oh… well, what do you think I said?"

Magus was silent for a moment. "I suspect you said nothing but the loveliest things."

"Odds are, you'll hear them again. Kindness bears repeating." She scooped up her bathrobe from the floor and wrapped herself back up. "I might need another shower, but first how about some chess?"

Chapter 34

Everything in the infirmary was covered with rubber sheeting. Mary was bundled head to toe in protective medical gear topped off with a plastic hood and a surgical facemask under a welding visor from Ingrid's 'mancave'.

Magus had guided her through the process of preparing the surgical equipment and changing out the AutoDoc's arm attachments for dissection purposes. Each spider leg surrounding the table was now tipped with slicing blades, gripping claws, and tiny rotating saws. Testing their operations, Magus commanded them in a slow rhythmic dance as they pantomimed their upcoming intentions with Mary's dead fellows.

"Are the refrigerated containers arranged to your liking, Mary? Each body part I hand you will need to be stored in the proper one."

"Yeah, I think they are good," Mary said, muffled and huffing from anxiety. Her welding mask was starting to fog at the bottom.

"Do you have various bags ready for the biowaste?"

"I've got several boxes of them here and the cart outside is ready to go to the incinerator."

"And are the items from the kitchen ready?"

Mary looked over to the counter at the large Cuisinart. "Yeah, that's all set up."

"Please remember that it is vital that you do not vomit on anything."

Mary nodded and reflected for a moment. "Honestly, I think I'll be okay. This is all just meat. They left a long time ago."

"Are you able to tolerate watching their forms come apart?"

"Yes. I think what makes a person so squeamish is that they sympathize with the damage being inflicted on others when they see violence. If I'm willing to tear my body apart, I have to be willing to overcome that and tear *these* bodies apart. I think I'll be fine."

"All right. Let's bring the first one in then. Where would you like to start?"

Mary sputtered as she fumbled with the question. "God… not that it makes a difference… well, let's start with Jack."

With the squeaky wheels of the gurney, Mary went to cold storage. Sliding Jack's drawer wide open, she tugged at the bag that held his body until she clumsily flopped it into position and wheeled it back.

Pulling up alongside the AutoDoc's table, she unzipped the body bag. She wasn't prepared to see his face and stopped halfway down his body, staring at the dead, pale coloring of his expressionless visage. It was as though an unpainted wax replica of him was in front of her, laying at attention.

Magus wisely remained quiet.

Reaching forward silently, as though fearful of waking him, her fingertips found the hair on his brow and stroked it gently.

"What you wanted was something I didn't have for you. I'm sorry." She pulled her hand back and began cutting the bag away from around and under him. With welling eyes, she focused on her task.

First, the bag was removed.

Next his clothing was sheared off of him.

The hair from his head was shaved off, as well as any substantial body hair on his chest, legs, forearms, genitals and underarms. He was surprisingly hairy.

Clumping it all up, she stuffed a small bag with it, labeled it, and placed it in the appropriate refrigerated unit. While doing so, the AutoDoc's arms spread wide to receive him at the center of its hydra-like nexus and Mary struggled to lift and move him into position.

Two of the arms began washing him off with a purple, foul smelling liquid while sponging him down. Mary got several of the bags ready, and steeled herself.

After a thorough rinse, the cleaning arms retracted, and the rest moved in. Saws spun with blades delicately gliding; thick, cold blood oozed out and down the sides of the table like dark lava from a sacrificial volcano. His skin was split in precise, un-living fashion while his restful stoic face remained stonily calm.

The feet were disassembled first, followed by the hands. Each tiny bone was pulled out, cartilage and sinew snipped clear, washed and seemingly polished, then placed on a tray for Mary to secure and label. Next came long piercing syringes from all sides, stabbing casually into his limbs and through his chest to collect as much marrow as possible.

It was now a flurry of activity, all the arms moving in a chorus of buzzing and snipping as skin was peeled and flopped aside, muscle isolated and handed to her for bagging. The organs were fairly solid from the freezer and easier to pluck out. Some of them went to her; others were merely cast aside onto the floor for her to dispose of.

Soon Jack's head and shoulders were all that remained unmolested, his bare spine still laid out on the table as the AutoDoc's mechanical tendrils sucked the marrow out of each vertebra before tossing it aside in order to secure the precious discs.

Two arms held Jack's head in place. Two perfectly coordinated saws took off the cap of his head with a tub above it, catching his brain the moment the sack holding it was ruptured. The ocular nerves, eyes, and remainder of the spinal fluid were gathered along with the tongue.

The remaining hollowed skull, like a drinking cup worthy of Vlad, rolled forward into an upright standing position.

And that is what did it.

Mary spun about and lurched out of the room to the trashcan that was waiting for just this. Luckily she lifted the welding shield in time before vomiting.

A few moments later she came back in with a fresh mask.

"Are you all right?" Magus asked.

"I'm good. That was the one time. I'm fine now."

Next came Gustavo, who may have weighed more stiff than loose. It took a full twenty minutes of grunting, resting, and grunting again as she dragged him onto the gurney while trying not to tip it over. After the shaving and cleaning ritual was repeated, Gustavo's blood was drained and stored in jugs and his fat was slurped out from most of his bodily deposits. Mary was instructed as to what chemical agents to add to the greasy fat collection prior to blending it in the Cuisinart.

As an aside, she resolved to find a new blender for the kitchen.

Next was his marrow, his isolated joints, his liver, and his heart which was surprisingly small for such a large man.

His skin was a bit floppier than Jack's and harder for Mary to gather up in her arms for disposal.

Ingrid was next. As the arms did their work diligently, her uterus, tubes, and ovaries were flopped carelessly onto the floor.

Mary nearly protested, but held her tongue behind her mask. Crouching down, she splayed them out respectfully with her gloved hands. It reminded her somewhat of the 'flux capacitor' from *Back to the Future*. Was the shape of a woman's internal sexual organs ingrained more so than expected? Instead of things merely being shaped like the outside of a woman's body (like cars or Coke bottles) could the triangle of a woman's womb be just as visible within culture with martini glasses and icons?

"Can we keep this?" Mary asked.

"To what end?"

"It just seems… wrong."

"You gave no protest of Gustavo or Jack's sexual organs being disposed of. Is there something different about Ingrid's?"

"Well…" Mary said. "Us girls have to stick together I suppose. But you're right. I just… it's a lot."

"We're almost done. You're doing wonderful, Ms. Mary. I am very impressed."

Ingrid's uterus was placed in a bag along with her disposed of intestines, fecal matter, and lungs. Her head was scooped out just as Gustavo's and Jack's were, and it was placed with theirs in the disposal cart for incineration.

Mary was about to push the loaded cart of ghastly remains away to be burned when Magus gently called for her to come back into the AutoDoc's laboratory.

She took in the scene with dazed eyes and an overwhelmed stupor. The rubber sheets had streams of blood swirling and converging under her every step and tiny lines of red streaked the ceiling from the work of the skull-saws.

"We need Mr. Rupert, still."

Mary simply stood there.

"I'm willing to bury him properly, but I'm not certain I'm willing to merge with him. I don't want him to come along."

"It is certainly your choice, but he has many substantial resources we can use given his fitness and long term health habits. Additional resources, especially of his quality, would behoove your metamorphosis."

Mary was far too drained to argue.

"Okay, fine! I'll nab him. My mother's worst nightmare is about to come true."

Gripping the gurney, she began down the hall.

"And what is that?"

"I'm going to have a black man inside me."

Chapter 35

Four days had passed and Mary had spent them in a sleepy and distant state of mind. She had read her favorite book again, practiced her yoga and some of the Tai Chi she knew, and watched several of Jack and Gustavo's silly movies without cracking a smile.

The kitchen was a wreck and she was in no mood to spend any part of her day doing dishes or laundry. The Flesh Mechanic's pod had taken in the human remains in proper order and through the proper ports, and Magus had given his full attention to the preparation of Mary's physical revolution.

The morning came, and she looked to the clock in the workshop. It was almost eleven a.m. Was eleven a.m. a good time to do this?

"It won't hurt," Magus assured.

"I'm not sure if I'm bothered by that thought anymore."

"Are you ready?"

"As I'll ever be."

The Pod hummed to life and split down the center. Inside was a cushioned mattress with vents and glowing light from all sides.

"It will be almost two months. I've made the systems within far more efficient and the programs for the nanites and nubots are substantially upgraded to maximize their hardware abilities. Some of the operations of the pod are too primitive to process what we intend to do, so I will take control of them directly."

Mary nodded, dropping her bathrobe to the floor revealing her joyless nudity.

"I want to be fast, flexible, and strong. I want to be the proto human… like I was forged on the anvil by a vengeful God."

"And you will be."

Mary stepped in elegantly, right toes first, and eased herself onto her back. The cushioning was comfortable and the chamber was warm without being smothering. With a silent, gliding motion the front of the pod collapsed closed just before her nose. As the glowing lights dimmed to pitch darkness, she felt her heavy exhalations blowing back into her face. Her heart was pounding so hard it sent tremors through her fingers and eyes.

With a muffled whir, an unseen gel began oozing from the sides. It slowly filled in around her with a warm, slippery thickness until it hit her ears. Oozing into and against her eardrums, she winced until it reached her eyes. Attempting a stoic facial expression in an effort to accept the oddity of it all, Mary tilted her head back jutting her chin into the air so she could breathe until the last.

It poured into her anus and vagina and the pores on her skin tingled. Her eyes were numb and she could hear nothing. Soon the mattress below her didn't even seem to be there anymore and she felt entirely suspended as her whole face was enveloped, nostrils flooding.

Instinctively her mouth opened and it poured through her teeth and around her gums, tongue, and down her throat and into her lungs.

She jolted, arms flailing in physical panic. Her eyes were open, yet she could see nothing. Suffocation was setting in, and her body was now convulsing, racked with uncontrollable fear and heaving.

Her clumsy arms tried to pound the pod, and her slow fingers fumbled about for a switch or a knob or a hatch handle. She had no doubt that she was dying. Had Magus made a mistake? Was it going wrong? Could she have been deceived this entire time? Was Magus an agent of the real Xeno, and it wasn't Mary at all?

The panicking thoughts swirled in a nightmarish blackout where Jack, Gustavo, Ingrid, and Rupert all had their heads cut off, emptied, and coffee poured into them. Their eyes opened and distantly beamed forward like headlights down a country road at night.

Something changed. There was an earthquake, a shuddering in the universe, and then the fluid started draining. Magus must have known it went all wrong and was aborting!

The fluid flushed away rapidly, leaving her on the cushioning, weak and heavy like a bather into an emptying bathtub. Sputtering as the gel rolled out of her nose and down the corners of her mouth, she began groping again for the front of the pod to open.

Everything tilted; her head now downward and dizzy while her feet seemed to be high into the air. Sliding, the top of her head pushed into some type of thick membrane wrapping her face, shoulders, and seemingly her whole body as the pod's sides rippled out in a fluid motion.

She slid onto something soft and stabbed desperately at the membrane with her fingers to free herself. Everything was slippery and the light of the workshop above was dimmed through the sack, teasing with the promise of freedom and air.

Clawing and flailing did nothing until she bit with her teeth, gnawing and tearing at what covered her face and suppressed her movement. And it began to give. Thrusting her hands out, she pulled and tore at the membrane, ripping it wide open into the stinging cold air. Blinded by the workshop's overhead lights, she clamped her eyes closed and tossed about in an effort to be free.

"Try and inhale now, Mary. Roll to your side."

Doing so, she found her lungs unwilling to give her air due to their being full of what felt like cement. Rolling to her knees and nearly toppling over, she spurted out the fluid in a long and consistent fountain onto the inflated mattress that had caught her when she slid out of the pod. Cramping her diaphragm, Mary spouted the fluid everywhere until her breathing took some level of air. Leaning down like a Muslim at prayer, she continued spurting and gasping until it was done, and she meekly rolled onto her side.

Eyes covered by her hands, knees tucked under her arms and feet tight to her bottom, she shivered and rasped with an exhausted wheeze. Finally, after enough time crawled by, she formed her lips into a question.

"What went wrong?" Mary wondered if the technology was broken or if her body had been rejected through some unforeseen medical conflict.

"Nothing went wrong," Magus replied with a bit of pride. "You look magnificent."

Mary pulled her hands from her eyes and pried them open. They were filmy and goopy and with several wipes of her fingers she could see. The first thing she saw were her palms.

They were huge, like God's, and the fingers appeared long and unnatural despite their thickness and strength. Her grip was wide, thick with muscle and padding, and her whole hand could easily cover her entire face.

Her face! She felt it and found her nose reduced to almost nothing, the nostrils recessed in a ghoulish manner giving her a skeletal appearance. There was no hair, her jaw was enormous, and her cheekbones wide and powerful. Her brow was pronounced and her eyes large and as she flitted her vision about, everything was suddenly sharper.

Flopping with exhaustion, she rolled flat onto her back in a coughing fit. Her muscled stomach coiled like a rubber band under the layer of sludge that still covered her and soon she drifted asleep, consciousness simply not being an option anymore.

Chapter 36

Mary jerked awake violently.

She was freezing and sore and each limb felt like it weighed a metric ton. Magus had turned the lights down low and as she peered about with weary eyes she realized that the world was far more vivid and textured than she remembered it.

In a hushed voice, Magus welcomed her to the waking world. "Good morning. Take your time finding your legs and your voice."

Shifting her legs, Mary realized that she had defecated while sleeping and it was smeared on her thighs. Looking down she saw that it was blackish and dark and clumpy.

"Shower," she croaked.

"There are several in the staging area for incursions. Can you make it thirty feet toward the carousel?"

Mary rolled onto her elbows and began dragging her rubbery legs behind her, using the worktable struts as handgrips. The semi-dried bio-gel that encrusted her flaked and slipped on her hairless, smooth skin as her shoulders rose and fell like slow pistons.

Slumping out of the room, her back muscles rippled with dormant power. With shoulders wider than most children are tall and arms as thick as legs she dragged herself towards the promise of cleansing water.

When gripping the final strut of the table to push past it, she took the time to observe her hands and their mechanics. Her fingers were huge, thick, and long with strong yet trim fingernails and stony knuckles. The palms felt rough and insensitive as though they had been ground callus by labor. Pausing, bringing the hand to her face once more, Mary spread her fingers wide to make sure this appendage was indeed hers.

Each finger obeyed, bending to her will. She covered her entire field of vision. Extended, her center three fingers felt solid and stable, like stabbing weapons. When she curled them all into a tightly compacted fist, her knuckles glowed white as the bones raised to the surface of the skin, causing the blood to flee.

What could that fist, when reinforced with her entire body behind it, *not* go through?

She continued crawling, faster now, with her shoulders alternating at a more steady rhythm. Then her knees began helping, finding a complimentary pace.

Between breaths she wheezed, "I am starving."

"You can consume the biogel for sustenance."

Mary disregarded the notion, and lifting to her hands and knees, she slinked toward the nearest of the two shower stalls that Wyatt and Rupert would use to clean off prior to suiting up. It spurted on with lukewarm water as she approached.

Flopping with a cough, she fell into the streaming water. Immediately the water flooded her sinuses and she shook her head violently side to side, spitting and snorting it out.

"What the—"

"You no longer have a traditional nose. It was a combat liability and the initial close quarter combat specs suggested its removal entirely since you will often have breathing apparatuses to filter air instead."

"How do I blow my nose?"

"With a tissue, sans the nose."

"Is that why my voice is so different?"

"I did my best to keep your vocal cords unchanged, however the restructuring of your sinuses and the considerable expansion of your diaphragm and ribcage has impacted it significantly. I am very sorry."

Inhaling another bout of water accidentally, Mary waved a free hand into the air to dismiss Magus' apology. Snorting, she sat up clumsily.

"No apologies. Ever. Got it, Mags?"

"Of course."

"I appreciate you trying to keep my voice intact. I can still hear me, a bit. I'm still in here."

"Exactly my intent. I wanted to ease any dissociative issues with your body, as well as stem any potential dysmorphia. Your eyes are still the same color, for instance, despite being thirty-eight percent larger."

"Not to mention sharper. You improved my vision!"

"The level of vision you now have is not obtainable by a human or even most animals, however light can be a challenge for you. I have dimmed and adjusted all lighting on board Janus at this point to accommodate you; however I strongly suggest contact lenses with light sensitivity to prevent your eyes from being harmed by flame or sudden bursts from light sources while you incur."

"Contacts. Like the ones Jack wears?"

"Yes, the AutoDoc stamps them for him."

"And they will be my size?"

"Correct."

"And not to ask another stupid question, but … we can have them produced in various colors, including reddish gold?"

"Correct. I show that Jack had even put in an order of special contacts for himself for Halloween."

Mary nodded, yet another piece sliding into place. Spying a grip bar on the wall, she steadied her arm with some effort and wrapped her fingers around it. It felt like it had been made for children. With a firm tug she pulled herself to her knees, leaning her forehead on the tiled wall as the water poured down her head and streamed down the long muscles of her back. Despite the wide shoulders, rocky musculature, and enormous feet and hands, she still had an elegant neck and slightly womanish hips.

"I'm still here," she murmured. With a determined tug she stood, knees wobbling as she rose to her full height. Squaring her shoulders and rolling her jaw she felt her joints gliding within the folds of her muscle, bulging and shifting under the surface.

"How do you feel?"

"I feel... *new.*"

Chapter 37

"You will need a mask for filtering air and ripcording."

"I don't want it covering my whole face," Mary mumbled with bits of peanut butter sandwich crumbling out of her mouth.

"It won't. It will cover your nostrils and grip onto your cheekbones with a flexible suction to attach under your jaw. You will be able to breathe, and still move your mouth to speak."

She swallowed hard. "How will this mask stay on?"

"There is an adhesive that was used for the same thing on the stealth suits."

"Gotcha," Mary said. "And the polymer that Wyatt and Rupert used will cover me, dry, and keep me disguised and creepy looking. Well… creep*ier*…" Mary's large eyes wandered to the front of the stainless steel oven that reflected her broadened visage. She shuddered at the sight of herself, and quickly looked back to the stack of peanut butter sandwiches on the kitchen floor that she had hastily made.

After her shower, she dragged herself down the main hallway while sliding her bulk along the wall, huge toes in the fancy carpet. The kitchen was her first destination, and all she could think of was peanut butter.

On her eighth sandwich, she voiced a concern. "Do I have diabetes?"

"Not at all. Your diet will be strange and erratic as your metabolism equalizes, but expect a substantial appetite from now on. I suggest a healthy and balanced diet that I can aid you in addressing, as well as at *least* nine hours of sleep per day."

"Easy enough."

"You will also notice issues with your endocrine system. Your adrenal output is substantially increased in both length of effectiveness in time and intensity. Your body might run away from you when frightened or angered, so be aware of your own actions and temperament."

Mary nodded sullenly.

"Mags, remember when I suggested you bounce me in and out of space time to feed you? Can we still do that, but with dropping me in and out rapidly in the Beta Line instead of here?"

"To what end?"

"I'm still just a body. Mortal, human, and untrained, and without any significant weapons except those carbines that I'm not keen on. For me to show up with a pistol or a rifle is absurd. I need to do it all, or almost all of it, with my hands. Especially from what we've seen already of what I'm going to do. I need you to be able to perform brief and rapid incursions into the same area."

"Firstly, I suggest becoming acclimated with your new physique prior to incurring."

Mary nodded again, stuffing an entire sandwich in her mouth.

"I worry, after all," Magus confessed.

"You need another fluid dump, Mags? I've been out of it for a while and you've been neglected."

"Not a concern at all."

"Let me take care of you as you've taken care of me."

After using one of her huge fingers to scoop the peanut butter jar clean, Mary wobbled her way back to the workshop. As soon as she entered, the stench of decaying biomass smacked her exposed nostrils.

"God!" she gasped, covering her face.

"Your sense of smell has also been significantly increased."

"Mind if I hose the floor down?"

"I was going to suggest as much."

The industrial hose was tiny, and her fingers felt clumsy around the knob and nozzle as she sprayed away the filth she had left. Tiny drains slurped the water up along the depressed edges of the room.

While the undersides of the two long and curved tables dripped, Mary stood over the pod with her shoulders slumped but otherwise standing tall. Her head cocked to its side, and with a lazy finger she freed the pod from its motorized harness.

With a deep and sharp breath, she scooped down, placing both hands under the pod's edge and pushed with surging might. Her calves bulged, her shoulders rippled like tectonic plates bursting forth mountain ranges, and her arms crevassed along her muscle lines from the strain. Blood coursed throughout her body like magma, making her skin prickly for a moment, and then there was a release. Mary's very being was fulfilled from the exertion.

Screeching along the floor, the pod slid directly back into its locker as she shoved it upright with a final nudge. Standing before her accomplished work, a smile crossed her face.

"Wow," she said. "I don't even think my heart rate elevated. How am I so fit? Shouldn't I be atrophied?"

"The nanites each delivered very specific impulses into your muscles to bolster them. Comparatively, you are in a significantly weakened state, so your diet and exercise will only increase your stamina and overall strength."

"What about my constitution? Illness? Cancer? Disease?"

"Given the breadth of travelling you intend to be doing, that will be hard to determine, but I did my best to make you resilient to what I could. You must take vitamins, however. Full supplements including vitamins C, D, and magnesium."

"*That* I know we have. Horse pills."

"I have also made sure you have been vaccinated to nearly every disease for which humans have a vaccine."

"That's a comfort. No polio for me."

Just as before, Mary prepared, emptied, and cleaned out Magus' tank.

Because of the enormity of her hands, she took care to be gentle and soon Magus was slipped back into his clean, comforting suspension. The pair had two months of chess games to catch up on and they played for hours. They chatted while they played and Magus filled Mary in on the political winds of change depicted in the data rod.

Tonight was movie night. Mary, dizzy yet stronger, walked back to the kitchen with Magus' tank under her arm. She was craving steak. They then sat on the couch while Mary ate each eight-ounce steak like it was a tiny beef tip, and *Somewhere in Time* played out on the screen in front of them.

Magus asked a difficult question halfway through the film.

"It's a fluttering in your tummy. High up, here," Mary responded, pointing a huge finger. "Above the belly button. That's where you feel excitement like that."

"That is love?"

"No, lust. Maybe 'smitten'. *Love* is when you think of the person twenty years after they are gone and you wish they were still around to nibble your shoulders."

"Did you feel that for Mr. Wyatt?"

"I miss him. But we never had that relationship. Truth is I think that flutter in me died a long time ago. And I killed it. Besides, he was married and still wore his ring. Everything about it was messy. Maybe after the mission on Janus was over, but who knows."

"Mary, it does occur to you that when you steer the Beta Line, you can alter many of the outcomes that you have witnessed in the Alpha Line, yes?"

"Certainly."

"Perhaps you and Mr. Wyatt could be together?"

"Wait, what? No. I'm not here to steer things my way, Mags. I'm not like Christopher there," she said, pointing at the screen as Christopher Reeve's character rubbed a penny between his finger and thumb.

"I apologize. I don't mean to suggest misuse of our power; it's just that my two favorite people would seem happy together. Upon viewing Janus' logs, you both would alter your stance when around each other in a telling fashion."

Mary smiled at the thought of the childlike Magus trying to make its two favorite adults become Mommy and Daddy.

"I know better than to ask you where Wyatt is, but if you ever get the desire to tell me how we can save him, please do so, okay?"

"Okay."

Mary's chewing lost its motivation as she fixated her mind's eye on the brushed steel reflection of herself in the oven once again.

"How recognizable am I, Mags?"

"I am far too biased to make an objective observation."

"Then let's test it out."

Chapter 38

He panted frantically through the humid night air as his trendy sneakers bounded on the black parking lot asphalt. Several gunshots rang out from behind him in a rapid and undisciplined pattern.

Deceptively handsome, he had always gotten what he wanted in life. Tantrums as a child earned him entitlement from his enabling mother and the sexual abuse at the hands of his sister made him so bitter that he felt validated to do the same to the world. In the end, he dreamt of dominating others, even in small ways.

Too often the tormented only want someone of their own to torment.

Janet had such a desperate smile. She was so self-conscious and eager to please. Coworkers walked all over her at the store yet, she never complained unless prompted, for fear of appearing 'like a bitch'.

"You're not a bitch," he purred, soothing her. "You're wonderful."

They would spend so much time after closing talking that they were often late leaving. And he was a very good listener. He knew what prompts to give, how to appear tender, and after observing how she turned her ankles and busied her fingers, he knew her weaknesses and soft buttons.

His preference was not to rape her. This time he had convinced himself to bend her to willingly be *his* in whatever capacity amused him. After an intentionally heart-felt and long post-hours conversation, he pretended his ride had stood him up over the phone.

Janet insisted on giving him a lift, despite his gentlemanly protests.

Once inside her car, she was willing to kiss. Her bosom heaved and her eyes couldn't meet his for more than half a second at a time, so he knew she was ripe.

He stroked her ear tenderly.

Janet snickered.

He ran the back of his hand along her face.

Janet blushed.

His fingers danced up her knee.

Janet blocked them meekly with her hands.

His hand thrust upward under her skirt, unable to settle for simple seduction.

Janet shook, pushing herself back into her seat.

His other hand curled into a fist, clenching her hair.

Janet made her one, singular protest.

He hissed at her, threatening her life.

He got what he wanted. Until *she* showed up.

It was her frigid roommate, the one that didn't respect him. He couldn't remember her name since in his head he only referred to her as 'cunt'. And she shows up with a gun! And shoots at him!

It was all clearly a misunderstanding. He would tell the cops, they would find the bullets lodged somewhere, and Janet would confirm the story. Or maybe he would say they were trying to rob him. That would pay them both back.

Rounding the corner to the back of the grocery store, his running eased a bit. His mind's anvil forged his story. Shuffling through his pockets, he searched for his cell phone, figuring he had best call the police first to get the drop on them. Cunt and Janet would pay. Janet had told him of her own mental health history, so he could play it several ways.

Pulling his phone out, he was about to dial when he realized someone was standing in his path. Looking up, he saw that the person was pale, taller than anyone he had ever seen, and without any clothing except a wrist band of some kind.

"I... I was just shot at," he stammered, still processing the large, vaguely familiar eyes of the bald thing in front of him. Wandering his vision downward, he was baffled to see the hints of a vagina despite the muscular stature and aggressive pose of what he thought was a man.

It stepped forward.

"Still recognize me?" it said in a thick, rich voice with hints of feminine gentility.

Shock, pure and unrestrained, surfaced to his face. His mouth was crimped in an effort to find a voice for his horror when Mary's open palms clapped closed on both sides of his head so hard that his skull was instantly misshapen, throwing one of his eyes onto his cheek.

He let out a wheezing spurt as his knees folded and he collapsed on the damp pavement. Blood trickled down the corners of his mouth while his lungs convulsed and pink fluid welled out of his ears. His mouth could no longer close properly, but it kept trying to do so for the sake of swallowing. Mary walked around him, observing his hideous suffering. She took the image in, testing herself to see if her resolve would falter.

It did not. She stomped repeatedly on his head until it was no longer a head.

Chapter 39

Splashing down, Mary quickly sank to the bottom of the catching pool. The red remains of the rapist's head caused a brief, dark swirl that cleared as she stroked toward the surface. Paddling to the edge of the pool with a single reach, she pulled herself out and took off the armband that had the call button for her ripcord.

"That was only a very basic functioning device. There were several aboard the station for emergencies. The mask I am currently building will employ the same function and will be activated by a clucking of your tongue."

Mary nodded vacantly, sitting at the edge of the pool, dangling her legs in the water. The dimmed lights made the domed ceiling dance with long strands of silver as the tiny waves slapped about.

"Are you all right, Mary?"

She remained silent for a bit before forming her confusion into words.

"I'm not sure how I should feel."

Careful not to slip, Mary stood and walked out. Travelling down the hall, she voiced her thought process.

"I'd always fantasized about what I would do to him. I used to daydream about rescuing Janet. And when I did it was unfulfilling. But… when I… ended *him* it was so much… better, somehow. How demented am I to get more out of punishing the guilty than saving the innocent?"

Allowing her legs to mindlessly carry her, she went into the rec room and began pushing all of the furniture, pinball machines, pool table, and folding card tables into the hallway. Special care was given to moving Wyatt's guitar.

"And that's it, then. The ethos of the Xeno, to put it distantly. Allow those who got away with their crime to be punished spectacularly for all to see and learn from. I save one person, and it just means they will need saving again, or it will be someone else needing the saving. But… set a brutal precedent, and each rapist will hesitate prior to unzipping because the boogyman might appear."

Standing in the center of the now empty room, Mary brought her heels together, one arm gracefully bent to place her hand in front of her navel and the other arm glided outward, fingers together, as her middle finger strayed slightly inside. Bending her knees, she squatted down in the traditional pose of a dancer.

"What use is dedicating your life to studying history if you aren't going to change it? What good would I be as a spectator?"

"To explore your thinking further, Mary, I suspect that may have been an issue with that first generation Magus we had spoken of. The one that expanded its borders of influence?"

"How so?" she asked while repeating the squatting motion slowly.

"What good am I as a sentience, being limited to monitoring and conducting port traffic?"

Mary smiled. "What a shit job that would have been, eh?"

She fired herself upward, straight and firm. She then rapidly repeated the up and down motion, pumping until she launched herself straight up. Landing, Mary spun on one heel, the other held well above her head in an elegant twirl.

As she practiced her form, watching her blurry reflection in the large television screen before her, she put more effort into each leap. She pumped herself with knees bending, and launched, milled her arms, and kicked higher. This time she brushed the ceiling with her foot.

The excitement of her success gave her pause. She spied the lamp dangling over the table in the alcove. Squinting, impulse took her. At a full run she sprung over the steps, landed a foot beside the table, rotated herself in midair, and with an outstretched foot, shattered the lamp in a glassy burst. Tinkling fragments rained as she landed on the other side of the table, all her previous grace suddenly gone. Tumbling, her elbow went into the wall, crushing several Italian revelers. With a perturbed grunt and a few tugs, she loosed herself from the plaster's grip and dusted herself off.

"Okay. I need work. Wyatt and Rupert had to have some training tapes or something. I'm going to dig those up."

"I will organize some and upload them to the cabinet."

"No. I can't fit in there anymore. Comfortably at least. Let's make this my playpen for now," she said, resting her knuckles on her bare hips. "Also, any chance I can get some clothes tailored for me in that tool shop? I'm not sure if naked is the way to go all the time."

"It is what I do."

Mary thought a moment. "You know, you're right. I really don't see why not. After all, clothing is a sign of vulnerability. We are beyond clothing. Who will judge?"

The various videos on hand-to-hand combat bored Mary, and she quickly surmised that combat effectiveness would come from both the desire to win as well as the ability to anticipate an enemy.

"That's it."

"What is?"

"I need to be where the enemy isn't. Sun Tzu. I need to be where the enemy isn't and I need to be able to do what he cannot or will not. I can blink in and out of time, like I said, and pattern my attack around the chaos I ensue. Why am I watching *videos*?" Storming toward the television, she pointed at it enthusiastically. "Start playing the video from Wyatt's suit at the RUF camp. Africa. Western Afri—there. There. See the footprints Wyatt is looking at? See that one there? And that one waaaay over there? I was blinking in and out of space time, perhaps fractions of a second apart. No wonder they can't hit me. There are spent shells all over the ground. I bet they shot *themselves*. No, this … this is how we do it. I was right. You yo-yo me in and out of the Beta Line. I bet that is how I moved around so much at that ice cream shop in Tulsa."

"Of course. I thi—"

"*And* you can incur me with momentum, I bet."

"Momentum?"

"Don't completely compensate for the Earth's rotation or maybe move me while incurring me so that I can plow into them and then incur out before hitting a wall."

"That would take tremendously challenging calculation as well as timing regarding your ripcord. I worry for your safety with such a strategy."

"We'll be playing chess against these people, but we'll only have the queen on the board while they have *all* their pieces at the start. The queen is tough, but *she'll* need to move more. *I* need to move more than them. Honestly, it would be far more dangerous for us *not* to use Janus to our fullest potential. I'm going to get shot otherwise. A lot."

"I can understand that."

"And we'll make it flashy and disorienting. Bring panic every time. Our technology and your ability and my physicality is so radically advanced … so alien to mid-to-early twentieth century that we will appear as being unbound by logic or physical law. Science, advanced enough, is magic to their primitive eyes."

"Will we limit ourselves to only the early-to-mid twentieth century?"

"Yes."

"Why?"

"Because prior to that, humanism and universal suffrage was still dawning. We had an excuse back then to be savages, raping and decapitating and pillaging. If we open the floodgate too much and try to tackle humanity's sins as far back as we can gauge, it will be overwhelming. We need to focus and steer from specific points in time. Modern history. Post-humanism."

"Where do we start?"

Mary gazed at the screen; the footprint loomed large. "The beginning seems the best place."

Chapter 40

Mary greeted Magus with a grin as she gingerly placed a wooden box filled with chess pieces on his workshop table. From under her arm, she drew forth a rolled white sheet and with a snap of her arm she unfurled it. Steadily her hand guided it open while it drifted over the table like a giant tablecloth.

The sheet had a clumsily painted grid on it. "So, each square in the grid is three square feet." Reaching into her box of chess pieces, she retrieved a white queen. "And this is me." She placed it at the center. "Each of these other pieces will be the civilians, witnesses, and targets we plan on engaging."

"I have actually anticipated this need and I have developed several UIs to meet the ends of planning tactical strategy for each incursion."

"Nice. We can use that, but for now this is better for my tiny human brain."

"Technically it is now *larger*."

"Yes, well, it doesn't always feel that way. But moving on: we will use this *other* white queen with the red paint on its top to indicate where I *will* be incurring next. So that way, for each incursion, I can plan a move ahead. And these battery packs and tools and things can be buildings and so forth and so on."

"To acquire a proper layout of the RUF camp, I had placed a probe in geosynchronous orbit above the camp's location to monitor it for approximately twenty five seconds," Magus said, displaying an aerial view of the camp overhead. "This way you can pattern your model more accurately."

"Thank you, Mags! I hadn't even thought of that. Ingrid scared me off the idea of putting in satellites post space-age."

"I knew exactly where I wanted it, and I could perform the math needed for the twenty-five second incursion. Also, within that data rod is a partial history of air and space traffic. I suspect Mr. Wyatt gathered such data for just this purpose down the road."

Mary nodded, inner sadness in her eyes. "I guess we're moving into his territory now." Gathering herself, she moved forward. "Is that mask ready?"

"Almost. I wanted to test its comfort on you prior to incursion. If, during this combat event, you need to fix or adjust it, please do not hesitate to tell me."

"Of course."

Mary took the lift down to Ingrid's disheveled cave. It was eerily silent. With a slow hand, she opened the machine room's door and found that all of the mechanical arms were at rest. At their epicenter sat what looked like a simple and subtle mask for the lower half of a face. A single overhead light illuminated it while the silent and still mechanical arms appeared to be genuflecting.

Reaching out to the mask and lifting it with both hands, she turned it over and over. "The last piece."

"The adhesive is in the prep room where you showered. It will be applied prior to the suit polymer."

Holding it to her face, it fit perfectly, covering her nostrils with a subtle filter.

"Click your tongue for me, if you please."

Mary did so.

"Thank you. That is all you need to do to ripcord out of the Beta Line. Is it comfortable?"

"It's barely there."

"The filter meets quarantine standards, however if you wish to fulfill the entire quarantine you'd have to—"

"I have no interest. Broke it for Florida, anyhow ," she said with her voice slightly muffled from the mask as she held it in place. "All right," she boldly announced, walking back to the elevator.

"All right?" Magus asked.

" I'm ready. Put me in the RUF camp before dawn. The children's tent is my first priority."

The suiting process was clumsy as Mary rubbed the polymer over herself without Rupert or Wyatt's precision. It was instead, war paint: messy and white. Blasting it with cold air, it clung to her..

The contacts slid easily into her large, rolling eyes. Under the firming polymer, her mask was seated comfortably and when she stretched, flexed, and limbered, long jagged cracks emerged along her muscle lines within the suit like rippling fault lines belying a cataclysm.

When the suit was satisfactory, she stood before the black pit that would lead to Africa. Rocking back and forth on her heels in anticipation, she relished the moment as she stared down the diving board.

"I'm glad to finally know. To know what I was born for."

"It is my personal opinion that such knowledge is fairly overrated," Magus chirped with a playful tone.

Mary walked briskly forward and her feet sunk into moist morning dirt. The trees rustled above and the dim blue light of predawn gave everything a magical luminescence. She looked about, her contacts giving her a golden filter for her perfect eyes to peer through.

The children's tent was to her right. A soldier slept in a chair in front of it. A barrel burned dully near the center of camp. There was a half-buried concrete bunker near the camp's center. A long bunkhouse at the south end of camp was the largest structure. Two off-road vehicles were covered with tarps next to it. Several birds could be heard heralding the morning. Everything around her was a series of details precisely and objectively displayed before her sharpened senses.

She clucked her tongue and was standing in the drained catching pool. With a leap and a grab she climbed out and ran back to the workshop.

"There's a sleeping guard by the left flap at the front of the tent. Here." She placed a black pawn on the grid in front of a tissue box that represented the children's tent. "Put me in front of him!" she commanded as she sprinted to the carousel.

Stepping out of nothingness, Mary appeared again, directly in front of the guard. His head jerked at her emergence, his breath frosting as he exhaled just prior to her bending his neck sideways like a chicken's. Lifting him, she clucked her tongue again.

With an effortless toss she flopped his limp body next to her onto the tiled bottom of the drained pool. Bounding out of the pool once more she ran back to the workroom.

"All right. I'm thinking one of two things. I clear out the camp prior to the children waking or I try and usher them to a safe distance. What do you think?"

Magus was silent for a moment. "I would advise removing the complication of civilian targets. Also consider that those children may become hostiles in the engagement. I would suggest pulling them out first."

Mary nodded in agreement. "Either way, Wyatt's HUD recorded that I had led them off into the jungle. The question is… how do I do that quietly?"

"I am unsure."

"Glad there are no children's bodies in those recordings. Assuming I didn't bury any of the kids after the engagement. Okay." Mary sighed. "Bring me into the jungle side of the tent."

Returning to the carousel, stepping forward into the black, Mary emerged at the closed flap on the far and secluded side of the children's tent. With a deft hand, she lifted it and peered in. A tiny boy, eyes white against his jet black skin, gasped and lifted a rifle much too large for his tiny arms. Mary's enormous hand wrapped around the weapon, steering it toward the ground. Leaning into his small face, she was sure he could see his reflection in her looming and lifeless eyes.

"*Shhhhhhhh,*" she cooed, lifting her free hand to his face and placing a giant finger across his lips. Thinking of what to say next, it dawned on her that there was a significant language barrier. What could she say? How would she convince this child and all the other traumatized, brainwashed, and most likely drug-addled children to follow her?

Glancing over the boy-guard's shoulder, she saw that the rest of the children were still fast asleep. Taking the rifle gently out of the child's hands, she bent the munitions clip out of place and tossed the thing outside of the tent. With a quick wit, Mary remembered that body language was universal and this was, after all, a child. Children can read bodies of adults precisely, especially if the adult can hurt them.

With a stroke of her hand, her fingers glided down his scalp tenderly. "You and all these children here are going to follow *me*," she said, more mindful of her tone than words. Remembering a gesture from the ballet of *The Pied Piper of Hamelin* she extended all her fingers of her one hand and wriggled them about in the air at the sleeping children curled on their tattered straw cots. Rotating her open hand carefully, she then curled her fingers closed in a waving gesture toward her chest as she backed out of the tent, guiding the boy by his shoulder out with her.

She knelt before him, her hands holding his, as she gestured her head toward the jungle. With a tender squeeze she released him, stepped inside, and came back out carrying the smallest boy she could find. She handed the child, still asleep and limp in the crook of her arm, to the boy-guard.

The boy had the idea, it seemed. Obeying with a glassy-eyed gaze, he went back into the tent, gathered the children in relative silence, and guided them out into the jungle's edge under Mary's gaze.

They looked up at her in wide-eyed bafflement. With open arms and gentle shooing, she began herding them into the trees and away from the camp as quietly as she could.

Someone was watching. She felt the back of her neck buzz with anxiety. A tall soldier in full fatigues was walking back from relieving himself, rifle slung lazily over his shoulder. Mary met his eyes and he saw her, their gaze connected.

She was gone.

She appeared behind him, snatching him up like she was a monster of legend.

She appeared in her previous spot with the children, most of them having seen what transpired. They neither screamed nor gasped, staring with wild amazement.

It saddened Mary to witness the things that a child can endure.

She ushered them deeper into the jungle until she felt there was sufficient foliage to protect them from any stray bullet. Kneeling before them, she cleared her throat softly and made a point of gently touching their hair, their shoulders, or their hands. Each boy had his full attention on her and she had to make it clear she cared for them and their safety.

"You will stay here until it is quiet in the camp," she said firmly. "Stay. Here." Her finger pointed downward at the ground at her feet forcefully. "Be safe, and when the camp is quiet go back for food and water and then… look, that way. *That* way. That way is the city. Go *there*."

Lifting from her knees, she vanished before them, her feet touching the tiles of the drained pool now slick with the blood of her second dead soldier. "I need to get in there and get them firing."

"Would you not rather use the stealth approach for the sake of safety?"

"No, I want it loud. I want to make sure those kids stay away. At least for a time. Besides, terror is the order of the day and the guerillas might do as much damage to each other as I would." Pulling a sheathed machete from one of the two bodies next to her, she swished it about. "This will do."

Jogging with excitement through the workshop, she glanced at the table cloth grid. " Put me in the middle. Same spot as the first incursion, but closer to their chow table. What's our overall time in the Beta Line so far? For the RUF camp this morning?"

"How much time you have spent in the line, or how much time has passed since you first incurred?"

"Let's consider… since I first incurred. In fact, put up a clock in the corner of that screen. Like a hockey game. I want to see how long this all will seem in the real world."

"Understood. You are currently at four minutes and twenty-seven seconds."

"Got it. We'll be done in fifteen."

Into the black once more, Mary was at the center of camp. Several soldiers were up and about in various states of dress. Two were looking inside the children's tent, their voices elevating. Another was sitting at the table nibbling on a round fruit. He dropped it as he spotted her. She spun about with the machete in hand and sunk its blade into the table's surface next to him. It made a splintering wooden *thunk*. With a cluck of her tongue she was gone.

"We've got two at the kid's tent, one at the table without a rifle, and four *maybe* five wandering around the half-underground bunker on the North side," she announced upon her return. Quickly she arranged the black chess pieces on the table cloth accordingly. Placing the white queen in front of the children's tent, she nodded at Magus. "Those two first. I'll be in for maybe four seconds." Then she placed the white queen with the red top. "Then put me here by the cars. They look like trashy jeeps under those tarps."

She incurred between the two men. One was crouched, sifting through the children's blankets while the other rubbed his eyes in an effort to fully awaken. Mary saw their breath frost. Goosebumps high on their skin, they gasped at her sudden presence. Gripping the nearest one by both wrists, she pulled him apart like a Christmas dinner cracker, one arm pulling free of its socket in his long sleeve as blood darkened his clothing.

He screamed as she hurled him through the tent's opening into the camp's main ground. As the green canvas rippled around her, Mary snatched the other man by his ankle while he was attempting to flee. He clawed the dirt as she dragged him to her, gripped his ribs between her knees, and twisted his head off.

Just after tossing his head out of the tent into the open yard, she clucked her tongue.

She landed on tiles, tossing the twitching headless body with the others. Running into the workshop, she adjusted her chess pieces and incurred again.

With adrenaline pouring through her body, she felt her shoulder muscles entwine around her back as the first jeep toppled over. Voices were shouting, soldiers were running, and cries of alarm were heard throughout camp. Mary gripped the second jeep, tossed it onto its side, and with a bull-rush shoved it along the ground and into the side of the bunkhouse. The entire structure shuddered.

She rip corded, hit the tiles, ran to the workshop, adjusted her chess pieces and props, and went back in.

By now they had realized that they were under attack. Some fired wildly into the jungle as others ran trying to co-ordinate each other. A few were in a full panic and two men tried to return one of the jeeps to its wheels. She ported next to them, kicked both men under the vehicle, and brought it down *hard*, crushing them. With a vicious tug, she rolled the jeep back onto its roof and then ported into the bunker. The captain, she assumed, based on his demeanor and red beret, was conferring with two other men when she appeared. Their conversation ceased when they felt Mary's chill hit just before she pounced on them.

Several soldiers gathered in front of the bunker door, banging on it, desperate for leadership, safety, or guidance. She swung the door open, flinging the misshapen head of their captain out at them. They fired blindly inside, threw grenades, and called for everyone to arm themselves while she ported out. She then proceeded to attack the bunkhouse on the other side of the camp, pulling half-dressed men out through the windows as they scrambled to tie their boots.

The catching pool was soon piled with bodies, some with heads wrenched backwards and several without heads at all. She continued to incur in and out, snatching soldiers up like weeds and adjusting her giant chess board between moves. The wooden box quickly filled with black chess pieces as the white queen devoured them; bouncing across the map.

There were a few stragglers now, and the smarter ones had run into the jungle in random directions. Mary dragged the last of them, a large and well-fed man too terrified to look up from his cowering, to the chow table. She flopped him onto it, and severed his hands off with two quick chops from the embedded machete.

He howled, cradling his fresh wounds to his chest as she dragged him to the edge of the jungle and rolled him clear of the camp. Machete still in hand, she returned to Janus and lopped off the hands of all the other bodies with the same blade and bundled them into a bed sheet from the infirmary to haul them back.

Piling them aesthetically on the chow table, she looked about with grim satisfaction until she shamefully realized that she had missed something vital. There was a wooden hut at the outskirts of the camp she had forgotten about almost completely. It was misshapen from warped wood and careless construction and had a metal roof. When she opened the rickety wire door, she saw the last occupant of the camp tied down to a bed.

The woman was clearly there for the sole purpose of rape. Her eyes had been put out with something sharp and hot months ago and all of her fingers looked like they had been broken and healed incorrectly. The woman's breathing rasped and percolated with disease and infection and as Mary stooped down closer she could see that all of the woman's teeth had been pried out with pliers.

Mary's knees weakened. The same long fingers that had twisted off heads and popped spines out of place just moments ago gently stroked the woman's brow.

"They are dead. And those that aren't dead will never be the same," Mary said apologetically. The woman didn't twitch; the stains of saliva and froth streaking from her infected eye sockets and chapped lips. With her hand spread wide, Mary covered the tiny withered ribcage to feel the woman's heartbeat. It was frantic, lumbering, and unnatural.

"When I rebuild the world, and steer it in a different direction, people like you will have a better place. This won't be tolerated. This won't be ignored." As quickly and tenderly as possible, Mary snapped the woman's neck. Prying the ropes that had bound her legs apart, Mary lifted the woman's body and swaddled her as best she could in filthy blankets strewn about. Cradled in her arms, Mary carried the thin bundle out into the growing sunlight that sliced through the canopy above. Within several strides, Mary was at the burn barrel and toppled it with a kick to awaken the embers inside. They spurted out onto the ground into a weak and smoky flame, and Mary laid her nameless charge face-up onto them. Fetching a half-full gasoline tank from next to a dormant generator, she poured gas over the body. The fuel soaked into the blankets, warping them to the frail woman's frame before lighting into a low blue flame.

Mary took a moment of silence to look on, and then clucked her tongue.

Bodies were piled around her clumsily as her feet touched down onto the tile for the final time that day. "What is our time in the Beta Line?" she asked while surveying the carnage.

"Eighteen minutes and forty-nine seconds."

"And how long have we been at this today? Planning, incurring, and rip-cording?"

"Eight hours, three minutes, and four seconds."

Mary nodded, prying off the mask and tearing at the suit's spongy surface to free her head. "Not bad for a day's government work. Any idea of what to do with the bodies? Should I cart them to the carousel and toss them through into the ocean or something?"

"Actually, once you exit the catching pool I was going to flood it with a chemical concoction to liquidate the remains and drain them."

"Wait, you can do that? Was the pool intended for that?"

"Yes."

Mary digested the thought for a moment. "I can't tell you how creepy that is."

"This room has a number of quarantine imperatives in place that we are currently ignoring, but the system still works and we can use it for a more... 'brute force' approach to cleanliness."

"Still creepy, but I suppose that is the business we are now in isn't it."

Chapter 41

The workshop was now a war room.

The largest of the monitors displayed the faces of targets and scrolled through photographic records of events for Mary to soak-in between incursions. Below the screen, at the nearest curved table, was her battle map filled with chess pieces, empty bottles, and upside-down Tupperware.

"I've got a hit-list already made for me via Jack's readings from Oracle. Can we get to that?"

"Sadly no, that is locked into Oracle… however I have accessed Mr. Jack's personal database and it appears he logged the times and locations of nineteen different cracks in the Beta Line. He hadn't logged them all and Oracle's search was still pending, so there is no certainty how many fractures there actually are, but would that be a sufficient start?"

"Can you scan the Beta Line for fractures?"

"I'm not certain. I will try. This may sound odd… but Mr. Jack's mathematical model for scanning the line was actually incorrect and fundamentally flawed. It is surprisingly difficult to replicate it given my nature. I might yield false positives."

"Take your time then, Mags. We have plenty to start with. Are one of his listed nineteen the Emmet Till murder trial?"

"Mr. Jack detailed a substantial fissure having occurred in September of 1955 within a town called Sumner, Mississippi."

"You know, I read a book about that boy when I was in middle school."

"It appears to have been a catalyst for the civil rights movement gain-ing media attention."

"When I read about Till's murderers… two grown men who tortured and murdered a fourteen-year-old boy, men who *stood* out front of that courthouse after shaking hands with the jury that set them free while smoking cigars and kissing their wives and calling the NAACP niggers … I fantasized about what I would have done to them. Or at least what would have happened out front of that tiny courthouse to bring justice."

"Their names were—"

"Unimportant. The two men are nothing and I'll end them quickly right in front of the cameras. I'm going after the villain in this event. The real monster that enabled it all."

And that is what Mary set out to do. A majority of the day was spent planning, Mary's mouth constantly chewing on thawed vegetables or dry nuts as she conversed with Magus.

"Was there a side door for black attendees?" she asked.

"As a federal courthouse, blacks were permitted to use the front entrance. I did find in several published journals and interviews that there was a side door used during this trial for non-whites, however."

"That makes sense. The trial lasted five days and to avoid strife the local sheriff may have forced black people to use a different door. He was a shit anyhow. He's lucky he isn't on my list. Yet. Give me the location of that door."

Mary studied the area, watched the celebratory interview by the front steps with the murderers and their pearly and perfect wives, and settled her large eyes upon the lovely Carolyn Bryant.

She slipped in her contacts, rubbed herself down with her war paint, and limbered up as it cracked and dried over her.

With a snap of searing cold, Mary incurred right before the cameras and reporters, snatched up the plump, bald murderer first and vanished. Landing in the empty pool, she slammed him down onto the tile under her as she glared at him. Coughing with panic and trauma, he was all eyes and terror as she loomed above. She wanted him to see himself in her rose-gold eyes.

"J. W. Milam!" she roared. "History has found you *guilty!*"

He screamed, unable to process what he was seeing. Snatching him up by his neck Mary hoisted him out of the pool and he landed with a thick thump by the room's exit. She leapt out next to him, seized his ankle, and dragged him down the hallway and back through the workshop toward the carousel. He flailed about meekly, trying to grip onto anything.

"Got the next incursion locked in?" Mary asked.

"Exactly as you asked. Forty meters in the air above the Tallahatchie courthouse."

"P-p-please... I don't... w-what..." Milam stammered as Mary arrived at the edge of the carousel's black void. Gripping his collar, she stood him up, leaning him over it. To him the yawning emptiness must have been horrifying.

"I'm going to say something to you, not because I want you to learn anything, but for my own satisfaction," she snarled through clenched teeth, one hand bunching his shirt and suspending him forward while the other clamped around his throat. "In the unaltered timeline you spend the rest of your days boasting to the press about how you killed that child because it was your patriotic duty. You had to stop that black boy from fornicating with any more white girls, and simply put, you got away with murder. However that won't be happening. I am taking that future from you. I am denying you every single day between this one and your eventual natural death much like you denied that boy."

"Please, no!" His plea was cut off with a convulsive yelp as Mary tore his left arm from its socket followed by his right. Mangled flesh held his limbs loosely to his body as she spun him about and snapped his pelvis with a blow to his groin via her knee. With a casual shove, she pushed him out.

"Change the incur location to the steps again. Now for Mr. Bryant."

Mary walked forward, landing on the brick steps. The crowd was now in full chaos and it struck Mary as a surprisingly quick reaction time for everyone. Though with the tension that must have been in the air post-ruling, it made sense.

Spying Roy Bryant running to his car, his wife's elbow in his hand, she incurred next to him and snatched him up. He also met the tile harshly, coughing and wheezing for air. Leaning her face into his, she snarled "*Guilty!*" With a similar grip on his ankle to that of his late friend's, Mary dragged him along the same route and he clawed and whimpered and huffed in much the same manner.

As Mary passed Magus, she moved her red-tipped queen on the grid and placed a small TV remote next to it. "This is his car. Incur him one hundred feet above it. Also, my next target is right next to—hey! Stop squirming, *you*. My next target is right next to that car and I want to snatch her up before our good Mr. Bryant lands."

She continued dragging him.

"Carolyn?" he exclaimed as Mary approached the carousel.

"Yes. Your wife. I will make an example of her. I will slaughter her like a baby lamb in front of every camera and wide-eyed reporter there. I hope Emmett's mother will be watching. Lord knows she can stomach seeing just about anything."

"W-why?" he yelped as Mary dangled him head-first over the void.

"I actually can't believe you can ask that question."

She released him.

"Incur location locked in next to that car? The one for me to land next to?"

"Is the vehicle facing the courthouse?" Magus asked.

"Yes. Put me by the passenger door."

Mary appeared directly behind Carolyn Bryant with her arms wide ready to snatch her prey. Glancing up she saw Roy falling directly toward the hood of his car, feet kicking as though he could gain traction to slow his descent somehow.

Filling her hand with Carolyn's long hair, Mary tugged her clear of the shattering glass of Roy's body smashing into the hood of his car, windows popping and bones snapping.

Carolyn screamed at the gory sight and when Mary twisted her about to meet face-to-face, she screamed greater still.

"Carolyn," Mary hissed as she dragged the woman by her hair back to the courthouse. She tossed the white-privileged beauty queen onto the steps, gripped an ankle with each of her massive hands, and stomped into her crotch furiously and repeatedly until her legs rotated loosely from their pivots. Focusing on a single leg, Mary knelt hard onto the woman's remains and wrenched at the hip joint, tugging and yanking as the flesh and sinew tore free.

Standing slowly, Mary hoisted the single pale leg high above her head to display to all those watching from behind parked cars and distant trees. Her sensitive ears heard cameras clicking.

Walking along the side of the courthouse with a deliberate stride, Mary came to the 'colored' entrance. Brushing the warm, bloody stump along the lintel of the doorway, Mary moved in a slow and graceful arc. Then both sides of the doorway were also painted, and once done Mary chucked the leg over her shoulder dismissively.

Stepping in, Mary turned toward the outside and lingered tall and visible for all to see. She slowly shut the door and then incurred out.

Chapter 42

"What are we in the mood for next? The Russian? I want the great white Russian turned *red* while he is in front of an audience that is too afraid to stop applauding. Looks like the fracture for him is in '48, Moscow. We could also hit China during the Japanese occupation a few years earlier, or Burma. Ooooooh the things I could do in Burma. Let's see those fissures and get to work. Where do I go?" Mary said with spry delight.

Incursions were planned and executed, occasionally filling up the catching pool with bodies for liquidation. Soldiers in uniform, infamous rapists and mysterious mass murderers alike fell under her thick fingers and grinding knees. Some she bashed apart with grace, and others she merely wrenched in half while gnashing her teeth in adrenaline-fueled rage. Bodies gave way under her knuckles and heels as Magus perfected the ability for her to incur from different angles and momentums.

Their chess games continued, sometimes even between incursions within the same combat action. Mary would need a snack break to eat a pound of spaghetti or gnaw a prime-rib, employing the leftover bones as trees for her battlefield model.

Movie nights kept their schedule as well, and Magus always had a bag of popcorn popped and leaned against his tank. Mary would invariably steal from it to sate her appetite, her fingers making a coy walking-motion as she snagged kernel after kernel.

Days gave way to months, and Mary changed Magus' fluid again, tenderly sporting her tiny, brainy friend about her shoulders as she walked around the station that evening. Upon returning Magus to the tank and connecting speakers, Magus chirped with delight.

"I felt like I was walking! It's amazing!"

"We'll make a daily habit of it, then? A nice stroll each morning?"

"Please!"

Christmas came and a fake tree was pulled out of storage, the hallways were decorated in a manic flurry, and Mary insisted on Christmas carols over the speakers for a week straight. Naked except for her Santa hat, she continued planning her incursions.

During one of their chess games, Mary's idle conversation went somewhere more tangible. "After this... after all this has been shifted and the generations get the hint that you can't get away with things... I think I would like to see a dinosaur. Or maybe listen to Buddy Bolden play in New Orleans. There was a church he used to play in at night until dawn... I forget the name—"

"St. John's Baptist Church."

"Right... right, I'd like to see them move the pews and turn the church into a dance hall while he bangs his heel against the side of the stage and plays. Dad used to love jazz. I'll hide in the rafters or maybe we can finally figure out the stealth suits. I'd like to go back to witnessing history again at some point, instead of steering it. I'm a human crew member right now, maybe the captain of the ship, but I won't be forever and I'd like to go back to being a human passenger at some point."

"Would you remain here, on Janus?"

"Until you get tired of it, and then we can have a cabin in the woods someday. Alaska looks nice."

"Would there still be movies?"

"You betcha."

Their game continued until Mary suddenly sprung to her feet and began bouncing up and down like an excited child at a toy store. "Okay, I'm ready for the big one," she said with a loud clap.

"The big one?" Magus asked, clearly confused.

"Yes. The big one. It's clear from the list that there is a fracture there and I've been thinking about it a lot lately. I think I finally figured out how to handle him. Let's get to work. I'll need anything you can find given that records are spotty of this incursion location given all the destruction that surrounded it."

"Were you saving this specific spot for later on the list?"

"Partly. In all honestly, I'm saving Tulsa, Leo Frank, and the KKK for last. Besides, I have to do the big one before I do Leo Frank. How else would I have the flame thrower?"

Hitler's Führerbunker was an impressive structure with a mysterious layout obscuring its bowels from record. "There are surviving escapees that chronicle Adolf's last days. I want them to be witnesses. I also want to try and prevent Goebbels from poisoning his children. Port me into one of his store rooms in his living quarters here… the one on the left, at night." Mary pointed to the screen. "I think I know what to do. We'll start there."

Like a monster in a child's closet, Mary emerged from the dark store room and tip-toed past six sleeping children sharing three beds, their tiny arms flung over each other among their flannel sheets and teddy bears. Once at the door leading to their parents' room, she opened it slowly and patiently, cautious not to let too much light onto the children's shut eyes.

She slipped in, closed and latched the door behind her, and crept to their mother and father's bed. With a quick jerking motion, Mary nabbed Mr. and Mrs. Goebbels' necks and snapped them cleanly. With shocked and vacant faces, they stared up at the ceiling looking like teenage lovers, their heads tilted together in false tenderness. Lifting a heavy dresser, Mary barred the children's door with it and then clucked her tongue.

"I might go back for them afterward. Any idea where an armory is in here? I want that flame thrower."

"One of the few schematics for the bunker that I have indicates several possible locations. Given the distance from the guard posts, I suspect

I know a location of one. It is safe to assume that a flame thrower would be there given its tremendous effectiveness within the bunker itself in case it was overrun by the Russians."

"Got it."

Mary incurred into a barely-lit room filled with racks of rifles, crates of munitions, and hooked to the wall hung three flame throwers. Snatching one up, she clucked her tongue and walked back into the workshop.

"There is just no way, unless I use my pinky, to fire this thing."

"I can easily manufacture modifications to it."

"Let me try something myself."

"May I guide you through a process of temporarily disabling the device so that you can safely remove the pilot nozzle and alter it to your hand?"

"Certainly," Mary said, sweeping off a clear space next to Magus for the task.

With fumbling fingers and frustrated curses toward German engineering as a whole, Mary eventually removed the firing mechanism and placed it on the table before her.

"It just needs a longer grip, like a gas pump handle or something."

"You can still take it down a level to the machine shop and I can alter it for you, Ms. Mary."

"Oh no, no, no. I've got this. There is a welding torch over there by Wyatt's side of the table and some scrap metal. Stand back, Mags! I'm going to *engineer*!" Her contact lenses protected her sensitive eyes from the blazing blue flame as she cut off the finger guard and welded on a shiny, ugly chunk of metal to the end of the trigger. After waving her hands furiously at it to cool it off, she lifted the nozzle, pointed, squinted, and toyed with the trigger.

"Good enough for government work."

Screwing the firing mechanism back on, she folded both straps over her shoulder and stood tall.

"Funny. The Nazi's always ranted about their super soldier. Wonder if I'll be white enough for them."

"Best ask."

Mary incurred into the main hallway, a doorway open to her left with several guards and two officers talking. They didn't even see her, although the nearest one felt the nip in the air from her endothermic incursion.

She set them ablaze.

People came running as an alarm went off. She incurred behind them and set them alight as well. The hallways filled with soldiers and secretaries scrambling about and for fear of hitting potential innocents, Mary held her fire.

She clucked her tongue. "Okay, Mags. Let's give them ten minutes to stew and then I'm going back in after the boss. He'll be in the deepest hole. I'll do a lot of tiny incursions I expect, so this could be drawn out."

"Safety is priority."

"Yeah... but keep in mind I still haven't incurred into Tulsa or Washington DC, so I either abandon this particular event or I succeed. Relax, good squiggly sir."

"I worry."

"I know."

The going was slow. The fire itself had hit in a vulnerable part of the bunker and troops swarmed there. The halls were cluttered with huffing soldiers and the echo of clomping heels. Occasionally, she'd lunge from a doorway and snatch one up, crunching his skull into the concrete wall to sow terror.

Deeper into the facility she incurred, a few steps at a time so she could see where she was going and direct Magus to her next incursion. On her battle-grid, the red queen crept ahead of the white inch by inch.

Smearing a final, handsome soldier against the low concrete ceiling, Mary kicked open two steel doors before her. Through either hubris or foolishness, they were unlocked.

Clucking her tongue the moment she heard the report of firearms, she directed Magus to wait a minute before incurring her inside the room. She landed on a large, elegant desk carved from dark wood with a leather top. Two men flanking her primary target were quickly dispatched; Mary not even providing them the reaction time to cry out.

Alone he trembled, pistol in hand, pointed at her standing on the far side of his desk. Seeing his finger tense around the trigger, she slapped it from him, shoved the desk aside and snatched him up. Sniffing deeply, she realized she couldn't smell him through her air filters. The question was genuine, though silly. What did Hitler smell like?

His feet clear above the ground; she lifted him to her eye-height and ripcorded out. Carrying him gingerly through the darkened halls, his feet dangled meekly. His eyes didn't dart back and forth and she sensed no particular panic in his grip on her forearm.

He just stared at her.

Mary soon stood at the edge of the carousel's void.

"Like so many people of every generation since yours, I've wondered how I would punish you. Honestly, it is brain-dead simple isn't it?" Mary thought for a moment. "Mags, translate that for me?"

A crisp German voice came over the speaker. Once done, Mary continued while Magus translated simultaneously.

"You were worried about pain, and made your Doctor test out cyanide on his own dog to show its effectiveness. Pain was your biggest fear. Pain at the hands of the Russians... because they have a special hell waiting for you now, don't they? That's why you commit suicide."

High pitched and small, a response came from him as he dangled from her grip. As Mags translated, Mary interrupted him.

"No. He has nothing to say. I don't need to hear it. My new incursion plugged in?"

"Ready."

Mary stepped forward and was in the courtyard outside of the Führerbunker during the dark night. The doors were open and much of the area was recently abandoned. Mary placed Adolf down gently, his feet finding the ground.

She vanished, and then appeared again with his large wooden desk high over her head. Gently, she placed it down before him, vanished again, and returned with his marvelous chair. Surprisingly, he did not run, but merely stood there and wet himself.

Vanishing and appearing once more, she had industrial cord gathered up into her hands. With a firm grip, Mary guided him into his chair and bound him thoroughly to it. He seemed comically out of place sitting at such a lovely bit of furniture in the middle of a deserted courtyard covered in the ash and dust from the week's past bombings.

Pointing a finger down toward the road, she spoke firmly and apathetically. "You watch that road there. In about two and a half minutes a bunch of Russians, all of whom have direct orders from Stalin himself to capture you for his pleasure, will come up. I had dozens of ideas of what to do with you myself, to be honest. But all in all, I doubt I could deliver the suffering that Mother Russia will upon you. I leave your fate to men even crueler than *me*."

Mary ripcorded, and sat Indian-style in the middle of the killing pool, its tile cracked and grout stained from the blood and impacts of her various prey.

"How many is that, Mags? How many combat events, actions, fissures, fractures, whatever… what is our total thus far?"

"Adolf Hitler was the nineteenth."

She nodded. "That leaves me with Leo Frank, Washington DC, and Tulsa. Bringing it to twenty-two. And after that we have no idea if there are more given our lockout from Oracle."

"Essentially, yes."

Mary sighed. "Well, I just killed Hitler in the worst way I could fathom… I think I need some ice cream."

Chapter 43

Mary allowed the alleged incident in the elevator to happen. She permitted the police to gather their simple and uneventful report. Crowds gathered outside the courthouse. Armed men of two distinct colors met in the streets as she watched from the rooftops. Eventually a weapon was fired. Fighting broke out. Lives were lost. Buildings enflamed. Biplanes overhead opened fire and dropped explosives on homes with children.

The black portion of Tulsa was burning, and the battlefield was clearly drawn between black and white. Being overwhelmed in numbers and fervor, the white tide strung up men upside down from lamp posts, shot them while they knelt on their knees, and tied them up and tossed them into their own burning homes.

Mary heard the occasional plane engine over the din of fire and gunshots from the top of The Hotel Tulsa. They were flying about, tilted in the air, so their pilots and passengers could spot any non-whites who were uppity enough to neither surrender nor die.

Time for work.

Picking two or three men from each roving pack, she would snatch them up, slam them into the tile, and slice off their ears with a fine paring knife. The tiny blade, handle pinched between her fingers, glided through their cartilage while her other hand enveloped their faces, muffling their screams of pain and terror.

To each she said after, "Every person who sees your missing ears will know *why*, and they will know the crimes you committed!" A healthy pile of ears formed in the corner of the killing pool and a gradual red line bled into the carpet as she dragged each of her subjects back through the workshop.

Prior to her first incursion into Tulsa, she had Magus blast machine noises over the speakers and switch the day-lighting to a blood red. The effect, combined with the lumbering monster that was Mary, was as terrifying as anything she could muster and each of her targets were horrified beyond human endurance.

By their heels she would drag them to the carousel, lift them upside-down to where their frantic eyes met hers, and then she would cast them out into the Beta Line to the recreational center next to the courthouse.

"I think I have enough by now. Time to bread-crumb Wyatt and Rupert," Mary said, disguising her dread. The work was easy, and like a beast of fairy-tale she daintily placed ear after ear down the hallway and into the street, occasionally being side-tracked to snag up a gunman from a posse in order to disperse them and add to her bread-crumb collection.

She led them to the soda shop. It was exactly as she had seen it from watching Rupert and Wyatt's video feeds over and over again, but now that it was with her own eyes and under the touch of her own fingers, everything was more vibrant. Her heart pounded. They would be here soon.

Could she wave her hands at them? Plead with them? Ask them to go back to Janus and shut down Oracle forever? It occurred to her that it was very well possible, and her body would obey whatever she wanted it to do... but the truth surfaced almost immediately in her heart.

She wanted this. She had dedicated her life to the study of history, evaluating it on a meta level as well as a direct and intimate scale. She was the best qualified person in the world she could think of to not only evaluate its importance, but to gauge how to change its course. A community hall packed with stumbling white rioters clamping their hands to the sides of their bleeding heads would echo throughout history, steering the course of future generations during the civil rights movement. "Don't you raise a hand against an innocent!" they would rasp at their grandchildren, finger pointing to the mangled flesh on the side of their heads. Their scars would be iconic, and enough of Mary would have emerged throughout history here and there to make her a plausible threat.

Mary wanted this. She would shoo away Wyatt, take out her anger on Rupert, and proceed with her other incursions. The work would continue. The world would fear the tall, white finger of God that would appear from nowhere and smite the villainous and cruel.

Because where was God, after all? A once vengeful and liturgical being described through capricious secondary sources had given way to a loving one… and as Mary looked out the shattered window of the burned and broken ice cream parlor, she knew a loving God wasn't what evil people needed to keep them on track.

She clucked her tongue and incurred upon the roof, tucked away behind a vent, and waited patiently to see the ashen dust kick up around her trail of ears that led to the back of the building.

Soon they arrived.

She let Wyatt and Rupert slip into the store and then as silently as able, she lowered herself onto the gravel lot beside the building. Her back to the wall, she slithered around the corner and hid behind the car she had seen in the footage.

Voices rang out in the distance. A moment later, three men came shambling up the alley, slumped with exhaustion as their rifles bobbed on their shoulders. Eyes to the ground in an early morning daze, they made for the back door of the store.

After they entered, Mary strained her ears, and soon heard them die. Tip-toeing from behind the vehicle, she stalked into the doorway. Blood was dripping down the smoky walls and the feet of the headless body before her twitched in a rhythmic pattern. Looking about, she estimated where Wyatt was and stood in plain view before him.

With the glow of distant fires, she could discern his outline; crouched and disciplined in his posture, chest barely moving. The urge to call his name occurred to her. Would he accept her? Judge her? Understand her motivation and that this all was thrust upon her? She never asked for this or set out for it, but she couldn't bring herself to commit the crime of squandering the greatest power in human existence as it lay available before her.

Would he understand that?

She would speak; say his name. Whisper it. She had led them there to listen to the cacophony of her gathered witnesses across the street, anyhow. This was the best time to illustrate her point. They would understand.

This could be different than the footage.

Forming her lips to speak the 'w' in Wyatt's name, something shifted in her peripheral vision to her right.

Rupert.

Rupert the idiot, as always, was just going to start shooting.

Remembering that in the video the Xeno barely escaped, Mary didn't hesitate to cluck her tongue.

Standing on the tile, she sighed. It was all for naught, and the thought of her destiny being directed or determined by Rupert infuriated her. Leaping out of the pool and storming through the halls and workshop she didn't even adjust the chess pieces.

"You know where to put me," she said flatly to Magus as she passed.

Incurring with a wall before her, she stormed it and burst through, groping for Rupert. Slippery as he was, she snared him up and drove his back into the opposite wall. She thought of Ingrid, of poor Jack's desperate face, and Gustavo face-down in the medical bay… repaid for his attentive care with meaningless murder. In a red haze, Mary drove her knee into Rupert's hip, snapping it, the jolt of the force shuddering through his whole body; the image of their heads sitting empty and eyeless before her vivid in her enraged mind.

Suddenly all she saw was white. Her nostrils tingled in her skull and dizziness hit. Rip-cording, she landed hard on the tile in a clumsy heap. Pain registered, her head throbbed well beyond its apparent size. Reaching both hands up she felt blood on the back of her skull.

The pain was immense and maddening. Thrashing her legs in agony, she kicked her pile of ears while she yelped in a distressed tantrum.

"Ms. Mary! What is it? Are you injured? Can you get to the AutoDoc?"

"*Fuck!*" was the first word she could finally form as she writhed. "He shot me! Wyatt shot me!"

"Where? In the head? It must have been a graze. Your thickened skull plates—"

"*Fuck!*"

"You need to get to the AutoDoc before you pass out, Ms. Mary. Please!"

Rolling to her knees and using her elbows to scale the side of the pool, Mary pulled herself out and like a drunken bull, tumbled into the hallway. She staggered into the infirmary, flopping on the AutoDoc table as its arms attempted to steady her.

Quickly, it snipped off her white, outer shell as she pulled her mask off, tearing away the white covering of her face. With her fingers in a pinching motion at the bridge of her nose, Mary pulled her contacts out and dropped them to the floor.

Tunnel vision was rapidly setting in as though she were looking at the sky while falling down a well, everything slowing as she descended. The busy arms above her blurred into a distant flurry as she drifted away.

It seemed like she had slept a century after travelling across worlds when she woke. Apparently, it had only been a minute or two.

"Ms. Mary? It is only a graze. You have a bad concussion, however."

She tested her fingers and toes to connect herself with her body again.

"It hurts. A *lot*."

"I suggest taking several days off and suspending this combat action until you fully recover. There will be significant swelling and I advise sleep, minimal ocular stimuli, and proper eating and rest."

"No argument there."

"Really? I was half-expecting you to protest."

"Absolutely not. I've been shot. In the head. By a master marksman that I underestimated. I won't be doing *that* again. I have to get that rifle out of his… heh," Mary snickered. "Yeah, I'll rest up. Ice Cream. Movies. And then I'll go back in, slap the weapon from his hands, make noises, land on that car, step on his rifle, and win a staring contest. We all know what will happen. It can wait a few days. I'd rather not get shot again. If I stick to the actions that I already did in the footage, I'll be just fine."

Chapter 44

After three days, Mary returned to Tulsa to complete her dance with Wyatt. Re-enacting what she had seen in his feed, she slapped his carbine away, hounded him, and while his featureless, clear form gazed up at her in horror, she regarded him in admiration.

He vanished before her. And she felt saddened knowing that she would only get to see him once more at Leo Frank's lynching.

"What about the horrors and the crimes that we don't know about?" Magus asked as Mary, head bandaged and empty ice cream bowl before her, reached to take her turn at the chess board.

"How do you mean?" she questioned, head barely able to think. Under her eyes were dark bruises that framed her bloodshot gaze.

"So much of what we know and see regarding our targets depends upon multiple sources as well as witness accounts. What about the many crimes that simply go unnoticed? So much suffering elsewhere exists and we are unaware of it. How do we impact these voiceless individuals?"

"I don't think we can. We can't save everyone, but we can make our presence known and influence those who would commit such acts. We would give them pause, at least."

"Would the monstrous truly bend their nature because of your appearance once every several years?"

She paused, deep in thought. "That's speculative. We need to do what we can within our ability, and hope some monsters would give pause."

"Perhaps some might attempt to provoke your appearance in order to be smote by the finger of God. As a demented honor, of sorts."

Mary blinked, her face quickly flushing red. "What the hell is *that* supposed to mean?"

"Please don't be angry, Ms. Mary. What I mean is that you have presented yourself in a god-like manner. You have painted the lintel and the posts red with the blood of the slaughtered. We heard prayer being sung from within the recreation center in Tulsa after their encounter with you."

"I painted the lintel to get the point across that the innocent and the oppressed would be *spared!*"

"Spared by whom?"

"Me! Us, of course."

"What is the goal, Ms. Mary? The final goal?"

Mary thought for a moment, her face calming. "To make the world a better place." She continued pondering her chess move.

"And we will accomplish that by continuing with the incursions and exacting impressionable punishments upon the guilty who escape redressing?"

"Yes."

"So, if people only change based upon external stimuli via you and me, how can we say the world is a better place when once we both die and cease our activities, it will continue down its path."

"Well, that's a good question. Two reasons: first, you underestimate how much of an impact certain events can have over thousands of years when it comes to people as a whole, and the second reason is that even if the world spirals back into genocide, racial executions, and religious warfare at *least* we gave the world a better state of being for a period of time. That *has* to be worth something, doesn't it?"

Magus seemed to ruminate over the idea, the tiny black eyes fixing into the distance. "Perhaps I am too far removed from humanity to understand. It just seems that we aren't building a better world… we are merely building a world influenced by you. You are an instrument, and through your application you may make things better, but the world will not intrinsically improve."

"Oh Mags," Mary said with genuine pity. "You are *not* removed from humanity. You have a friend to play chess with." She beamed. "And I am sorry I got angry. I'm not trying to fulfill my own hubris. I swear it."

Magus said nothing for a time, merely floating motionlessly. Finally the gentle voice came once more over the speaker. "Rook three squares over, if you please."

Magus' observation of Mary's executions throbbed in her skull for the duration of the game. Joylessly, she planned her incursion into Georgia, took up her flamethrower, and when her enormous feet felt the cushioning brambles and needles under them, it was all so far removed that the arcing flame over the crowd didn't even register to her. Passively, her heart thumped as each white face was turned to black howling singe.

A crisped body crawled toward her from the burning crowd, arm outstretched toward her leg. Her ears perked, barely catching what escaped his charred lips before she instinctively crushed his head in with her heel.

"We did it for you," he had rasped.

His words didn't click. Mary heard them, processed them, understood exactly what they implied, but nothing changed in her heart or her mind. Looking about for Wyatt's tree, she double-checked to make certain that it wasn't on fire. Eyes scanning upward, searching for his obscured form, branch by branch she found nothing.

With a crushing loneliness in her chest, she clucked her tongue, knowing that she would never see Wyatt again.

Chapter 45

"You know, I used to study at George Washington University in DC. The District is an odd city. Bipolar. Even the streets didn't know where they were going," Mary said as she organized her battle grid into a long street, each building a heavy battery or piece of painted Tupperware. "So, I'll appear beyond Wyatt and Rupert's vision over here. I'll come in, do my thing, and then about ten seconds afterward you'll incur the probe right in front of me."

"Understood."

"And you'll omit the compensation for the Earth's rotation, correct?"

"Correct. In doing so, the probe will be moving at substantial speed down that road, just as illustrated by Mr. Rupert's and Mr. Wyatt's captured footage. I advise that given the tremendous heat that will be produced from the friction of the probe's rapid speed upon arrival, that you consider ripcording quickly to avoid debris and flame."

Mary nodded. "I've already seen the aftermath, so I'm not worried about missing it."

The air crisped from her incursion and she stood twenty meters before the front of the Parade with her arms outstretched welcomingly. The lead banner was held by a handful of children, their hoods pointed and their tiny masks hoisted up to show their beaming faces. No doubt their mothers had worked hard at sewing their tiny ghost costumes of hate.

Several adults that flanked the lead children noticed her first, and their hands reached out cautiously to tug on their little one's collars and capes. The parade ground to a slow halt, mouths agape. The parents looked to each other. Their children looked to the parents.

"What?" Mary asked indignantly. "Is it because I'm part black?" The cold air snapped, nipping her fingers and toes and prompting her eyes to close, as she felt the probe incurring. Turning her head to shield herself from the incoming blast, her tongue curled to the back of her top row of teeth, preparing to 'cluck.'

Wyatt.

Mary had forgotten how simply handsome he was, his mustache a combination of classic and roguish. His flannel plaid shirt suited him and as he ran towards her from the side of the road she felt her heart flutter.

Her tongue dropped, and shifted in her mouth to delightedly form his name. It occurred to her far too late that he was there to kill her.

Spearing her with a long, metal flashlight that sported two prongs on the end, her whole body felt on fire, wrenching her off of her feet and twisting her about. Slumping to the ground, she only had the presence of mind to lift her hand feebly in an effort to deflect the next blow to her head as Wyatt clubbed her temple.

The road caught her harshly as she flopped over. Clucking her numb tongue, she found that nothing happened and she was still there with Wyatt lifting his blunt instrument once more to strike.

A sonic shockwave knocked him off of his feet, tumbling him over her as every window in sight exploded from its frame, trees immolated, and dirt flew. A cloud blew over them quickly and as she rolled onto all fours, Mary looked to where Wyatt had landed and saw he wasn't there.

She clucked her tongue again. And again. Nothing happened. Her filter was making a wheezing sound as she panted, panic setting in. Screams and wails drifted to her through the obscuring cloud that now blocked out the sun and engulfed her.

Boots clomped around to her left. She spun to meet them, but nothing was there. They came again behind her and pivoting she lunged with her fists outward, meeting nothing.

Something stung her. A gunshot. Another. And another. Her thigh was bleeding as was her shoulder. Crouching low, adrenaline surging and masking her pain and fear, Mary's fight or flight instinct took over completely.

Flight was not an option, so she chose fight.

Barreling directly into the cloud, charging toward the north, she leapt over several disoriented bystanders and burst through the nearest wooden door. Standing in what seemed to be a general hardware store, she scampered about the tall metal shelves trying to find a spot for an ambush within the aisles. Placing her hands against a shelf, she aimed it toward the entrance and waited for Wyatt to follow her inside.

And follow he did. With an angry shove, the entire standing rack of shelves came down, spilling tools, pitchforks, and shovels about. Wyatt bounced back spryly, dodging the debris with his revolver raised.

It was a weathered weapon, nicked and dulled by years of trusty usage, and it leveled with Mary and entered another round into her chest. Stinging into her pectoral, she gasped for air as she lifted a paint can and hurled it into Wyatt's stomach. He doubled over, revolver hanging loose in his one hand, as she crawled over the collapsed shelving and slammed into him.

They tumbled like manic lovers, both flailing and swinging as they rolled into another shelf, knocking heavy items loose onto their heads.

She snarled.

He was silent.

Everything about Wyatt was suddenly slippery and her grip couldn't close in around him despite her size and speed. He writhed under her, drove his sharp elbow into the crook of her arm, and slid free from her assault. His deft hands gripped her left one, both his thumbs driving into the base of her own thumb, and he ground down into the nerve.

She howled in pain as his legs wrapped around her huge arm, boots against the side of her neck and face, and he began twisting. She could feel her sinew being tested to its extremes and tunnel vision began setting in from the pain.

With a desperate jerk, Mary used her shoulder to hoist him and bring him down onto the wooden floor. The impact was hard, bouncing tools around them into the air. She did it again, Wyatt's face starting to lose its controlled demeanor. A third time pried him lose, but not before she felt her shoulder pop and her thumb snap.

She rolled from him, and he from her. Wyatt coughed desperately while snatching up a claw hammer, sharp end first, and raised it to bring it into her.

"I can save your son!" Mary rasped, hands raised.

It stunned him for a fraction of a second, the startling offer giving him a faint moment of hesitation. Mary repositioned her hips, making herself less vulnerable. Then a flash of furious rage crossed Wyatt's face, terrifying her to her core. The calm man, the disciplined man was simply *gone* and she now faced his entire wrath.

As the claw hammer came down, renewed with a broken father's hatred, she kicked outward as hard as she could, delivering a blow above his crouched right knee. Something in it caved, spinning Wyatt about, and landing him onto the deadly end of a pitchfork. He slumped, spit, and with unseen strength, he pulled it from his midsection and turned it toward her. Mary was swiftly up on her knees and wrenched it from his grasp, throwing it aside.

Interrupting his search for another weapon, she gripped his shirt and dragged him in closer. Both his hands immediately clasped something on his belt but she gripped his wrists and held them tight, preventing him from operating whatever it was.

She assumed it was his ripcord.

"No!" she shouted, head-butting him. Stunned, he flopped back. "I press it! Not you. You're coming with *me*," she commanded, lifting his shirt and seeing a device much like the one she used to ripcord out of

Florida.

He weakly swatted her hands away with surprising effectiveness. "Dammit, Wyatt!" she chastised with frustration. "You're hurt and I can help you!"

"M-Mary?" he asked, blood pooling around his teeth as he looked up at her.

"Yes. Now stop being an ass so I can ripcord with you in my arms. Magus has the AutoDoc and we can fix you up."

Wyatt's grip around the ripcord strengthened, barring her fingers from getting to its call button.

"What is wrong with you!? You're bleeding to death. Wyatt, please!"

"Mary," he called to her as though whispering from across a field.

"Yes?"

"The pod… and the worm…"

"Magus. It has a name. Magus."

Wyatt blinked in acknowledgement.

"Now come with me. I can fix—"

"I'm so sorry, Mary. I'm so sorry."

"No big deal, you fucking bastard. Now let go. *Please*!" Try as she might, his fingers held a grip that she couldn't penetrate with her fumbling, numb, damaged hands.

"It's my fault. The pod, the worm, all of it. I did this to you. Oh God…"

She abandoned her efforts for the ripcord, resolving to let him pass out before using it. With a relinquishing sigh, she lifted her good hand and pulled her mask off, yanking it over her face and removing the suit's head-cover with it.

She smiled, face bare, and pulled out her contacts one at a time.

"Still, your eyes . . ."

"Magus made certain to keep them."

"Always a pleaser, that one."

"Wyatt, come back with me. Please? Please come back? I'm lonely. I miss you. I was so worried. You could play guitar again."

He shook his head, face gradually becoming paler. "I can't be part of this."

"I'm making the world better. I'm making justice tangible!"

"We have no right to do that."

"But we have the ability and the power and the knowledge!"

"But not the *right*," he whispered, a gargle creeping into his words.

"Wyatt?"

His grip loosened.

"Wyatt!?"

His eyes unfocused.

Mary hit the rip cord, screaming in pain as she tried to land on her feet with Wyatt in her arms. Her thigh was filled with what felt like acid, and her shoulder gave way, nearly dropping him.

"Mags!" she screeched. "AutoDoc! It's Wyatt!"

With every effort she could make, desperate and frantic, she hoisted him out of the tiled pool, lifting herself out with a wincing grunt. Only able to half lift him, Wyatt's heels dragged and she limped into the infirmary and pushed him onto the table.

The arms instantly came alive, pulling the remains of Wyatt's shirt aside and slicing his boots off, leaving their leather in ribbons on the floor.

"He was stabbed, in the stomach."

"In the liver," Magus corrected over the speaker. "And his chest cavity was perforated."

"Save him. Just save him, Mags. Please?" Mary cried as she slumped onto the floor.

"I will try. I will. You need attention as well."

"Him. Him first," was the last thing she managed to say as her descent down the well hit bottom and she passed out.

Chapter 46

Mary drifted back into the world of the living. Looking up, she saw a sheet over Wyatt's body, his head covered. Her misery was only slightly interrupted by the dull pain that gnawed her shoulder and the sharp, stinging that accompanied her attempts to move her thumb.

"Mr. Wyatt is gone, Mary. I'm sorry. Please believe me that I am."

"I know, Mags. I know. It isn't your fault. None of this is."

"I had designed the device that he used to disable your ripcord mask."

"I figured."

"And I was required to circumvent Oracle's lockout to activate Janus' carousel. Only I could manage the math to incur Wyatt merely a quarter mile from his previous self."

"I know."

"I did not know the Xeno was you at the time of my promise to Wyatt. I did not know you."

"Sweetie, I know. Calm down and stop confessing. It's done. It is over."

Silence met her last statement. With her good hand on the counter, she grunted as she stood, one arm curled into her midsection, and she stood over the dead body shrouded in white.

"It's done. I'm done."

Magus continued his silence.

"When I was in Georgia, some fuck crawled up to me saying that they lynched Leo Frank for me. That it was me. I inspired them to enact 'justice'. How many times had I incurred prior to 1913? Two? Three?"

"Three total. Only once in the United States."

"And that is all it took. The people outside of the Tallahatchie court-house knew what I was from the get go. Maybe Hitler did, too. Maybe a few of them at the RUF camp. Oh God... that recreational center in Tulsa isn't filled with examples... it is filled with the anointed! They must see themselves as disciples, proselytizing the word of whatever fucking vengeance they feel like!" Clasping her hand against her face, she screamed with so much shocked rage that no sound came out. It was a stifled, smothered, agonizing call of despair. Trembling, she lowered her hand after her lungs were spent. "We're done. We're done. No more. We're done." She wiped tears from her eyes.

"No more incurring?" Magus asked overhead.

Mary thought a moment. "Only two more. Only two. And we do them *now.*"

"May I treat your injuries first?"

"No, you may not. I also need you to look something up for me. Where Wyatt's boy was buried. We go there first."

Carrying Wyatt's body, swaddled in white against her chest, she stepped through the carousel and found herself in a small cemetery in the middle of the night. The grass was uncut and moist from a fresh evening thunderstorm.

She placed her precious bundle down gently. Lacking a shovel, Mary clawed at the grass and roots with her strong arm and began digging in the spot next to a humble headstone that proclaimed 'Vanderwood' as its charge.

It wasn't long until Mary was almost completely drained of energy. The grave was shallow, and clearly someone would notice it come morning. Exhaustion and defeat kept her from caring too much, however. Odds are the grave would be re-dug despite all the questions and Wyatt would be next to his son.

Gathering up the front of the sheets as best she could, Mary lowered him in, his bare feet sticking out. Intent on covering them, she dabbled with the sheets until she was satisfied.

Mary hovered there, unsure of what she could possibly say, and who could possibly hear it.

"I… wanted to make things better. That's all. Make things better. I hated people who got away with it. Got away with rape, murder, or even lesser crimes like… like just cruelty or delinquent parenting or abusing children. I wanted the presence of justice to be something people could believe in."

She paused, her hand reaching out to begin filling in the improvised grave.

"I was selfish," she finally settled on saying. "I was just selfish."

Slowly over a period of a quiet hour, she filled the dirt back in. Pressing the call button wrapped around her wrist, she returned to Janus.

"Welcome back. I was worried," Magus said.

"One last incursion, but there are some things we need to do first."

"Such as?"

"You are going to reprogram every probe on this station and launch them with a very specific set of instructions. We'll discuss it over chess. And ice cream. And maybe popcorn."

With one hand, she fixed herself a sundae worthy of Ingrid's standards, and briskly limped to her spot in front of Magus' tank. After several moves, Mary began explaining in great detail what she wanted.

Each probe was to be deployed into various locations and time periods all over the solar system, even during uncharted time periods in the future. The new programming for the probes would broadcast a detailed warning as well as select footage of Wyatt and Rupert's various incursions involving the Xeno. The warning would contain her entire story that transpired onboard Janus.

"Something this horrible has to be known. And if we do this, perhaps others who develop similar technology will heed the warning."

"Are you certain that we wish to limit this to the solar system?"

"What would you suggest?"

"Given that sentient life invariably exists on other planets through-out the galaxy, we might consider sprinkling the probes throughout the Milky Way."

"I'll leave that to you. I hope context can be derived from the video feeds, at least."

"I will script the probes with basic binary language detailing elements of relevant culture so that an intelligent species might hope to decipher them accurately."

Mary nodded in approval. "How long will that take?"

"I've already written everything, in every language that could express the concepts, and currently Janus is updating the probe's firmware and data stores."

Mary nodded again in approval.

"How long will all those incursions take?"

"Approximately three days, given the limitations of the carousel and Janus overall."

"Sounds like a lot of time for chess and movies. Ever watch *Quantum Leap*?"

The time passed lazily. The first morning, Mary had Wyatt's bullets removed, her shoulder placed completely into its socket, and her thumb set.

"You also have several cracked ribs and your previous head injury is agitated by blunt trauma."

"Yeah, it's safe to say I had my ass kicked."

The days passed with Mary telling school yard jokes for Magus' amusement, several long games of pacifistic chess, and long walks around the station with Magus coiled around her shoulders. After their excursion around the living quarters, Magus was hooked into his speakers once more. He immediately asked, "Did you still want to listen to Buddy Bolden, or see a dinosaur?"

"No," Mary said, contented. "I'd rather spend time with a friend right now."

"Thank you for still being my friend."

"Why wouldn't I be?"

"If I had broken my promise to Mr. Wyatt, and told you where he was, things could have been different. Because I kept my promise, he died."

Mary sighed. "I could say many things to argue that, but I think we'd best just stop thinking about what *could* be for a bit. Wyatt is okay with what happened. I think I am too. Besides, when the probes are done, we have a single incursion left. I'll need your help doing some chemistry in the infirmary to accomplish that last incursion …and then after all of that is done I have a horrible favor to ask of you."

Chapter 47

Greetings.

My name is Magus Kami, or 'Mags' to my friends. You may call me 'Mags' since I am a friend.

Contained within this simplistic probe is a detailed account of a series of cataclysmic events that occurred of which I was not only a witness, but also a participant. It is vital that this information be observed, studied, digested, and shared among all that can comprehend its substance. Simply put, this is of value.

The individual in question, Mary Forsythe, has killed her past self during her college years within what we dubbed the 'Beta Line' by delivering a deadly concoction into her leftover beverage from the night prior. This concoction was deliberately designed to remove any suspicion from being applied to her current lover while still effectively killing her.

Mary felt that the day after her engagement to her lover was an ideal time to end her life. This accomplished a multitude of goals.

Initially, upon her younger self's death in the Beta Line, that Beta Line no longer had a Xeno and therefore a potential *third* time line was spared similar trauma.

Secondly, since the probability of temporal causality as dictated by a Mr. Jack Miller suggests, since a single Mary assassinated her past self, *many* Marys in alternate time lines did the same. This most likely caused a mass removal/prevention of Xenos from literally trillions of time lines via one poisoned coffee cup.

Thirdly, Mary was certain that her lover could move on despite her death, given that in her own primary (Alpha) timeline he already had.

This was a consideration given that she did not wish to victimize him even further.

Upon returning to Janus, after her last incursion to assassinate her younger self was successful, her request to overload the faux gravity well at the center of Janus was granted. This, presuming I am correct, effectively crushed Janus into a point no larger than a meter across.

In short, I am dead. As is Mary and many of her iterations thereof. And this probe contains the details, motivations, and events behind the overall event.

Permit me, if I may, to contemplate.

Again, given Mr. Jack Miller's perplexing theory that all that *can* happen in the mutli-verse *will*, it is safe to assume that this broadcast probe will be found. Some of you may listen, some of you may not. Some of you may do both depending on how many timelines are considered in the speculation. Somewhere, Mary and I spent the rest of our days playing chess and watching entertaining films. Somewhere Mary did not take a sip of her coffee. Somewhere she did, and perhaps another occupant of Janus became the equivalent of the Xeno.

Somewhere, I was terminated by my Chinese manufacturers, or Mr. Wyatt rescued another Magus from another vat. Somewhere, Mary stayed to her destructive course of purging, humanity spiraling into an unknown course. Perhaps she made minimal impact. Perhaps she made all the difference. Perhaps members from each of those timelines will eventually meet in the spaces between, where countless floating husks of Janus, no longer than a meter, drift in the void.

All in all, I had a chance to be. I made friends. I existed, influenced and *was* influenced by the world around me and built a relationship with existence. As trivial as it may seem, I find that a fairly delightful thought.

I wish you well, and to exist with intention.

Mags

31883595R00184